Praise for A[illegible]
the Montalbano Series

"Camilleri's Inspector Montalbano mysteries might sell like hotcakes in Europe, but these world-weary crime stories were unknown here until the oversight was corrected (in Stephen Sartarelli's salty translation) by the welcome publication of *The Shape of Water*. . . . This savagely funny police procedural . . . prove[s] that sardonic laughter is a sound that translates ever so smoothly into English."

—*The New York Times Book Review*

"Hailing from the land of Umberto Eco and La Cosa Nostra, Montalbano can discuss a pointy-headed book like *Western Attitudes Toward Death* as unflinchingly as he can pore over crime-scene snuff photos. He throws together an extemporaneous lunch of shrimp with lemon wedges and oil as gracefully as he dodges advances from attractive women." —*Los Angeles Times*

"[Camilleri's mysteries] offer quirky characters, crisp dialogue, bright storytelling—and Salvo Montalbano, one of the most engaging protagonists in detective fiction." —*USA Today*

"Like Mike Hammer or Sam Spade, Montalbano is the kind of guy who can't stay out of trouble. . . . Still, deftly and lovingly translated by Stephen Sartarelli,

Camilleri makes it abundantly clear that under the gruff, sardonic exterior our inspector has a heart of gold, and that any outburst, fumbles, or threats are made only in the name of pursuing truth."

—*The Nation*

"Camilleri can do a character's whole backstory in half a paragraph." —*The New Yorker*

A PENGUIN MYSTERY

© Elvira Giorgianni

THE SICILIAN METHOD

Andrea Camilleri, a bestseller in Italy and Germany, is the author of the popular Inspector Montalbano mystery series as well as historical novels that take place in nineteenth-century Sicily. His books have been made into Italian TV shows and translated into thirty-two languages. His thirteenth Montalbano novel, *The Potter's Field*, won the Crime Writers' Association International Dagger Award and was longlisted for the IMPAC Dublin Literary Award. He died in 2019.

Stephen Sartarelli is an award-winning translator and the author of three books of poetry.

Also by Andrea Camilleri

Hunting Season
The Brewer of Brewston
Montalbano's First Case and Other Stories

THE INSPECTOR MONTALBANO SERIES

The Shape of Water
The Terra-Cotta Dog
The Snack Thief
Voice of the Violin
Excursion to Tindari
The Smell of the Night
Rounding the Mark
The Patience of the Spire
The Paper Moon
August Heat
The Wings of the Sphinx
The Track of Sand
The Potter's Field
The Age of Doubt
The Dance of the Seagull
Treasure Hunt
Angelica's Smile
Game of Mirrors
A Beam of Light
A Voice in the Night
A Nest of Vipers
The Pyramid of Mud
Death at Sea
The Overnight Kidnapper
The Safety Net
The Other End of the Line

THE SICILIAN METHOD

ANDREA CAMILLERI

Translated by Stephen Sartarelli

PENGUIN BOOKS

PENGUIN BOOKS
An imprint of Penguin Random House LLC
penguinrandomhouse.com

Originally published in Italian as
Il metodo Catalanotti by Sellerio Editore, Palermo.

LIBRARY OF CONGRESS CATALOGING-IN-PUBLICATION DATA

Names: Camilleri, Andrea, author. | Sartarelli, Stephen, 1954– translator.
Title: The Sicilian method / Andrea Camilleri ; translated by Stephen Sartarelli.
Other titles: Metodo Catalanotti. English
Description: New York : Penguin Books, [2020] |
Series: Inspector Montalbano mystery series |
"Originally published in Italian as Il metodo
Catalanotti by Sellerio Editore, Palermo"—Title page verso.
Identifiers: LCCN 2020013715 (print) | LCCN 2020013716 (ebook) |
ISBN 9780143134978 (paperback) | ISBN 9780525506638 (ebook)
Classification: LCC PQ4863.A3894 M4813 2020 (print) |
LCC PQ4863.A3894 (ebook) | DDC 853/.914—dc23
LC record available at https://lccn.loc.gov/2020013715
LC ebook record available at https://lccn.loc.gov/2020013716

Printed in the United States of America
1 3 5 7 9 10 8 6 4 2

Set in Bembo Std
Designed by Jaye Zimet

THE SICILIAN METHOD

1

He found himself in a clearing beside a thicket of chestnut trees. The ground was covered by a special kind of red and yellow daisy he'd never seen before, but which filled the air with a wondrous scent. He felt like walking on them barefoot and was bending down to untie his shoes when he heard a loud jingling of bells. Stopping to listen, he saw a flock of small brown and white goats come out of the woods, each of them wearing a collar of bells around its neck. As the animals drew near, the jingling became a single, insistent sound, sharp and unending, growing in volume until it began to hurt his ears.

Awakened by the pain, he became aware that the sound, which persisted even into his waking consciousness, was nothing more than the monumental pain-in-the-ass telephone. He realized he would have to get up and answer but was unable; he was still too numb with sleep and all cottonmouthed. Reaching out with one arm, he turned on the light and looked at the clock: three a.m.

Who could it be at such an hour?

The ringing persisted, giving him no respite.

He got up, went into the dining room, and picked up the receiver.

"'llo, 'oo ziss?"

Those were the words that came out of his mouth.

There was a moment of silence, then a voice: "But is this the Montalbano home?"

"Yes."

"This is Mimì!"

"What the fuck . . . ?"

"Please, Salvo, please. Open up, I'll be there momentarily."

"Open what up?"

"Your front door."

"Wait a second."

He started walking very slowly, like an automaton, in fits and starts. When he reached the door, he opened it.

He looked outside.

There was nobody.

"Mimì! Where the hell are you?" he called into the night.

Silence.

He closed the door.

Wanna bet it was all a dream?

He went back to bed and rolled himself up in the covers.

Just as he was drifting off to sleep again, the doorbell rang.

No, it hadn't been a dream.

Montalbano went to the door and opened it.

Mimì then pushed it forcefully from the outside. The inspector, having no time to step aside, took the full thrust of the door bodily and crashed against the wall.

As Montalbano had no breath left with which to curse, Mimì couldn't figure out where he was and so called out: "Salvo, where are you?"

The inspector then kicked the door shut, leaving Mimì once again outside.

He started shouting: "Are you going to let me in or not?"

Montalbano opened the door again and stepped aside in a flash, standing stock-still as he watched Mimì come in, eyes shooting daggers. Mimì, who knew his way around the house, quickly raced past him and into the dining room, where he opened the sideboard and took out a bottle of whisky and a glass. Then he collapsed into a chair and started drinking.

Up to that point Montalbano hadn't breathed a word and, still without opening his mouth, he went into the kitchen to make himself his usual mug of espresso. He'd realized, upon seeing Mimì's face, that the guy had something very serious to tell him.

Mimì joined him in the kitchen and sat down in another chair.

"I wanted to tell you . . ." he began, but stopped, only then noticing that the inspector was naked.

And Montalbano, too, realized only then, and so he dashed into his bedroom and grabbed a pair of jeans.

As he was putting them on, he wondered whether it might be best to put on an undershirt as well, but decided that Mimì wasn't worth it.

He went back into the kitchen.

"I wanted to tell you . . ." Mimì began again.

"Wait. Let me drink my coffee first, then we can talk."

The mugful's effect was just barely sufficient.

The inspector sat down opposite Mimì, fired up a cigarette, and said: "Okay, you can talk now."

As soon as Mimì started telling his story, Montalbano—perhaps because he was still sort of half-asleep—felt as if he was watching it on a movie screen, as if Mimì's words immediately turned into moving images.

It was late at night. The street was rather broad, and the car advanced silently and ever so slowly, drifting past the other cars parked along the sidewalk. It seemed not to be rolling on wheels but sliding on butter.

All at once the car took off, lurched over to the left side, swerved, and parked in an instant.

The driver's-side door opened and a man got out, carefully closing the door behind him.

It was Mimì Augello.

He pulled the collar of his jacket up to his nose, tucked his head down between his shoulders, took a quick look around, and then, in three short hops, crossed the road and found himself on the opposite sidewalk.

Keeping his head bowed, he took a few steps straight ahead, stopped in front of a door, reached out with one hand, and, without even looking at the names listed, rang one of the buzzers.

The answer came at once: "Is that you?"

"Yes."

The latch-lock clicked. Mimì pushed the door open, went inside, and closed the door behind him in the twinkling of an eye, then started climbing the stairs on tiptoe. He'd decided he would make less noise on foot than by taking the elevator.

Reaching the fourth floor, he saw a shaft of light filtering out from a door ajar. Approaching it, he pushed it open and went in. The woman, who'd apparently been waiting for him in the entrance hall, grabbed him with her left hand while, with her right, she closed and locked the door with four turns of the key in the top lock and two more in the bottom lock, before tossing the keys onto a small table. Mimì made as if to embrace the woman, but she stepped back, took him by the hand, and said in a soft voice: "Let's go in the other room."

Mimì obeyed.

Now they were in the bedroom, and the woman embraced Mimì and pressed her lips against his. Mimì held her tight, returning her passionate kiss.

At that exact moment, the two lovers froze and looked at each other with eyes open wide in terror.

Had they really heard the key turning in the front-door lock?

A fraction of a second later, they had no more doubts.

Someone was opening the door.

In a flash, Mimì dashed over to the balcony, opened the French door, and went outside, as his lady friend quickly reclosed the door behind him.

He heard her ask: "Martino, is that you?"

A man's voice from inside the apartment replied: "Yes, it's me."

And she: "Why are you back?"

"I called in a replacement; I'm not feeling very well."

Mimì didn't wait to hear any more. He had no time to lose, and felt utterly trapped. He could hardly spend the night cringing outside the window and had to think of a way to get himself out of that uncomfortable, dangerous situation.

He leaned out to look below.

There was a balcony exactly like the one he was on: old-style, with a cast-iron railing.

If he climbed over the railing he could reach the one below, keeping his hands fastened on the bars of his railing and lowering his body down, little by little.

At any rate, there was no other escape route.

And so, wasting no more time, he stood up on tiptoe, looked to the left and right to make sure no cars were coming, and, seeing that all was quiet, climbed over the balustrade, rested his feet on the outer ridge of the balcony, and crouched down. Then, lowering his legs while hanging on with all the strength in his arms, he managed to touch the railing of the balcony below with the tips of his toes.

Arching his back and swinging his legs forward, he then executed an athletic leap and managed to land on his feet on the third-floor balcony.

He'd done it!

He leaned his back against the wall, panting heavily and feeling his clothes sticking to his sweaty body.

As soon as he felt ready for more acrobatics, he leaned out again to survey the situation.

Below him was another balcony exactly like the other two.

He calculated that, once he got to the second floor, he would be able to grab onto a large metal pipe that ran parallel to the main door of the building and from there drop himself onto the street.

He decided to rest a little longer before attempting his descent. When he took a step back, his shoulders touched the balcony's half-open shutters. In terror he feared that his movements might be seen or heard by someone inside the room. Turning ever so slowly on his heels, he then noticed that not only were the shutters open, but so was the window. He stood stock-still for a moment, trying to think. Might it not be better, rather than risking a broken neck for the second time that night, to try to go through the apartment without making any noise? On the other hand, he thought, he was a cop, after all, and if he were somehow caught, he could always come up with some kind of excuse. Carefully pushing the shutters and window aside, he stuck his head into the room, which was in total darkness. No matter how hard he listened, holding his breath, all he could hear was absolute silence. Summoning his courage, he opened the window even more and stuck his head and upper body inside. He held completely still, ears peeled for any sound, a rustle, a breath . . . Nothing. The wan light from the street was enough to let him know that he was in a bedroom—which, he realized, was unoccupied.

He advanced two more steps and then an accident happened: He crashed into a chair and tried to grab it before it fell to the floor, but didn't manage in time.

The noise it made was like a cannon blast.

He froze, turned into a statue of salt. Someone would now turn on the light, start screaming, even . . . But why was nothing happening?

The silence was even deeper than before.

Was it possible he'd been lucky as hell and there was nobody home at that moment?

He stopped and stood still, looking around to confirm this impression.

His eyes were growing more accustomed to the darkness, and because of this he thought he could make out a large dark shape on the bed.

He brought his vision into better focus: It was a human body!

How could the person possibly be sleeping so deeply as not to have heard the racket he'd made?

Mimì drew near. Touching the bed ever so lightly with his hand, he realized that it wasn't made. There was merely a sheet over a mattress. He kept feeling around, drawing closer to the dark shape, and finally came up against a pair of man's shoes, then the cuffs of trousers.

Why had the man gone to bed fully dressed?

He took a step alongside the bed, reached out, and started touching the man's body, running his hand over the perfectly buttoned-up jacket. Then he bent down to hear the man's breath.

Nothing.

And so, plucking up his courage, he laid his palm decisively on the man's forehead.

And withdrew it at once.

He'd felt the chill of death.

The images vanished.

Mimì's words suddenly became the sound of a film reel spinning empty.

"So what did you do next?"

"I stood there without moving, then headed for the door, still in total darkness, opened it, went out and down the stairs . . ."

"Did you run into anyone?"

"No, nobody. Then I walked over to my car, got in, and drove here."

Montalbano realized that, despite the mugful of coffee he'd drunk, he was in no condition to ask Mimì the questions he needed to.

"Excuse me just a minute," he said, getting up and leaving the room.

He went into the bathroom, turned on the cold-water tap, and put his head under it. He stayed that way for a minute, cooling his brain off, then dried himself and went back into the kitchen.

"I'm sorry, Mimì, but why did you come here?" he asked.

Mimì Augello looked at him in astonishment.

"So what should I have done, in your opinion?"

"You should have done what you didn't do."

"Namely?"

"Since, as you said yourself, there was nobody in the

apartment, you should have turned on the light and not run away."

"Why?"

"So you could look for other details. For example, you told me there was a dead man on the bed. But how, in your opinion, did he die?"

"I don't know. All I know is that I got so scared I ran away."

"That was a mistake. Maybe he died a natural death."

"What do you mean?"

"What makes you think the poor guy was murdered? Since you described him as all dressed up and lying on top of the bed, it's possible the man came home, felt really bad, and had just enough time to lie down and die, maybe from a heart attack . . ."

"Okay, but what's the difference?"

"There's a world of difference. Because if you were dealing with a man who died of natural causes, that's one thing, and we at the police can pretend we know nothing about it; but if the man is a murder victim, that changes everything radically, and it is our duty to intervene. But, before replying, Mimì, think it over carefully. Try to concentrate and tell me if you had any sense, even the slightest inkling, of whether the man was murdered or died on his own."

Mimì struck a pose, brow furrowed, elbows on the table, and head in his hands.

"Try to draw on your lifetime of experience as a cop," Montalbano urged him.

"Well, frankly," said Mimì after a pause of a few seconds, "I did notice something, though just barely. It might just be the power of suggestion, I dunno . . ."

"Try telling me anyway," Montalbano encouraged him.

"I could be wrong, but when I went up to him to touch his forehead, I thought I smelled something strange and sickly sweet."

"Maybe blood?"

"What can I say . . . ?"

"That's not enough," said Montalbano, getting up.

At that moment, however, he froze, staring at Augello, who still had his face buried in his hands.

Then he leaned across the table, grabbed Mimì's right arm, twisted it, quickly looked at it, then thrust it back at him so that it struck him in the face.

Mimì was shocked.

"What the hell's wrong with you?"

"Look at your right cuff."

Mimì did as told.

The edge of the sleeve's cuff had a faint red streak. Clearly blood.

"See? I was right!" Augello burst out. "And that answers your question: He was murdered."

"Before going any further, I need some information," said Montalbano.

"Well, here I am."

"First of all: Was that the first time you'd gone to meet this woman at her home?"

"No," said Mimì.

"How many times, my son?"

"At least six, four of them good ones."

"And what does 'good' mean?"

"Salvo, it means . . . well . . ." replied Mimì, somewhat resentfully, "it means 'good' in the sense of . . . complete. Know what I mean?"

"Yes, I do. And the other two times?"

"Let's just say they were partial and exploratory. But, Salvo, what do these questions have to do with anything? Do they seem so important to you?"

"No."

"Then why are you asking me them?"

"It's an alternative option. Haven't you realized that?"

"Alternative to what?"

"At this hour of the night, I'm faced with two options: babbling away as I've been doing or bashing you in the face. Therefore I advise you to answer my questions and stop making a fuss."

"Okay," said Mimì, resigned.

"Are you sure that during all this coming and going to and from her place, nobody ever noticed you?"

"Absolutely certain."

"What's this lady's name?"

"Genoveffa Recchia."

Montalbano started laughing heartily.

Mimì got upset.

"What the fuck is so funny?"

"I was just thinking that if she ever rang the station, Catarella would surely end up calling her something like 'Jenny the Wreck.'"

"All right," said Mimì Augello, getting up. "I'm leaving. Have a good night."

"Come on," said Montalbano. "Don't get pissed off. Sit down and let's continue our discussion. What does this Genoveffa do?"

"Let me inform you, first of all, that she goes by 'Geneviève.'"

Montalbano started laughing again.

Mimì looked at him sullenly, but kept on talking.

"Secondly, as far as what she does, Geneviève is a housewife."

"So, apparently, poor thing, since she gets bored during the day, finds a way to amuse herself at night."

Mimì's gaze turned darkened further.

"You're wrong all down the line. Geneviève is very active and involved in many things. For example, she runs a theater workshop for kids."

"Does she have any?"

"Kids? No."

"And what's her husband do?"

"He's a doctor at Montelusa hospital, and works the night shift every Thursday."

"So you have one night per week for your nocturnal escapades?"

Mimì rolled his eyes to the heavens for help in the face of Montalbano's incessant mockery.

Apparently his prayers were answered, because the inspector then asked: "Do you by any chance know the name of the dead man?"

"Yes, I looked at the doorbell on the landing. His name is Aurisicchio."

"Know anything else about him?"

"Not a thing."

Silence fell.

"What's wrong? Did you lose your voice?" Mimì asked anxiously.

"The fact is, you've created a big problem for me."

"And what would that be?"

"How are we going to swing it so that we come to

learn, officially, that there's a murder victim in that apartment?"

"I think I have an idea," said Mimì.

"Let's hear it."

"What if the man committed suicide?"

"It's a possibility, but that wouldn't change anything."

"Of course it would! It would change everything, because if the man killed himself, we, the police, can forget about him until someone discovers the body."

"Mimì, leaving aside your deep sense of humanity, your brilliant idea actually complicates things. The only thing to do at the moment, in my opinion, is to arrange things so that, in one way or another, we come to know that there's something strange in that apartment, requiring us to go and have a look."

"And that's just it."

"At any rate," Montalbano continued, "bear in mind that the first person to set foot in that apartment has to be you, Mimì, and you have to do everything within your power to touch as many things as you can with your bare hands."

"Why?"

"My friend, between pushing open the shutters when entering the apartment, grabbing the chair to keep it from falling, and turning the inside lock on the front door, do you realize how many fingerprints you left in that place?"

Mimì turned pale.

"*Matre santa!* If this ever gets out, that'll probably be the end of my marriage and career. What can we do?"

"For the time being, your only choice is to get the hell out of here. I'll see you at the station this morning at eight. Is that okay with you?"

"It's fine with me," said Mimì, getting up and heading for the door.

Montalbano didn't see him out; he went back into the bedroom and looked at the clock: almost four a.m. What to do now? He didn't really feel like going back to bed, but he didn't feel like getting dressed, either.

By now the coffee had kicked in.

All he could do was stay up and go for a walk along the water's edge at daybreak. And so, just to ward off any unexpected bouts of sleepiness, he went and prepared a second mug of espresso.

2

He walked along the wet sand for over half an hour.

He hadn't bothered to put on a shirt or jacket, and so the light, early-morning breeze that had risen made him shudder with cold.

He kept on walking for a while, but then the wind suddenly picked up and the dry sand began to swirl and stick to his skin. It was time to go back.

As soon as he turned around, a sheet of newspaper flying through the air struck him in the face and wrapped it up like a fish at the market.

He removed it and instinctively began to read.

It was the front page of the *Giornale dell'Isola* from the day before.

In the faint morning light he read the front-page headline: ALARMING EMPLOYMENT FIGURES.

The subhead went:

SICILY THE REGION WITH THE LOWEST EMPLOYMENT RATE IN EUROPE: BELOW 40%.

Then, to the right, another headline:

WHAT WILL HAPPEN IF WE EXIT THE EURO ZONE?

In the middle of the page was the announcement:

NEW SECURITY MEASURES TAKEN AGAINST TERRORISM.

As he was rolling the sheet into a ball, the inspector stopped. At the bottom of the page was another headline saying that the name of the comic who'd founded the

Vaffanculo Day party would no longer appear on their emblem but only that of the movement itself. Big deal.

Dress it up however you like, a pig is always a pig, he thought.

They would keep on saying NO to everything, in the hope of one day gaining power and ending up like everyone else.

Montalbano hoped he would never see the day.

He finished rolling up the ball of paper and tossed it into the sea. Reading all that bad news made him feel unclean.

He wanted to rid himself of the feeling at once. Despite the fact that cold shivers were shaking his body every few seconds, he looked around and, seeing there wasn't a soul about, took off all his clothes and stepped naked into the water. He very nearly had a heart attack, but withstood the shock, and when he was chest-high in the sea, he started swimming.

At eight o'clock that morning, Montalbano and Augello took one look at each other and realized things were hopeless.

Without saying a word, they headed side by side into the little room with the coffee machine.

They drank two cups each, and then, still silent and standing one beside the other like a pair of carabinieri, they went back into Montalbano's office.

They sat down face-to-face and stared at each other for a long time in silence.

Then Montalbano asked: "Have you come up with a solution for discovering the body?"

"Nah, nothing so far."

"But we can hardly just leave it there until it turns into a skeleton. Let's call Fazio and see if he can think of something."

"Wait a second," said Augello, giving a start. "I don't think it's such a good idea for Fazio to know what happened to me last night. My reputation is at stake."

"Gimme a fucking break, Mimì! Your reputation's already a public disgrace!"

"Oh, all right," said Augello, resigned. "Go ahead and call him."

Montalbano picked up the receiver and said to Catarella: "Get me Fazio, would you, Cat?"

"'E ain't onna premisses yet, Chief, bu' I wannit a tell yiz 'at a lady jess called all upset an' tremblin' an' she said—"

"You can tell me about it later, Cat. For now, get me Fazio, on the double."

"Straightaways, Chief, bu', ya see, 'iss lady was all upsit an' said—"

"I told you to get me Fazio!"

"Whate'er ya say, Chief."

Seconds later the phone rang.

"Hello, Chief, it's Fazio."

"Are you on your way here?"

"No, Chief, I'm on duty at the labor unions' demo."

Montalbano intoned a litany of curses.

"And when can you wriggle away?"

"This is gonna take at least another two hours, Chief."

The inspector hung up. Fazio wasn't going to be any help.

The door suddenly flew open and crashed cataclysmically against the wall. Catarella appeared with his hands in the air.

"I gotta beg yer partin', Chief, bu' yisterday I putta bitta erl onna door 'inches 'cuzz 'ey was squeakin . . ."

"What is it, Cat?"

"Chief, I wannit a tell yiz 'at a cleanin' lady housekipper awriddy call twice all upsit an' tremblin'—"

"Why trembling, Cat? Can you see her?"

"No, Chief, I can't see 'er, bu' when she talks 'er voice is all a-tremblin'."

"Okay, go on."

"An' so this lady, 'oos name is Giusippina an' som'n like Lo Voi or Lo Vai, says 'at when she went to clean up 'er boss's 'ouse, she foun' 'im layin' down dead on 'is bed mattress all dead 'n' all—"

"Stop right there," said Montalbano. "You can tell this lady we're on our way. Thanks, you can go now."

"Holy shit, what luck!" Augello bellowed as soon as Catarella left the room. "The solution came all by itself. Somebody found our corpse. So what do we do now?"

"Now, Mimì, you and I are going to get in the car and go to the site of your nocturnal exploits."

Fifteen minutes later they parked in front of number 20, Via Umberto Biancamano.

Mimì got out first and led the way for Montalbano.

They stopped outside the front door.

"I repeat, you must touch everything you possibly can while we're in the apartment, and for starters, just to overdo it, go and ring the buzzer."

Mimì pressed his forefinger long and hard on the button with the name Filippo Aurisicchio next to it.

No answer.

He tried again, keeping the buzzer pressed even longer.

Nothing.

"But the cleaning lady must be there! Why doesn't she answer?" asked Mimì.

"Maybe the buzzer doesn't work."

At that moment the front door opened. A man of about forty stopped in the doorway.

"Do you need to come in?"

"Yes, thank you," replied Montalbano.

The man let them in, then went out as the front door closed automatically with a loud crash.

"This time we'll take the elevator," said Montalbano.

Mimì, who now knew what he had to do, opened the elevator door and made sure to push the button for the third floor.

When they arrived, just to leave as many possible and imaginable fingerprints, he rang the doorbell to the apartment with his thumb.

Once again, there was no reply.

"Maybe this cleaning lady is running some appliance and can't hear us."

A few minutes later Mimì rang again, this time with his middle finger, but there was only silence by way of reply.

The two became convinced that the only person in the apartment was probably the dead man.

"Maybe the cleaning lady got too scared to wait with the corpse and is waiting for us somewhere else. Call Catarella and ask," said the inspector.

Mimì took out his cell phone.

"Hey, Cat, did the cleaning lady say where she was waiting for us?"

"Yeah, righ' where the moider 'appened. At nummer toity-eight, Via Almarmaro."

"What the hell are you saying, Cat? The murder was in Via Biancamano."

"I don' know nuttin' 'bout no Mancabiano. The lady tol' me asplicitly it was Via Almarmaro, nummer toity-eight."

"But there isn't any Via Almarmaro in Vigàta."

"Wait a seckin' an' I'll take anutter look at the piece o' paper. I'll spill it out f'yiz."

In the end Mimì was able to grasp that Cat was talking about Via La Marmora. Montalbano watched him turn so pale it was frightening. He got worried.

"What happened? What did Catarella say?"

"What the hell are we gonna do now?"

"What does that mean, 'What the hell are we gonna do now'? Speak!"

"Salvo, Catarella's corpse is not the same as ours. There are two of them. One here, and the other in Via La Marmora."

"Holy shit!" said the inspector, this time leading the way himself.

As they were driving along, Mimì said: "So we're back to square one, with the colossal hassle of trying to figure out how to discover our dead guy."

"Mimì, your dedication to law enforcement really touches my heart! We have two killings on our hands at the same time, and all you can think about is covering your own ass. For the moment, stop worrying about it. Our dead guy is already dead, and he won't be moving from his bed anytime soon."

The front door at Via La Marmora was open. Inside the doorman's booth was a shabbily dressed woman of about sixty who, as soon as she saw them, sprang to her feet and came towards them.

"You're with the police, aren't you?"

"Yes," said Montalbano.

"Oh my Gah, whatta fright! My Gah, my Gah, my Gah! It was just awful! I nearly got a heart attack!" shouted the woman.

Two or three people walking by on the street stopped to see what was happening.

Montalbano took a deep breath and, bringing his mouth almost right up to the woman's left ear, he howled: "What flooooor?"

The shout did the trick. The woman calmed down enough to say: "Third floor. But the elevator don't work."

"What's your name, signora?" Augello asked as they started climbing the stairs.

"Giusippina Voloi."

The whole way up the stairs the woman never stopped crying and shrieking.

"My Gah, why! Why do these terrible things always happen to me? Why's the Lord always put me through these ordeals? An' just the other day, my brother-in-law slipped an' fell, an' last week my sister broke her arm, an' now *ragioniere*

Catalanotti has to go an' get killed so that I'm the one that finds him . . ."

Montalbano went up to the lady's ear again and said: "Oooopen up, pleeeease!!!"

The woman looked at him and shook her head.

"See wha's happenin' to me? I left my keys inside. So what are we gonna do now? Ah, I'm such a wreck!"

Montalbano cursed.

The woman fell silent.

"Mimì, see if you can find the building superintendent, who should have an extra key."

"Of course he's got one! An' you'll definitely find Bruno in the bar next door."

Mimì ran downstairs in a flurry, and Montalbano sat down on a stair and gestured to the woman to come and sit beside him.

According to the good cop's manual, this would be the right moment to ask the cleaning lady a whole slew of questions. But he didn't feel up to it, because he was sure he wouldn't be able to stand the woman's whiny, shrill, quavering voice.

And so he just sat there in silence, smoking a cigarette. Then, since the woman wouldn't stop whimpering without managing to say a word, he sprang to his feet, went down one flight of stairs, and sat down on the same step, but one floor below.

He'd barely taken three drags when Mimì returned, triumphantly holding the keys in view. And so, by the grace of God, they were able to enter the apartment.

"Over here, over here," said Giusippina, "he's in the bedroom."

One look was all it took for Mimì Augello to have to lean against the wall for support, so great was his surprise. Even though the previous night he'd barely gotten a glimpse of the corpse, he felt as if he was now seeing an exact copy of it.

The dead man was all dressed up, in jacket and tie, wearing shiny shoes and a handkerchief in his breast pocket.

If not for the handle of the dagger-shaped letter opener sticking out of his chest near the heart, he could have simply been a well-dressed gentleman resting for a moment on his bed before heading off to a wedding or a baptism.

As Montalbano was bending down to look at the dead man's face, Mimì went up to him and whispered: "He looks to me like a spitting image of our cadaver."

The dead man was about fifty years old and well shaven, with his eyes closed in such a way that he appeared to be sleeping. His face was handsome and untroubled, and he looked as if he was having a wonderful dream.

Montalbano noticed at once that there was too little blood on the man's shirt and jacket, which seemed rather strange to him.

He turned to Augello.

"Mimì, give Fazio a ring. Tell him to blow off the fucking demo and come here. Then summon the circus."

As Mimì was leaving, Montalbano noticed that Giusippina was no longer in the room. But he could hear her whimpering in the distance. Following the sound of her voice, he came to a bathroom.

He was immediately assailed by a cloud of scent so sickly sweet and piercing that he started sneezing. Giusippina had not only drowned herself in perfume, but was now, between whimpers, in the process of dolling herself up.

Seeing him enter, the woman excused herself.

"My dear Inspector, now that the newsmen and cameramen are gonna be here shortly . . . a woman's gotta present herself in the proper fashion. Just think, a little while ago my cousin saw her picture in the newspapers after a terrible car accident that killed two people, and there she was, poor thing, passing by, looking like somebody's maid!"

"I understand," said the inspector. "Listen, I need to ask you a few questions. Where can we go to talk?"

"In the living room. Just follow me."

"First of all," Montalbano began, sitting down on the couch, "I would like to know the dead man's first and last names, age, and profession."

At the sound of the words "dead man," Giusippina resumed her irritating litany of whimpers, but Montalbano interrupted her at once, among other reasons because an overpowering scent of perfume had filled the room and he could barely breathe.

"That's enough!" he shouted.

The woman fell immediately silent, then said, all in one breath: "Carmelo Catalanotti, born and raised in Vigàta, about fifty years old, let's say, and profession . . ."

The woman fell silent.

"Profession . . . ?" Montalbano repeated.

"Well, that's just it, Inspector. He didn't really seem to do anything. Round about ten o'clock in the morning he would go down to the Café Bonifacio and sit at a table. He would stay there till twelve-thirty or so, then come home an' eat whatever I made for him, an' which he always complimented, an' then he would nap for a couple of hours, an' afterwards he would go out, an' after that I have no idea what he did. An' sometimes he would go away for a few days."

"Do you know where he went?"

"No, sir, I don't, and I'm no busybody."

"But," said Montalbano, feeling a little awkward, "how did he make his living?"

"I know he had a few properties an' maybe, just maybe," the woman ventured, "he did some kind of trafficking."

"Please be more precise."

"But . . . I don't know what to say. When he was at the café, always at the same table, every so often somebody would come up to him, sit down an' talk to him, an' then leave. Then somebody else would arrive, they'd talk an' talk for a while, an' then that person would leave, too."

"But how do you know this if you worked only part-time? What did you do, follow him into the café?"

"No, Inspector, it was my cousin Amalia who told me all this. She's got a little bakery right in front of the Café Bonifacio."

"Was he married?"

"No, sir. His mother and father are dead, an' he didn't have any brothers or sisters."

"Did he have a girlfriend?"

"Not even."

"But did he bring any women home with him?"

"That he certainly did. I never met any of the sluts, but the next morning I always realized that they'd been there, from all the wet towels. An' sometimes they'd forget, I dunno, a lipstick, or another time, a pair of panties . . ."

"Okay, okay," said Montalbano, cutting her off. "What was he like personally? What kind of character?"

"He was sweet as honey, Inspector. But, sometimes, when he got mad, he became a little devil. It was scary."

Mimì returned.

"I've alerted everyone. And Fazio's on his way. Have you finished with the signora?"

"Yes," said Montalbano.

"So what do you say we go and have some coffee while waiting for the circus?"

"Good idea," said the inspector. Then, turning to Giusippina: "You, however, mustn't move from here."

"So who's goin' anywhere? I'm supposed to be watchin' the place," said the woman, adjusting her hair in front of a mirror.

The men started down the stairs, but while descending the last flight they heard some animated shouting.

"What's going on?" asked the inspector.

"You wait here. I'll go and see," replied Mimì.

He returned almost immediately.

"The entrance hall is full of people. Apparently the doorman spread the word. We'd better not let them see us."

They went back to the apartment and knocked on the door. Giusippina opened up.

"Hey! Why'd you come back?"

Montalbano didn't answer the question but merely asked: "Giusippì, think you could make us some coffee?"

"Sure! No trouble at all! An' I make damn good coffee, too! C'mon in!"

They sat down in the living room. Augello leaned over to the inspector with a conspiratorial air and asked softly:

"So what do we do now?"

"What do we do? We wait for our coffee and the circus to arrive."

"No!" Augello retorted. "I was referring to our cadaver."

"Man, what a pain in the ass! Anyway, what do you mean 'our cadaver'? You discovered him, and you can keep him. He's all yours!"

"So much for friendship!"

Giusippina came in with the coffee. She set two cups down on the coffee table and went back out.

Montalbano took a first sip and literally spit it out onto the carpet.

"This is just hot piss!" he exclaimed.

Mimì merely started drinking his calmly. Then he clicked his tongue and said: "Tastes fine to me."

Montalbano didn't have time to reply before there was some loud knocking at the door.

"Open up! Police!"

Mimì got up to open the door, with Giusippina following behind. Montalbano, too, had stood up and now saw a woman he didn't know coming towards him.

She was about thirty years old, tall and slender, with tight, curly hair cut short. Her eyes looked like two long fissures arising from a perfect nose. As soon as he saw her, the inspector felt a sort of shooting pain in his stomach.

"You're Montalbano, aren't you?" she said to him, holding her hand out. "I'm Antonia Nicoletti, chief of Forensics."

"Since when?" the inspector asked, feeling a bit tongue-tied.

"Since last week."

Meanwhile, Mimì, who'd led his just-arrived colleagues into the bedroom, returned in a hurry to introduce himself to Antonia.

"I haven't yet had the pleasure of meeting you. I'm Inspector Augello, my compliments." And as he was saying this, he gallantly took the woman's hand and kissed it. Then he said: "May I have the honor of showing you into the other room?" he said, putting a hand on her shoulder.

Antonia didn't move.

She looked at Montalbano with her two green fissures and said: "Aren't you coming?"

"No, I'd rather wait here. I'd just get in the way."

Only then did she remove Mimì's arm from her shoulder and say: "Okay, let's go."

The doorbell rang, and this time Montalbano went to open. Before him stood Dr. Pasquano.

"You're a little late."

"Why do you say that?"

"Because the forensics team are already here and working, so you'll have to wait. If you like you can come into the living room with me and drink some excellent coffee."

"Sure, why not?" said Pasquano.

Montalbano led the way and then went into the kitchen, where Giusippina was. When he returned, he saw the doctor sitting in a chair and fussing about.

Pasquano was holding a medical bag, which he set down on his lap, opened up, and started searching, fumbling through scalpels, scissors, gauze, and various medications before finally pulling out a small, waxed-paper bag from which he extracted a totally squashed cannolo. He didn't lose heart, however, and, maneuvering with one finger, restored it to its original form.

He then brought the finger to his lips and licked it. "Would you believe I didn't have time for breakfast this morning?"

"No," said Montalbano.

3

The doctor did not retort, but only finished eating his cannolo and then, looking at Montalbano, asked: "Why is it you haven't told me anything yet about this corpse?"

"Because I feel a little uneasy about it," the inspector confessed. "There's something that doesn't add up."

"Explain."

"I'd rather you have a look at him first."

"How was he killed?" asked Pasquano.

"Stabbed in the heart with a letter opener shaped like a dagger. Or so it seems. Only the handle of the weapon is sticking out."

"What does that mean?"

"It means that it's exactly like a drawing in a horror comic. The dead guy's lying there, all dressed up, in jacket and tie, even shoes. We realize he's dead only because he's got a blade stuck into his heart, otherwise he looks merely asleep. So my impression is one of, well, fakery. Theater."

Antonia appeared in the doorway.

"Ah, Dr. Pasquano. You're already here? If you want, you can get to work now."

Pasquano wiped his mouth with the sleeve of his jacket, grabbed his medical bag, and went out.

Antonia sat down in the chair the doctor had vacated.

"No coffee for me?"

Montalbano sprang to his feet, went into the kitchen, told Giusippina to make more coffee, and returned in a jiffy.

When he sat back down, he moved his chair a little closer to Antonia.

"Why aren't you in the other room with your men?" she asked.

"They know perfectly well what they need to do. As soon as they're done taking pictures and looking around, we'll pack up and go."

She waited a moment and then said: "In my opinion, this case is going to be a tough nut for you to crack."

"What do you mean?"

"There's something about it that doesn't seem to make sense."

I agree, thought Montalbano. But he said: "Namely?"

"I don't know, I just have this impression that it's faked. As if it was staged."

Giusippina, preceded by the sickly sweet scent of her perfume, set a cup of coffee down in front of Antonia, who started sipping it.

"Where were you working before you came here?" the inspector asked.

"In Calabria."

"And was your transfer to Vigàta a promotion or a punishment?"

"A layover."

"I don't understand."

"I wasn't getting along with my colleagues, and so they found a temporary solution for me. I'll soon be going to Ancona. But it's a long story . . ."

"Feel like telling it to me over dinner?" asked Montalbano, not believing what he'd just said.

"I'm sorry, but I don't go out to dinner with strangers."

"But I'm not a stranger, I'm a colleague!" Montalbano insisted.

"Then I'm sorry, but I don't go out to dinner with colleagues."

Montalbano didn't know what else to say.

At that moment Pasquano returned.

"At first glance, I have to say I feel like I'm in a 'Murcan movie. It looks like the man was killed by a stab wound to the heart, but appearances are often deceptive."

"But when, in your opinion, was he killed?"

Pasquano opened his mouth to answer, then closed it again. He shook his head.

"I can't say anything before the autopsy."

He took his leave of Antonia with a bow, and was about to go out when Augello suddenly appeared in the doorway. The doctor pushed him aside with a thrust of the shoulder and continued on his way without even saying hello.

Augello gave him a dirty look, but then his expression changed at the sight of the girl. Putting on his best smile, he said: "Antonia, your men are asking for you. They've finished."

She stood up and headed for the bedroom.

Mimì didn't take his eyes off her, then came over to Montalbano and, without saying a word, patted him twice on the shoulder.

"Let's hope a rash of killings breaks out in Vigàta, so we get to see this Antonia more often," he said, smiling.

Montalbano bristled at these words.

"No need for any 'rash,' Mimì. All we need is for someone to find your cadaver in order to see her again."

Mimì quickly deflated and dropped heavily into a chair.

Montalbano stood up.

"I'm going back to the station. You wait here until the prosecutor arrives, whenever he decides to come. Give my regards to Antonia."

He went out of the apartment and was standing on the landing, waiting for the elevator, which was working again, when the door opened and Fazio appeared before him.

"Go into the apartment and have a look at the body."

"Will you wait for me?"

"No."

He got into the elevator and went down.

In the entrance hall, he found himself facing some forty-odd people—newsmen, rubberneckers, photographers, and TV cameramen—making a tremendous racket.

"What happened?"

"How was he killed?"

"Have you found any clues?"

Montalbano shook his arms in the air, then used them to carve a path through the crowd and finally walked away without answering any of their questions.

It was almost noon when he sat down in his office.

It was almost twelve-thirty when Fazio returned.

"So what was your impression?"

"What can I say, Chief? The man died from a stab wound, but it's an awfully strange stab wound 'cause his shirt and jacket weren't stained enough. And Forensics found no trace of blood in the other rooms. It's possible the man was killed somewhere else and then taken home and left all nice and dressed up in his bed. Which leads me to ask: What does all this mean?"

"I don't know what to say. Let's wait for the results of the autopsy, and then we can talk about it. Tell me about the demonstration instead."

Before answering, Fazio twisted up his mouth and threw up his hands.

"Once again, Chief, what can I say? You know, at the demonstration there weren't just workers from the factories that are being closed, there was also just regular people, and that's the real tragedy. There were kids with no hope of ever finding a job. I even recognized some of my son's former schoolmates who're now married with kids, clerks and university graduates who've lost their jobs with no chance of getting them back. If things go on this way, their only choice will be to emigrate, like they used to do."

"I know, Fazio. And that's the least of it, because if these people suddenly decide to let out all the rage they've got inside, the whole thing could end very badly. If you're in no position to feed your children, you're ready to do just about anything."

The inspector fell silent for a moment. Something had occurred to him.

"Do you have stuff to do here?"

"Nah."

"Then come with me."

On their way out, he said to Catarella: "When Augello gets back, tell him I'll see him this afternoon."

When they got to the car, he opened the passenger-side door and said to Fazio: "Get in."

"Where you taking me?"

"You'll see soon enough."

Twenty minutes later, Montalbano pulled up outside number 20, Via Umberto Biancamano.

"Let's go."

Fazio obeyed.

Montalbano took him by the arm and gestured towards the building in front of them.

"See that third-floor balcony?"

"Yeah."

"It gives onto a bedroom, and on the bed there lies a man, murdered, all dressed up, with even his shoes on. In short, an exact replica of the murder victim you saw in Via La Marmora."

As he was talking, Fazio's face became transformed, jaw dropping, eyes bugging out.

"Are you kidding me, Chief? Are you serious?"

"I'm not kidding."

"But how do you know this?"

"I know it straight from the mouth of that womanizing asshole, Mimì Augello. Join me for lunch and I'll tell you a story to end all stories."

Upon entering the trattoria, Montalbano asked Enzo: "Is the little room free?"

"Yessir."

"Anybody in it?"

"Nobody."

"Then we'll eat in there."

"As you wish, sir."

They went in and sat down.

"Do me a favor, Enzo," said Montalbano without asking Fazio what he wanted. "Bring us two servings of *pasta con le sarde*, and while we're waiting, we'll have some octopus *a strascinasale* 'cause I'm hungry as a wolf."

Enzo went out and Montalbano started telling Fazio about all that had happened the previous night.

When he'd finished, Fazio drank down a whole glass of wine in a single gulp.

"That's a little better," he said. "I think the most important thing to do at this point is to find out as much as we can about Inspector Augello's corpse. Do you know what his name is?"

"Wait, I think I remember . . . Yes: Aurisicchio."

"Okay," said Fazio. "As soon as we're done eating, I'll start looking."

The moment the inspector stepped into his office, Mimì Augello came in behind him.

"The fucking prosecutor made us wait a whole hour before the body could be taken away."

He tossed a set of keys onto the inspector's desk. Montalbano put them in his pocket.

"And what can you tell me about the conclusions Forensics came to? Or were you hypnotized the whole time by Antonia's ass?"

"I can see the honest and upright Inspector Montalbano is himself not indifferent to the young lady's world-class posterior. Oh, and on the subject of women, I wanted to let you know I'm going back tonight."

"Going back where?"

"I got a call from Geneviève."

"And who's she?"

"Come on, she's my lady friend who lives on the fourth floor. She said her husband is feeling better and will be working the night shift out of turn tonight, so we can try again."

Montalbano looked at him with genuine admiration.

"You've really got guts, Mimì! After everything that happened last time . . . and the dead man lying on the bed downstairs . . ."

"Ya gotta strike while the iron is hot, Salvo," said Augello. Then he continued: "At any rate, Forensics have nothing to go on for now. They're hoping to find a few fingerprints on the letter opener, but there doesn't seem to be much chance of it. In my opinion, given the lack of blood, the guy was killed somewhere else. Which leads me to ask: How the hell did they manage to transport the body all the way to the apartment he lived in? In one way or another, they must have taken him out of the car, dragged him to the front door, put him in the elevator, and dragged him into the flat. Now, don't you think they ran a huge risk?"

"Get to the point, Mimì," said Montalbano.

"The point is that it's highly likely he was killed in some other apartment in the same building. In which case the risk would have been minimal."

Montalbano sat there and stared at him, waiting.

"And so, in my opinion," Augello resumed, "we have to sift through everyone who lives at Via La Marmora, the doorman included."

"Okay," said the inspector. "You go first."

"You're not coming?" asked Augello, surprised.

Montalbano decided it was better, for the moment, not to mention what Fazio was up to.

"No. I have to wait for an important phone call from the commissioner. I'll come and give you a hand in a couple of hours."

Augello left, and Montalbano reached out and grabbed the first document for signing.

He was quite surprised to see Fazio reappear before him after only an hour, smirking as if he was bringing big news.

"So, wha'd you find out?"

Fazio sat down.

"I can affirm without a shadow of a doubt that Inspector Augello's cadaver is not Signor Filippo Aurisicchio."

"And what makes you so sure?"

"I talked with the guy on the phone, personally in person. So I got the idea to go back to Via Biancamano, and I was lucky enough to run into somebody I know, who asked me what I was doing in the neighborhood, and I told him I needed to talk to Mr. Aurisicchio. My friend gave me a confused look and said: 'But Aurisicchio moved out of Vigàta last summer! His apartment's been sitting empty, waiting for someone to rent it.' And then he gave me the guy's phone number and said he was now living in Ravenna. So I called him up at once and pretended I was someone interested in his apartment."

"And wha'd he say?"

"He told me he moved out of the area for work-related reasons, and that he'd turned the apartment over to an agency."

"Do you know the name of the agency?"

"Of course: Casamica."

"So give 'em a ring."

"Already taken care of."

To avoid getting upset, Montalbano decided to pretend he hadn't heard Fazio.

"And wha'd they tell you?"

"They told me to call back in four days, when the boss who has the keys returns."

"But what kind of fucking agency is that?"

"Apparently Aurisicchio is very jealously protective of his apartment, and so he left his keys with the agency's boss, who's in Stromboli, and made him promise that he would be the only one who could open and close the place."

"Well, we can't wait that long. We absolutely have to find a solution."

"Maybe an anonymous phone call . . ."

"No, Fazio, that's out of the question."

"Why?"

"Just think for a second. If we find out about the corpse from an anonymous phone call, then we'll be forced to investigate and discover who it was that made the phone call. And what will we tell the prosecutor?"

"We could write a letter instead."

"The problem's the same as with a phone call."

"So we're going to have to discover the body ourselves?"

"Yes. But how are we going to get inside? We need an excuse."

Fazio didn't know what to say.

Montalbano suddenly had an idea.

Fazio, who knew the inspector well, realized from the change of expression on Montalbano's face that he'd found a solution.

"Tell me what you're thinking."

"I can't at the moment. I have to talk to Augello first. In fact, you know what I say? Come with me; we'll go and see him together."

"Where is he?"

"He's at Via La Marmora, questioning the tenants in the building."

The phone rang just as the inspector was getting up.

"Chief, 'ere's summon onna line say's 'ey're the chief o' F'rensix. Bu' t' me they soun' jess like a goil."

"Put her on."

"Ciao, Salvo, I just wanted to give you the first results we've got, which unfortunately will also be the last. There were no fingerprints on the handle of the letter opener. The killer either wore gloves or wiped them off."

"Thank you, Antonia, for calling me right away."

"You're welcome. Thank *you*. I'll be seeing you."

Beep . . . beep . . . beep . . . went the telephone.

And Montalbano felt sort of bad about it.

When they were outside the building on Via La Marmora, the inspector asked the doorman: "Do you know what apartment my colleague is in at the moment?"

"Yes, Inspector. He's done the attic and the fifth and fourth floors. Now he's with Signura Musumarra on the third floor."

"Go and take over for him," Montalbano said to Fazio. "Continue the questioning and tell Augello to come downstairs 'cause I need to talk to him."

He didn't have time to light a cigarette outside the door before Mimì appeared.

"Good God!" said Mimì. "What is this? Aside from a pretty forty-year-old in the attic apartment, the average age of the tenants here is practically over a hundred . . ."

"Never mind that. Did you manage to find anything out?"

"No, it's as if nobody ever even sees their neighbors in this place. A waste of three hours. What did you want to tell me?"

"Let's go and have some coffee."

They sat down at a table apart from the rest.

"I had an idea of how to officially discover your cadaver," the inspector began immediately.

"And what would that be?"

"Tonight, you must go the same route you did the other night."

"You want me to lower myself down onto the floor below?"

"Exactly. You can tell your lady friend that you lost your wallet the other night, and you're sure it happened on your journey to the third floor, so you have to go back and look for it."

"That means I'm going to miss another night!" Mimì Augello said in despair.

"No, Mimì, you can pull out the story of the wallet after you've done what you need to do."

"Wait a second," said Augello. "The minute I find that body there, Geneviève is automatically going to be in a pickle because I have to somehow justify the fact that I was in her apartment."

"I've thought of that, too," said Montalbano. "The official version we'll give is that the lady called you at the police station because she thought she'd heard someone climbing up onto her balcony, so you went out to have a look and your wallet fell onto the balcony below. Got that?"

"Well, okay," Augello said in resignation. "I'll give it a try."

When they came back to the front door at Via La Marmora, Augello said he was going to go and give Fazio a hand.

"You're not coming?" he asked.

"No."

When Mimì headed upstairs, Montalbano went into the doorman's booth and, seeing a vacant chair, grabbed it and sat down silently beside him.

The doorman laughed.

"What are you doing? Do you want to take my place?"

"No, I just would like to exchange a few words with you."

"You're the boss."

He was a ruddy-faced man of about sixty, with a cheerful expression and a big Turkish-style mustache.

"And what is your name?"

"Bruno Ammazzalorso."

"That's not a name from around here."

"No, in fact my father came here from the Abbruzzi when I was just a little baby."

Bruno Ammazzalorso, the killer of the brown bear of the

Abbruzzi!, thought Montalbano, smiling to himself, musing that if the man had phoned the police station, Catarella would have put the call through, saying, "There's a jinnelman 'at killed a brown Abbruzzi bear onna line."

Then he asked: "How long have you been the doorman here?"

"Ten years."

"And was Signor Catalanotti already living here?"

"Yessir, he was."

"Tell me about him."

"Look, Inspector, he was a strange guy, but I don't hardly know nothin' about 'im. He never got married. He was a bachelor when I got here, and he stayed a bachelor."

"But did he have a girlfriend?"

"Dunno, I can't say. There was both women an' men goin' up to his place. An' maybe some of 'em stayed the night . . ."

"Did he have any relatives?"

"Not that I know of."

"All right, go on."

Ammazzalorso took a look around, leaned down towards the inspector, and, lowering his voice, said: "If you really wanna know the truth, I think there was a misunderstanding."

"What do you mean?"

"Signor Catalanotti never went to work an' didn't seem to have any other kind of steady job, either. But he was never short on money! Hell, it practically danced in his pockets. Every morning he'd go out to the café nearby, all slicked up, and then would . . . well, he'd receive visitors."

"Try to be a little more precise," said the inspector.

"Sometimes you'd see women and men coming in to

talk to him. But you could tell they weren't his friends. What did they say to him? What was all that talking about? Who knows! Then, at exactly one o'clock, he would get up and come home for lunch. He'd take a little nap—or so I was told by Giusippina—an' afterwards I dunno what he did. Sometimes he'd go out again and then come back at eight o'clock on the dot, or else he'd just stay home. I also know he had stuff to do in the evenings."

"And do you know where he went?"

"I ain't got the vaguest idea."

"But were there any days when he just stayed home?"

"Not too often, but, yeah, sometimes. But then he would have people come an' see him at home."

Montalbano assumed the same conspiratorial air as the doorman and said: "Let's talk man to man, eye to eye. Surely you must have had some kind of idea of what Catalanotti was doing."

"Of course I did."

4

"Feel like telling me about it?" asked the inspector, grinning complicitly.

Ammazzalorso sat up, leaned back against the chair, and assumed a proud expression.

"Inspector, I ain't in the habit of makin' trouble for people."

"What more trouble could you possibly make for poor old Catalanotti, now that he's dead?"

"That's true. Well, all right. What I can say is that, in my opinion—but it's just my personal opinion—the guy was dealin' drugs."

"And what made you think that?" asked Montalbano.

"I dunno. Just because."

"But do you remember how old the people who used to come to see him were?"

"No kids. Mostly forty years old and up."

Montalbano got the impression this drug story was neither here nor there. Just a doorman thinking ill of a tenant.

He stood up, shook Bruno Ammazzalorso's hand, and headed for the stairs.

Two flights of stairs he could handle.

As soon as he reached the landing, Augello and Fazio popped out of the apartment across from Catalanotti's.

"Any news?" he asked them.

"Wha'd I tell you?" replied Augello. "It's like a typical residential building in Stockholm."

"There's another possibility," said the inspector. "That everybody knows everything, but nobody wants to tell us."

"Well, that would change things, and in that case we would be dealing with a typical residential building in Sicily," said Fazio by way of conclusion.

"We were on our way to the floor below," Augello said to Montalbano.

"Best of luck," replied the inspector. Then he removed the seals, took the keys out of his pocket, and unlocked the door to the dead man's flat.

Catalanotti's apartment consisted of a spacious entrance hall, to the right of which began a corridor, with one wall, on the left, entirely covered by a very long white wooden armoire before giving onto the bedroom and the bathroom next to it. Also off the entranceway were three other doors: one to the kitchen, beyond which was a second bathroom; another to the dining room, which also served as a sitting room; and the third to a rather small study that nevertheless featured a sofa that took up an entire wall.

Montalbano stopped for a moment.

The study's walls were lined with shelves jam-packed with books and magazines, and on the desk, which featured two large drawers, sat an old computer, a printer, a few sheets of paper, and a telephone.

He retraced his steps as far as the bedroom, and here he noticed something he'd failed to see before. Between the bed and the window was a sort of small door that looked like it gave onto a closet.

He tried to open it but was unable. It was locked.

Montalbano was suspicious. With an armoire that took

up the whole hallway, what need did Catalanotti have for a closet in the bedroom?

He tried again to open the door with a key he'd found on a bedside table, but it didn't work.

At this point, he became obsessed.

He had to see what was inside, whatever it took. Taking three steps back to work up a head of steam, he charged, raised his foot as high as it would go, and kicked the door hard.

He heard the sound of something breaking.

When he tried again to open it, the door wobbled. Another kick would do it. And indeed . . .

He found himself looking at a sort of bookcase stuffed with more books, magazines, and folders.

Stuck on the spine of each folder was a strip of white paper with the name of a person written on it: "Giovanni," "Maria," "Filippo," "Ernesto," "Valentina," "Guido," "Maria 3," "Andrea," "Giacomo," and so on. A long row of folders was occasionally broken up by an object dividing one section from another.

He grabbed three of the first folders that came to hand, one right next to the other, and brought them to the bed. He opened the first, the one with the name "Maria" on it.

Inside was a close-up photo of a blond girl sitting down and reading something.

Then there were two sheets of paper, one printed from a computer, the other covered with handwriting.

The first was a dialogue of four or five lines.

He read them:

—*What?*

—*The truth.*

—*Starting today, you will have to resign yourself to living without any illusions.*

—*I've lived with illusions my whole life. I've never been able to do without them.*

—*It's you who wanted it to come to this, at all costs.*

—*Until today, illusions gave me the strength to go on, they helped me to live. I don't believe in anything else. I've had no other kind of help.*

At the bottom of the page were two initials: DC. Montalbano had no idea what the hell any of this was about. He moved on to the handwritten sheet, in the middle of which stood out the name *Maria.* Written in parentheses were the words *first meeting.* Then it went on:

It was very hard to get her to open up.

It took several hours. She appears to be quite ready for friendship, but as soon as I try to go beyond the first threshold and elicit more personal information on her intimate life, she shuts up like a clam.

I've come to the conclusion that it's not an inborn personality trait. She must have undergone some extremely negative experience that conditioned her manner of behavior. And that's exactly what interests me about her. I think she's still a virgin. She's an actress, or at least considers herself one, and it's possible the key to opening her up is in fact the theater. When I asked her a specific question—that is, how far would she go to defend herself against a sexual assault—she gave a confused answer. So I became even clearer: Would you be capable of killing your attacker? And she didn't answer, but only looked at me. Then she wanted to recite a passage from Antigone. *She reacts in unexpected ways.*

She's very interesting to me. I will keep meeting with her, as often as possible.

This time Montalbano understood even less than before.

He picked up the second folder, the one called "Giacomo," and opened it. Here, too, he found two sheets of paper, along with a photo of a man in a hat, standing with his mouth open as if he was singing. The inspector read the first page, printed from a computer.

—What conclusion? You speak as if you knew a lot more about Martin's account than we do.
—All I know is that there must have been a reason for him to do what he did.
—Maybe Martin killed himself because he thought I'd taken the money.
—The money again! If you think Martin killed himself because he thought you'd taken his money, then you didn't know your own brother. He laughed when I told him. He found it amusing. He found a lot of things amusing.

Montalbano's confusion increased.

Who were these people? The handwritten sheet for "Giacomo" said:

Rarely have I met a person with no intention of ever renouncing any pleasure life might have to offer him.

During our fourth meeting I clearly realized that he would not hesitate to do harm to others so long as he might derive some pleasure from it.

His main concern is money, in that his pleasures are expensive. Very expensive.

When I asked him whether, if he came across a check for an enormous amount of money that he could cash without any risk, he would try to pin the blame on someone else, he said he wouldn't be capable of doing such a thing.

I had the impression he was lying. I will meet with him again, because if I were somehow able to establish that he'd lied to me, Giacomo would be ideal for my purposes.

Same two initials at the end: DC. Montalbano felt bewildered, lost in a foggy abyss, with the folder on his lap.

He made a snap decision. He got up, grabbed the three folders, put them back in their place, closed the closet as best he could, and went into the study.

He sat down at the desk. The sheets of paper lying there were blank. He made a mental note to look inside the man's computer.

Then he opened the first drawer on the left.

It contained a great many accounting books. Montalbano took out the one for the current year, 2016, and started looking through it.

When he closed it half an hour later, he had learned that Catalanotti owned quite a few houses, lots, and warehouses that he legally rented out. If he wasn't a rich man, he was pretty close.

The inspector then opened the right-hand drawer. Here, too, were many accounts books, and these also had the year written on each. He took out the one for the present year and had a surprise. Each page had a different name at the top.

At the top of the first page was the name Adalberto Lai. Under it was a declaration:

JANUARY 8, 2016

I, the undersigned, Adalberto Lai, declare that I have received the sum of fifteen thousand euros (15,000 €) from Mr. Carmelo Catalanotti, and hereby pledge to repay, within six months of the present date, the sum of fifteen thousand five hundred euros (15,500 €) to the same Mr. Catalanotti.

In witness whereof,

Followed by his signature.

Under the signature, and this time in Catalanotti's ornate calligraphy, was another declaration.

JUNE 10, 2016

I, the undersigned, Carmelo Catalanotti, hereby declare that I have received, on this day, from Mr. Adalberto Lai, the sum previously agreed upon. I have no further claims.

This was followed by both Catalanotti's and Lai's signatures.

He flipped the page. The next one had the name Nico Dilicata at the top.

It turned out that on January 14 this Nico had borrowed fifteen hundred euros, then paid back sixteen hundred three months later, and barely twenty days later had requested another loan, this one for a thousand euros, which he hadn't yet repaid, however.

The next pages were all of the same nature.

When he closed the registers, he came to the conclusion that Catalanotti was a moneylender, a loan shark, but that while the interest rates he charged were indeed high, they weren't that high. A loan shark with a heart, one might say.

Montalbano opened the computer and immediately noticed that in the folder called "Loans and Sundry" were copies of the paper documents, all in perfect, precise order.

At this point he stood up and started looking at the books about the room. They were novels of some quality, as well as journals and other books, most of them to do with the theater.

In conclusion, Catalanotti's character seemed to consist of several different people: a cultured reader, a middleweight loan shark, and a fairly moneyed man who, for whatever reason, was quite interested in the personal and psychological makeup of others.

The latter was the most mysterious aspect.

He was stubbing out a cigarette he'd just smoked at the window when the doorbell rang. It was Fazio and Augello.

"We thought you'd already gone home to Marinella," said Mimì. "Signora Contarini, on the second floor, kept us for more than two hours, talking about her grandson, Ninuzzo, who can't get a job, and asking me to recommend him for work with the police."

"Aside from that, did you find anything out?"

"All the tenants in this building are exactly alike. Nobody knows anyone. Apparently they don't even have condominium meetings."

"Well, I'm done here, too," said Montalbano. Then, turning to Fazio: "Put the seals back up over the door."

As Fazio was doing this, Montalbano said softly to Mimì: "Don't forget what you have to do tonight."

Mimì nodded in assent.

They descended the stairs. Ammazzalorso wasn't there anymore. Apparently eight o'clock had come and gone. Montalbano got in his car and headed home.

When faced with the marvelous platter of fried shrimp and calamari that Adelina had made for him, he had a moment of hesitation.

His eye drifted over to a piece of paper hanging on the refrigerator.

Just one week before, when Livia had last come and stayed with him, she'd left him a note with a few words, though enough that to him they sounded like a death sentence.

The note said, precisely:

> *Remember* [written in red felt pen] *that your metabolism has decidedly changed* ["decidedly," too, was in red and underlined twice].
>
> *You don't need many calories to reach your daily requirement.*
>
> *NOT ALLOWED:*
>
> *Carbohydrates (bread, pasta . . .)*

Sweets (especially cannoli and cassata)

Fried foods (especially sarde a beccafico, *whitebait fritters, and baby octopus (the kind you like so much)).*

Alcohol: not more than one glass of red wine per day.

Then there was a drawing of a death's-head and, underneath it, also in red felt pen:

NO MORE WHISKY EVER

Adelina had asked him to explain this message. And he'd replied with a shrug.

The aroma rising from the frying pan got the better of him.

He went out to set the table on the veranda and started eating straight out of the pan.

When he'd finished, he refilled the glass of wine he'd had during the meal and downed it in a single gulp.

At that moment the phone rang. It was Livia.

"I've just finished eating dinner," she said. "Have you eaten yet?"

"Boiled shrimp with a smidge of olive oil and a splash of lemon. Whole wheat bread, and half a glass of wine. I'm following your rules, as you can see."

"Great! Just keep it up. I mean it. I wanted to tell you that I'll probably be able to come down in a couple of days."

"That would be wonderful, but I have a new murder on my hands since this morning, and the whole thing's looking a little complicated . . ."

Livia cut in.

"That's all right. We can try again next week. I might even take an extra day."

They chatted awhile longer about everything and nothing, then said good night. Ever so slowly, Montalbano made his way over to the television set and sat down in the armchair.

Nicolò Zito, the chief newsman at the Free Channel, was reporting the news of Catalanotti's murder, describing the victim as a well-off man who, most important, had never had any run-ins with the law. The inspector changed the channel to a variety show.

It immediately sparked his interest. The lead dancer was a perfect copy of Antonia . . . who was certainly a fine-looking woman, but, Jesus, was she ever unpleasant! Certainly not very approachable . . .

Why, Montalbano asked himself, *do you by any chance want to approach her?*

The answer came at once, from the heart:

Sure, why not?

He didn't allow himself any further questions.

Turning off the TV to avoid seeing any more of the lead dancer, he went and smoked one last cigarette on the veranda, then decided it was time for bed.

It was late at night. The street was rather broad, and the car advanced silently and ever so slowly, drifting past the other cars parked along the sidewalk. It seemed not to be rolling on wheels but sliding on butter.

All at once the car took off, lurched over to the left side, swerved, and parked in an instant.

The driver's-side door opened and a man got out, carefully closing the door behind him.

It was Mimì Augello.

He pulled the collar of his jacket up to his nose, tucked his head down between his shoulders, took a quick look around, and then, in three short hops, crossed the road and found himself on the opposite sidewalk.

Keeping his head bowed, he took a few steps straight ahead, stopped in front of a door, reached out with one hand, and, without even looking at the names listed, rang one of the buzzers.

The answer came at once:

"Is that you?"

"Yes."

The latch-lock clicked. Mimì pushed the door open, went inside, closed the door behind him in the twinkling of an eye, then started climbing the stairs on tiptoe. He'd decided that he would make less noise on foot than by taking the elevator.

Reaching the fourth floor, he saw a shaft of light filtering out from a door ajar. Approaching it, he pushed it open and went in. The woman, who'd apparently been waiting for him in the entrance hall, grabbed him with her left hand while, with her right, she closed and locked the door with four turns of the key in the top lock and two more in the bottom lock, before tossing the key set onto a small table. Mimì made as if to embrace the woman, but she stepped back, took him by the hand, and said in a soft voice: "Let's go in the other room."

Mimì obeyed.

Now they were in the bedroom, and the woman embraced Mimì and pressed her lips against his. Mimì held her tight, returning her passionate kiss.

"I'm sorry," said Mimì, "but there's something else I still have to do."

"Something else?" she asked teasingly.

In the meantime Mimì had got up and was quickly getting dressed.

"I have to find my wallet, which I think I lost during my escape last night."

"But I haven't found anything here."

"That's just it. I fear it may have fallen out in the apartment downstairs."

"So what are you going to do now?"

Mimì hopped athletically towards the French door giving onto the balcony and opened it.

"Not to worry! This shouldn't take more than ten minutes."

Pulling a small flashlight out of his pocket, he leaned out over the railing, lit the torch, and, hamming it up, carefully examined the balcony below.

"I don't see it down there. I'm gonna have to climb down," he said, vanishing from the woman's sight.

As soon as he found himself on the third-floor balcony, he noticed that the French door was still ajar.

The idea of having to deal with that corpse again made him grimace, but he steeled himself and opened the door all the way.

Remembering perfectly well the spot where he'd bumped into the chair the last time, he felt around with his hands but encountered no obstacle. Clearly someone had put the chair back in its place. He turned the flashlight on, at a low setting, and left the room without looking at the bed. At a glance the apartment seemed an exact copy of the one above.

Advancing on tiptoe, he had a look around: another bedroom, a study, a room with a collection of seashells, two bathrooms, and a kitchen. There wasn't a living soul about. He went back into the bedroom and aimed the beam of his torch at the bed.

The flashlight fell out of his hand. But Mimì was in no condition to pick it up.

What he'd seen had turned him into a statue of wax.

Or, rather, what he hadn't seen.

Wasting no time, he grabbed the flashlight, headed for the door, opened it, closed it behind him, descended the stairs, opened the main door, ran to his car, ducked inside, and shot off like a rocket in the direction of Marinella.

From the depths of sleep's ocean Montalbano rose with effort to the surface, having heard a bothersome sound, which continued to bother him immensely.

He was trying to unstick his eyelids when he realized he was hearing the telephone ring.

Feeling around, he turned on the light and looked at the clock.

A little past two.

He got up, crashed into the chair at the foot of the bed, crashed into the doorjamb of the bedroom, crashed into the doorjamb of the dining room, crashed into another chair, crashed into the coffee table, and finally, still feeling around, found the telephone and picked up the receiver.

"Clo," he said.

"Open up, Salvo, open the door! It's me, Mimì! Open the door!"

What could have happened to him?

Before opening the door, the inspector went into the kitchen, put his head in the sink, turned on the faucet, then set about making himself some coffee when a large boom made him jump into the air.

A bomb! he thought.

He ran into the hallway and opened the door.

Mimì had braked too late, and the nose of his car had crashed into the door like a ram's head.

"Back up or you won't be able to come in," the inspector said to him.

But Mimì didn't even hear him. He got out of the car, jumped over the hood, and after another jump found himself inside the house, shoving Montalbano aside with one hand and dashing into the dining room. As the inspector was going back into the kitchen, he noticed Mimì guzzling whisky straight out of the bottle. When the coffee was ready, Montalbano poured it into his customary mug, and at that moment Mimì came in and collapsed into a chair.

5

"And so?" Montalbano asked, sitting down in front of him with his steaming mug of espresso.

Augello gestured with his hand to tell him to wait a minute. He had to catch his breath.

The inspector started sipping his coffee, then, seeing that Mimì still remained silent, repeated loudly: "And so?"

Mimì stammered a few words in reply.

Montalbano didn't understand a thing. "Would you like to try speaking a little more clearly, please?"

"There . . . there . . . there wasn't anyone there," Mimì stuttered.

"What? You mean Genoveffa didn't show up?"

"No, not Genoveffa! Geneviève is still waiting for me with open arms . . ."

"And so?"

"And so *he* wasn't there."

"He who?"

"Salvo, our cadaver was gone from the bed."

"So where was he?"

"He wasn't anywhere, for Christ's sake! He's disappeared!"

"Somebody took him away?"

"Of course! It's not like he could have walked away on his own two feet!"

Montalbano ran a hand over his forehead.

"Wait a second. Wait just one second. Are you sure he was dead when you first saw him?"

"I touched him! He was stiff as a board! What, don't you remember I stained my shirt with his blood?"

"But did you look in the other rooms?"

"I looked, I looked! There was nothing, Salvo! Our cadaver is no longer there."

"So, in short, and in conclusion, this cadaver—which I would like to remind you is yours and yours alone—was parked for a while on that bed, then somebody came to get him and took him away, God only knows where. But this does solve one problem for us."

"Which?"

"It's no longer up to us to discover the corpse. It's sure to turn up somewhere else, whereupon we will be duly notified."

"So all we have to do is wait?"

"Yes, and while waiting, I bid you good-bye. I'm going back to bed. Don't forget to get the nose of your car out of my front door."

He got up and went out of the room, leaving Mimì sitting there with his head in his hands.

When he got to the station house, he was immediately, and literally, assailed by Catarella.

"Ahh, Chief, Chief! 'Ere'd happen a be a jinnelman 'at wants a talk t'yiz poissonally in poisson an' 'is name is Rosario Rosario."

"Is he on the line?"

"Nossir, 'e's onna premisses."

"Okay, send him in to me in five minutes, and send me Fazio as well."

"I'm incapacitated to sen' 'im t'yiz in so much as 'e aint onna premisses, 'cuz 'e 'adda bistake hisself to Montelusa haspitol."

Montalbano got worried.

"Why, did something happen to him?"

"Nat to hisself poissonally in possion, Chief, but 'iss mornin' when 'ey shot—"

"Who shot? Why am I only hearing about this now?"

"Chief, ya got no ideer 'ow many times I tried a call yiz at home on yer lann line. It jess rang an' rang, but nobody answered. An' yer sill phone was toined off . . ."

Only then did Montalbano remember that while he was sleeping in a cataleptic state he thought he'd heard a concert of bells.

"Okay, go on. Who'd they shoot?"

"They shat a dilicate kid, an' so Fazio went to the haspitol to go an' see this dilicate kid."

"Did you see him, too?"

"Did I see who?"

"Well, if you're telling me this kid was delicate, it must mean you saw him, no?"

"Nah, Chief, I din't see 'im. 'Is family's dilicate."

"What the hell are you saying, Cat?" Montalbano said in despair, turning away and heading for his office.

As he sat down, he heard a light knock at the door and then a voice.

"May I come in?"

"Yes, come in."

In the doorway appeared a man of about forty, thin as

a rail, with black hair combed straight back and a mustache that looked like a pair of rats' tails.

He was visibly upset.

"Good morning. My name is Rosario Lo Savio. I'm an engineer."

Montalbano stood up, they shook hands, and the engineer sat down in front of the desk.

"What can I do for you?"

"I heard yesterday that Carmelo Catalanotti died. He was a friend of mine."

At this point the man's voice broke. Two tears rolled down his face, and he pulled a handkerchief out of his pocket and wiped them away.

"I'm sorry. I came here because I think I was the last person to see him alive."

Montalbano corrected him.

"The last person to see him alive was surely his killer, don't you think?"

"Yes, of course. So I was the next to last," the man said.

"Tell me your story."

Before answering, Lo Savio took a deep breath.

"I'm a member of Trinacriarte, the most important amateur theater company in our province, and Carmelo was, too. The day before yesterday we ended our rehearsal around midnight, and when I got in my car, it wouldn't start. So Carmelo kindly offered to give me a lift and drove me home."

"How was he, do you remember? Was he upset, or any different from his usual self?"

"No, he was perfectly normal and calm."

"Did you have any impression he might have had an appointment?"

"I don't think so. He wasn't in any hurry, and I remember that when we reached my place, we even lingered awhile, talking about the play we're planning to put on. I mean, that we *were* planning to put on."

Another pair of tears.

"Tell me something about your theater company. Where do you work? How many—"

"Trinacriarte," said Lo Savio, interrupting him and puffing up his chest with pride, "was founded in 1857 by the now unfortunately forgotten Vigatese playwright Emmanuele Gaudioso, then disbanded for three years after the unification of Italy, because of—"

As the prospect of having to listen to more than a hundred years of the company's history didn't exactly appeal to Montalbano, he couldn't restrain himself.

"I'm sorry," he said, interrupting him, "this is all very interesting, but please come to the present day. Actually, let me ask the questions."

"All right."

"How many people are there in your company?"

"Well, we have eighteen members, ten men and eight women."

"Is there a director or manager?"

"We have a directorate with three members, one of whom was poor Catalanotti."

"And who are the other two?"

"One is Elena Saponaro, a bank manager, and the other is Antonio Scimè, a lawyer."

At this point Lo Savio made a sort of grimace. He was about to say something but held back. Montalbano didn't let the opportunity slip by.

"Tell me about this Scimè," he said.

"No, actually, he's a fine fellow, but also a pain in the neck."

"How?"

"When he was young, he attended the National Academy of Dramatic Arts and got a degree in acting. Apparently—though we've never had any direct confirmation of this—he had his debut in a play starring Vittorio Gassman and never really got over it. Every five minutes he finds ways to remind us, and himself, of his Roman days living *la dolce vita*."

"Aside from being part of the directorate, what else did Catalanotti do? Did he act? Did he direct the plays?"

"Aside from being Trinacriarte's primary subsidizer, he was also an excellent character actor and a very serious stage director, always extremely well prepared and having his own particular idea of the theater."

"Tell me about that."

"For him, the theater was the written text. Everything had to arise from the text. Even the costumes, the sets, the lights, they all had to come from the written drama. And his work with the actors was the foundation."

"Meaning?"

"It's a bit complicated to explain, but I'll try. Carmelo wanted for every actor, in interpreting his or her role, to start from something deeply personal in his or her own life. Some trauma or moment in one's life, say, a love gone wrong, some private, profound, intimate experience that could be used to serve what the text requires."

"Let me get this straight. So, if there's a widow in the play, he wanted a real widow to play her?"

"No, Inspector. He wasn't so literal as that. He would start to dig into the actor's intimate life, in search, for example, of the equivalent of a feeling of absence similar to what a widow might feel, and he was very good at it, very skilled. He was able to knock down the defenses of the person he was dealing with until he could draw out something similar to the feeling he was seeking: a recent death, a divorce, or sometimes something as simple as moving into a new house—a traumatic experience, in short, that had something to do with what was needed—in this case, something to do with loss, with the void that one feels in those situations."

"I see. So he was sort of a cross between a psychoanalyst and a confessor."

"No, I would call him instead a sort of corrected Stanislavsky, revised and updated."

"I'm sorry, but did all the actors consent to being subjected to this sort of psychological investigation?"

"No, not all of them. A few rebelled, and so Carmelo didn't pick them for the part."

"Did these sessions take place in front of the whole troupe?"

"No, only afterwards. First there was a long preparatory phase that Carmelo always wanted to do tête-à-tête."

No other specific questions to ask came into Montalbano's mind other than the usual bureaucratic ones, to which Lo Savio was unable to give any answers, since Catalanotti apparently never confided in anyone. He still didn't know, therefore, whether the man had any enemies, or women with grudges, or treacherous family relations.

As he was saying good-bye to him, extending his hand across the desk, Montalbano asked Lo Savio: "What are you rehearsing at the moment?"

"Shakespeare's *The Tempest*."

"And was Catalanotti part of it?"

"No, he was preparing another mise-en-scène. But he didn't miss a single rehearsal."

"What play did he want to put on?"

"A play by a modern British playwright. But I'm not familiar with it."

There was a pause, then Montalbano asked: "I'd like to see a few of these rehearsals. Where are you based?"

"One of the actors has made a former timber warehouse available to us. It's at number 15, Via Lombardo."

As he was writing this down on a scrap of paper, Montalbano asked: "Do I need to call ahead?"

"Don't worry about it. We're there every Monday, Wednesday, and Friday, from 9:30 p.m. until late."

When Lo Savio left, Montalbano started thinking about something the man had just said, that is, that the troupe got together on every other day of the workweek.

He picked up the telephone.

"Cat, I want you to call Bruno Ammazzalorso at Via La Marmora for me."

He could tell that Catarella was completely flummoxed.

"Cat! You still there?"

"Yeah, Chief."

"Everything okay?"

"I dunno 'ow to do it."

"To do what?"

"To call a Mazzalorsamamamora."

Montalbano felt lost. He took a breath and tried a different approach.

"Find me the phone number for the doorman of the building where the murder happened."

"Ah, okay, okay, Chief. Iss a lot easier 'at way."

Indeed, five minutes later he had the number.

"Signor Ammazzalorso? Inspector Montalbano here."

"What can I do for you, Inspector?"

"I need some clarification. You told me Signor Catalanotti went out every evening. Is that right?"

"Yessir, that's right. Every evening."

"You mean every single evening?"

"As far as I know, sir, every single evening."

He thanked him and hung up. The question arose by itself: So where did Catalanotti go on the evenings he didn't devote to the theater?

At that moment Fazio came back.

"Tell me everything," said the inspector.

"The kid who was shot in the leg is named Nico Dilicata. He's twenty-eight years old, got a degree in literature but is presently unemployed like almost half the kids around here. He's made all kinds of job requests, entered competitions, taken training courses, but so far nothing. And so every morning he goes out looking for any kind of job he can find."

Montalbano remembered the news item about unemployment he'd read in the paper that had flown in his face the day before on the beach.

"So," he said, "in short, a good kid who had the misfortune to be born here!"

"An excellent kid, and from a good family. They're all there at the hospital at his bedside, but nobody has any idea why anyone would want to shoot him."

"But how did it happen?"

"This morning, right as he was coming out of his house on his way to the port, somebody shot him in the left leg."

"Were there any witnesses?"

"No, around here you can never find witnesses for love or money. The best part is that Nico maintains he never heard the sound of the gunshot. He says it must have been an accident, that he was in the wrong place at the wrong time."

"And do you believe him?"

Fazio grimaced.

"Chief, I could be wrong, but, at first guess, my gut feeling is that it doesn't really make sense."

"Meaning?"

"Meaning that it seemed to me that this Nico Dilicata was singing only half the Mass to me."

"Wha'd you say his name was?"

"Domenico Dilicata, known to friends and family as Nico. Why do you ask?"

"I'm under the impression I've heard that name before."

"That may be, but this kid's never had any run-ins with the police."

"Well, okay, I'll see about that. But now I want you to listen to a nice little story."

"I'm all ears."

"You remember Augello's cadaver?"

"Hell, yes! Which we need to discover."

"Good. Now the situation's become even more complicated."

"How so?"

"The cadaver can no longer be located."

As Fazio's chin dropped down to his chest, he simultaneously almost fell out of his chair.

Having trouble speaking, he finally managed to ask: "What does that mean?"

"It means that when Mimì Augello went back into the apartment on Via Biancamano, his cadaver was gone."

"So somebody removed it. That means there's somebody who has the keys to that apartment."

"Elementary, my dear Watson!" said Montalbano. And he continued: "Try to find out as much as you can about this Nico, but also you absolutely have to call the guy from the agency and find out if there's a copy of the keys to Augello's cadaver's apartment floating around."

"I'll call him straightaway," said Fazio, running out of the room.

One minute later Mimì Augello came in, wearing a face fit for the Day of the Dead.

"Greetings!" said the inspector, looking at his watch. "Do you know what time it is?"

Mimì got the message.

"The fact is, I didn't get any sleep last night."

"So the thought of your vanished cadaver wouldn't let you sleep?"

"Not at all! I just couldn't leave things unfinished like that. Just think, Geneviève waited out on her balcony for two hours, getting more and more desperate, wondering what had happened to me. I had to go back and comfort her, at the very least."

"And did you happen, at the very least, to tell her about your cadaver?"

"Come on, Salvo. No, I didn't tell her. I only said that when I went into that apartment I sensed that something was amiss, and so I carefully inspected the place, and then went to the police station to do some research. At that point Geneviève confirmed that there wasn't anyone living in the apartment, but that, come to think of it, she had in fact heard strange noises there, some stirring about and muffled voices . . ."

"And so?"

"And so nothing, Salvo. That was all she could tell me. But then I went back to comforting her."

Fazio came in, looking crestfallen.

"The woman at the real estate agency couldn't tell me anything," he said.

"Why don't you try calling the apartment's owner again?"

"Already done. Aurisicchio assured me that nobody has any copies of the keys. Other than the head of the agency, of course."

Seeing, then, that they were unable to reach any sort of conclusion whatsoever, the inspector decided that the only solution was to go and eat lunch.

As he got in the car, for whatever reason he no longer felt like going to Enzo's. And so he headed for a restaurant called Catarinetta, about which he'd heard some good things and which was halfway between Vigàta and Montaperto.

He'd barely gone three miles when he saw the first sign, which told him to turn right onto an unpaved road.

He drove for another half an hour or so, turning first left, then right, in keeping with the signs, and ended up in the open countryside. All around him were vineyards, and in the distance, as far as the eye could see, were almond groves with a few peasant houses sprouting here and there among them. It was an enchanting landscape that soothed the heart and soul. And yet a dark thought entered the inspector's mind. Who knew how many mafiosi on the lam were hiding out in houses just like those, so innocent in appearance? He remembered how, so many years before, a little boy named Giuseppe Di Matteo had been kidnapped and hidden in just such a house before meeting an atrocious end, the kind of fate that made one ashamed to be a human being. But he didn't want to think about that. He pulled up outside the restaurant, got out of the car, and went inside.

The place consisted of a small entrance area that gave onto a large room with twenty or so tables, all of them full. Discouraged, he watched the people eating their fill, talking loudly and laughing, and turned his back to leave when a waiter came up to him.

"Were you looking for someone, or did you want to eat?"

"I wanted to eat, but . . ."

"If you're patient enough to wait half an hour . . ."

Montalbano was about to say no when the bathroom door, which was right next to the entrance, opened and he saw, from behind, a woman come out. He stood there speechless for a moment, just looking at her, because he recognized that body from somewhere . . . Then suddenly he realized it was Antonia, the new chief of Forensics. For a moment he couldn't breathe. Meanwhile she, not having seen him, headed for a table. Following her with his eyes, Montalbano noticed she was alone.

His feet, of their own accord, took him in her direction. Raising her eyes, she looked at him, and Montalbano was convinced she was not happy to see him.

"Hello."

"Hello," Antonia said drily.

"Were you waiting for someone?"

"No. Why do you ask?"

Montalbano stammered.

"Well . . . it's just that . . . the place is full . . . there aren't any empty tables . . . If you would allow me . . . I'm pretty hungry."

Antonia said nothing and simply gestured towards the chair opposite hers.

Montalbano sat down and looked at the menu on the table.

"Have you ordered?"

"Not yet."

"Did you already know this place?"

"Yes."

"Is the food good?"

"It's decent enough."

A silence as heavy as a boulder descended on them.

Montalbano ran through a hundred different subjects in his head at lightning speed but didn't find a single one that seemed fitting, so he just grabbed the menu and started looking at it. At first glance he became certain there wasn't so much as a single scale of fish in that restaurant.

"What are you going to have?" he asked Antonia.

"Pasta with ricotta. It's very good here. How about you?"

Montalbano remained silent for some thirty seconds or so, then made up his mind.

"Me, too."

They sat there in silence until the waiter came round to take their orders.

For her second course Antonia ordered lamb chops with potatoes, and Montalbano, naturally, did likewise.

In the silence that followed, Montalbano wondered why he felt so awkward in front of the young woman.

Was it that very unsociable reserve of hers which made him feel so ill at ease, or did his unease stem instead from the fact that Antonia had the same effect on him as a magnet?

6

His gaze fell on her beautiful hands. She wore no rings.

He never knew from what depths came the question his lips fired at her across the barrier of silence separating them.

"Are you single?"

The woman's irritation was clearly visible, etched across her face.

"Why do you ask?"

Montalbano sank back into the depths, which this time provided no answer to her question.

The barrier of silence turned into an iron curtain.

A few moments passed before he was able to say: "I'm sorry, I didn't mean to pry . . ."

This time she was the one to speak.

"I've been living alone for the past ten years. That doesn't mean I don't feel attracted to men, but I still haven't met one I've liked enough to want to have around every day. How about you?"

The inspector hadn't anticipated her rejoinder.

"I live alone, but . . . but . . . I'm not single."

He was expecting Antonia to ask him to explain, but the girl remained silent. And so he concluded that for her, there was nothing more to discuss on the matter.

The inspector, however, didn't feel like dropping the subject and was about to open his mouth when he was overwhelmed by a loud yell from the table to the left of them.

Sitting next to a tiny, frail woman was a fat, sweaty man waving his ring-studded fingers as he vented his anger on a waiter standing stiffly in front of him.

"What? I come all the way from Fela, driving miles and miles because of all the good things I've been hearing about this goddamn restaurant and their *pasta con quadumi*, and now you tell me that the goddamn European Union says you're not allowed to make it anymore?"

"Yessir, that's right, but what can I say? These aren't our rules; they're dictated to us by others. We can't do anything about it . . ."

The fat man got up, grabbed the frail little woman, and dragged her out of the restaurant, cursing.

"What's this *quadumi*, anyway?" asked Antonia, as the waiter was setting down a dish of cavatelli with ricotta in front of her.

"*Quadumi* are cow innards. In Sicily we cook them many different ways."

Antonia grimaced in disgust. They started eating without continuing the conversation. Then, violating his own rule about not talking while eating, Montalbano asked: "What did you find in Catalanotti's car?"

"Nothing of any importance. There weren't any significant biological traces. We can say for certain that he wasn't killed or transported anywhere in that car after his death."

Rather than listen to what she was saying, Montalbano was spellbound by her movements. In her every gesture there was a grace, a lightness, and . . . what else? . . . yes! a harmony.

That was the right word. It was as if her rapport not only with her own body but also with the space around her—not just the small immediate space in which she found herself, but a vast, limitless space—were perfectly synchronized. The woman seemed, in short, to be in harmony with the world itself.

A question came spontaneously to his lips.

"But how do you spend your evenings, Antonia? Do you go out? Go to the movies? Watch TV?"

"I hardly ever go to the movies. I'd rather read."

This piqued Montalbano's curiosity.

"I really like to read, too. Who are some of your favorite authors?"

"There are so many. At the moment I'm reading a story by a Sicilian author I really like, whose name is Giosuè Calaciura. Do you know him?"

Montalbano didn't know the writer, but he knew all about his publisher, a lady who had set up a publishing house in Palermo that put out the loveliest books, which were a real pleasure to look at and to read.

And so, talking about books, they discovered they had many things in common. Maybe even too many.

The first one to realize this was Antonia. And she immediately pulled back.

"But now I have to go. Your treat?"

Without waiting for an answer, she got up, shook his hand, and went out. Montalbano didn't take his eyes off her until she was out the door.

As he was driving back to Vigàta, for no apparent reason the name Nico Dilicata resurfaced in his memory and he remembered where he'd seen it.

He had to check it out at once, and so, instead of heading for the station, some twenty minutes later he was pulling up outside Catalanotti's place. The front door was closed. He took out the keys he had in his pocket, found the right one, then went to the third floor, removed the seals from the apartment door, unlocked it, and went in.

Once inside the apartment, he shot into the study, sat down, opened the right-hand drawer, and took out the register of loans. He'd remembered correctly: on the second page appeared the name of Nico Dilicata.

He continued examining the notebook carefully.

In the end he discovered that, aside from Nico, two other people had failed to return the borrowed money with interest: Luigi Sciacchitano, who had owed three thousand euros, and Saveria di Donato, who'd borrowed twenty thousand. He turned on the computer and got further confirmation that everything in it had been duly noted and put in order in Catalanotti's registers.

He jotted the two names down on a scrap of paper and went out.

This time the front door of the building was open. Ammazzalorso was at his post and seemed surprised to see the inspector there.

"'Scuse me for asking, Inspector, but in the movies I always see the police spending hours and hours looking into every little nook and cranny in the house. How come the cops here come and go after just a few minutes?"

"We use different methods in our neck of the woods," the inspector said with assurance.

Whatever those might be, he thought as he was saying it. But, in any case, the honor of the Sicilian police was safe.

By the time he got back to the station it was half past five. He sent immediately for Fazio, and then handed him the scrap of paper when he showed up.

"Try to find out as much as you can about those two people."

"Why? Who are they?"

"They're two of the people Catalanotti lent money to who were unable to pay it back."

"Are you thinking Catalanotti was maybe killed by someone who couldn't pay?"

"Why, my dear Fazio, do you somehow think that never happens? And while we're on the subject, I can tell you that Nico, too, is in the same situation."

"And who's Nico?"

"He's the kid who was shot in the leg."

"I'm sorry, Chief, but are you saying that Nico Dilicata could be a murderer who, after committing his crime, was shot in revenge by some accomplice of Catalanotti's?"

"I don't know, Fazio. But in any case I want to talk to the kid. Think they'll let me into the hospital at this hour?"

"Why not, Chief? The bullet only grazed him. It's nothing serious."

"Let's go."

"There's a problem," Fazio said once they were in Montalbano's car, heading to Montelusa.

"And what would that be?"

"Nico's in a big room with eight other beds, all occupied. How are we going to talk to him without the others hearing?"

"We can ask the doctors to give us a private room, and you can bring him in."

"Okay."

Half an hour later Nico Dilicata was sitting in a wheelchair in front of the inspector. The head nurse had given them a tiny room full of hospital supplies and smelling so badly of medications that it nearly gave the inspector a heart attack. Nico was brought in by a nice-looking blond girl, who, before leaving, bent down and kissed him on the forehead.

"That's Margherita, my girlfriend," Nico explained after she left.

Montalbano introduced himself and immediately asked: "How are you feeling?"

"Well, I'm on painkillers at the moment, so I'm feeling better."

"Can you tell me in some detail what happened?"

"There isn't much to tell. I already told Signor Fazio everything."

"And I'm asking you to repeat it to me."

"Very early this morning, probably around six-thirty, I was on my way out the door to go to the port . . . I sometimes get work unloading crates of fish to earn a little money—"

"Excuse me for interrupting," said the inspector, "do you always go out of the house at that hour of the morning?"

"Most of the time."

"Go on."

"As I was closing the door, with my back to the street, I felt a really sharp pain in my leg. I couldn't stand anymore and so I slid down on one knee, bracing myself against the door. When I turned around, the street was deserted. And that's about all I can say."

"Who came to your aid?"

"After some time I managed to struggle to my feet by leaning against the wall, and I rang the buzzer. Margherita came right down with Filippo, and they drove me to the hospital."

"I'm sorry, but I don't quite understand. Do Margherita and Filippo live with you?"

"Yes. When my parents moved to Catania, they left me their apartment. And so, just to earn a little money and to cover expenses, I rented a room to my friend Filippo, who's lucky enough to have a job."

"I see. Do you have any idea who it might have been?"

"No idea. No idea whatsoever."

"Not even a hunch? Someone who might have something against you?"

"Certainly not to the point of shooting me."

Montalbano decided to throw down his ace.

"Do you know a certain Carmelo Catalanotti?"

"Yes. Why?"

"He was murdered in his own apartment."

Nico turned pale.

"No . . . I didn't know . . ." he stammered. "When?"

"We found him yesterday morning."

"I'm so sorry. He was a good person. I mean . . ." and he trailed off.

"Go on," said Montalbano, prodding him.

Nico then said something the inspector would never have expected.

"I owed him some money. So what am I supposed to do now?"

"But was it a friendly debt, or was it—"

"We weren't friends. He'd lent me some money at interest, but it wasn't too high. He wasn't a loan shark, and I wouldn't call him a usurer, either."

"It's against the law, just the same."

"Inspector, I'm sorry, but nowadays it's really hard to say what's against the law or within the law. Every day we read in the papers that the very people who are supposed to enforce the law are under investigation—"

Montalbano cut him off sharply.

"Sorry to say, but I myself don't have any doubts. I know what's legal and what's not. And unauthorized lending is illegal."

The youth said nothing. His admission of his debt might simply have been a very shrewd move, but it was also naïve. And so the inspector decided to continue the questioning, but then he didn't have the time, because the door opened and Margherita came in, followed by a male nurse, who said: "I have to take the patient back to the ward."

Nico was whisked away in a flash.

Margherita was about to follow behind him when Montalbano stopped her.

"Could you stay a little longer?"

"Sure," said the girl.

Nico's voice then called from the hallway.

"But come soon, Margherì."

"Please have a seat," said the inspector.

Margherita sat down.

"What is your name?"

"Margherita Lo Bello."

"Are you from around here?"

"I was born in Messina, but my family moved to Vigàta when I was three."

"Have you known Nico for a long time?"

The girl looked at him.

"May I ask why you want to know?"

"Quite simply because I didn't have the time to ask him, so now I'm asking you. How long have you been together?"

"Two years," she said.

"And for how long have you been living together?"

"For three days."

"Why so short a time?"

The girl smiled bitterly.

"I had a nasty quarrel with my dad. He practically threw me out of the house."

"Mind telling me the reason for the quarrel?"

"I'd rather not."

"Do you have a job?"

"I have a math degree. I tutor kids to get by. I'm hoping to find some steadier work soon. Nico and I are doing everything we can to try to make our lives better . . ."

"Do you plan on getting married?" asked Montalbano.

"I'm not terribly optimistic, Inspector. The way it's been going for us, with me and my tutorials and Nico unloading crates at the port, how could we possibly support a family . . . ?"

"I'm sorry, but isn't living together practically the same as being married?"

"Inspector, I was forced to go and live with Nico. If it had been up to me, I would have waited until we got married."

Montalbano found this girl from another age very much to his liking.

"Tell me about the shooting."

"I was going out to the balcony to wave good-bye, but just as I was opening the window, the intercom buzzed. It was Nico calling for help. I screamed, waking Filippo up, and then I went downstairs."

She stopped for a moment and looked at the inspector.

"Do you know who Filippo is?"

"Yes."

"When Filippo came down to the entrance, I told him to go and get his car, and then we drove Nico here to the hospital."

"So you didn't hear any shot, either?"

"No."

"And you didn't see anyone?"

"No, nobody."

"Do you have any idea who it might have been?"

Margherita hesitated ever so slightly, but they both noticed.

"No. No idea at all."

"Okay, you can go now. Thanks," said Montalbano.

As they were walking down the hospital corridor, Montalbano said to Fazio: "Are you in agreement that Margherita only sang us half the Mass?"

"Yeah," said Fazio.

"Then I want to know everything there is to know about this Lo Bello family. Try also to find out what the spat between the father and his daughter was about. I'm going home now."

Not that he was really so hungry, since he still had that strange hospital smell on him. The first thing he wanted to do was to take a shower.

When he was done, his appetite returned with a vengeance. It was past nine o'clock.

He had a thought. Maybe they were organizing some kind of commemoration for the late Catalanotti at Trinacriarte that evening. Why not pay them a visit?

As soon as he got into his car, his entire backlog of fatigue came crashing down on him, burying him under its weight. He immediately felt like going back inside and getting into bed, but his sense of duty won out.

He turned on the ignition and drove off.

Only after ten minutes behind the wheel did he realize he hadn't the slightest idea where Via Lombardo was located. He felt completely muddled from lack of sleep.

Then he saw a sign announcing the forthcoming opening of a shopping center right on Via Lombardo. Under the sign was an arrow pointing straight ahead. He followed it. A hundred yards later, there was another arrow telling him to turn right. He did. In this way, going from arrow to arrow, he found himself outside of town, on the road to Montereale. And there, on the left, was a sign for Via Lombardo. All that was visible of the much-announced shopping center was a sort of skeleton of concrete. At that rate, the forthcoming opening wouldn't be for at least another two or three years.

At number 15 was a warehouse with a steel-reinforced door. He pulled up and got out of the car.

By the glow of the headlights—since it was pitch-dark all around—he noticed that beside the door were a doorbell and a plate that said TRINACRIARTE.

He rang. There was no answer.

He waited a moment before ringing again. The warehouse was big, and it might take them awhile to come to the door.

Two or three minutes later, he tried again. And, once again, there was no answer.

He became convinced there was no one inside the warehouse, and that they'd probably canceled the rehearsal as a gesture of mourning.

He got back into his car, and as soon as he'd closed the door, he saw the door of the warehouse open. Getting out of the car, he was immediately accosted by the man who'd opened the door.

"Who are you? What do you want?"

"I'm Inspector Montalbano, police."

"Oh, I'm sorry. Please come in," said the man, stepping aside.

They went in. Montalbano found himself in a sort of reception area created from old, and probably fake, Chinese screens.

The man, about sixty, was completely bald and looked polished from head to toe. He held out his hand to the inspector.

"Hello, my name is Antonio Scimè. I'm a lawyer and also on the board of directors of Trinacriarte. What can I do for you?"

"I don't want to interrupt your rehearsal . . ." said Montalbano, feeling a bit awkward.

"Don't worry, that's not a problem. We're not working today, we're organizing a celebration for our friend, Carmelo."

"You mean the funeral?" asked Montalbano.

"No, there's not going to be one. Carmelo always made

it clear that he never wanted a religious funeral. If you'd like to come inside . . ."

"With pleasure," said the inspector, and as he was following the man, he remembered that he should phone Pasquano for the results of the autopsy.

Inside the warehouse, a parquet had been set up with some fifty or so chairs, with about ten people presently sitting in them. On a raised floor that served as a stage, there were two women and three men sitting behind a long table. Among the men, the inspector spotted Lo Savio, the engineer. Upon recognizing Montalbano, Lo Savio came rushing up to shake his hand, then invited him to come up on the stage with them and sit wherever he liked. The two women were introduced to him as Elena Saponaro, also on the board of directors, and Giovanna Zicari, lead actress. The other two men turned out to be Filiberto Vullo, lead actor, and Calogero Granturco, the troupe's administrator.

Naturally, as soon as Montalbano sat down in the last chair of the row with the others, silence descended on the gathering. Nobody knew where to start.

After a brief spell, Lo Savio stood up and began speaking.

"We are gathered here today to determine how we might best pay homage, with dignity, to our dear friend, who passed away so tragically."

The lead actress then interrupted him, also rising to her feet.

"I don't think there are any words, or any songs, or any hymns in the world that could measure up to the lofty merits of our friend, who was a truly great stage director, and a giant of a man, whose accomplishments I would like—"

"Enough of this farce!" a female voice yelled from the seats in the audience.

It was a young woman who'd been sitting in the parquet but was now standing. Montalbano recognized her at once. She was the Maria from the photo in Catalanotti's folder.

"Why do you call it a farce?" Scimè asked, challenging her.

"Because," the girl replied, getting more and more upset, "you never appreciated Carmelo's true worth when he was alive, you always considered him too strange . . ."

"Because he was!" a tall beanpole of a man called out, also from the floor.

"That's enough of that!" Scimè cut them off. "We always gave him everything we could, but he was never satisfied!"

The girl resumed talking.

"The best way for you to commemorate him would be to remain silent," she said, then she turned around and left the room.

In the dead silence that followed, only Montalbano's voice could be heard, asking: "Excuse me, but who is she?"

Scimè once again provided the answer.

"Maria del Castello. She was hoping to work with Carmelo. And he probably would have picked her for the next play he was preparing."

"I'm sorry I interrupted your meeting," Montalbano resumed. "I really don't want to waste any of your time. I only came to get the names, addresses, and, if possible, the telephone numbers of everyone in your company."

The lead actress, clearly put out by all the interruptions, turned her chair three-quarters away from the audience. Lo Savio did the same. Scimè came to the rescue.

"If that's all you want, it's no problem. I can bring everyone's name to you personally tomorrow morning. I'll come to your office at police headquarters."

"All right, then," said Montalbano. "Thank you so much. Sorry again to disturb you. I'll let you get back to work now."

He shook everyone's hand and went out of the warehouse with Lo Savio leading the way.

He got in his car and began to drive off. In the beam of the headlights he recognized Maria at the side of the road.

She was walking fast, all hunched and enclosed within herself. Montalbano pulled up beside her.

7

"Need a lift?"

"No," she said without turning her head.

"I'm Inspector Montalbano."

The girl then turned and looked.

"Then all right," she said. "Thank you."

Montalbano opened the door and she got in.

"Tell me where you want me to take you."

She gave him an address. The inspector knew the street.

"So, you worked with Catalanotti?"

"I was hoping to, but . . ."

"Go on. I'm interested."

"Carmelo put me through the hardest tests, like he always did. I put up with it because I really liked the role and I wanted it for myself, but in the end he decided I wasn't up to the task, and so that was the end of that. But that doesn't prevent me from appreciating the guy's genius. Nobody in our company was on the same level as him. They're all just amateurs."

"So how did you react when you found out he didn't pick you?"

"I certainly can't say I was happy about it, but I decided I understood the reasons for it. Well, here we are," said Maria, cutting the conversation short and getting out of the car. "Thanks for the ride. Good night."

"Listen, could I ask you for your cell phone number, in case I need to talk to you?"

The girl told him the number, the inspector wrote it down, and they said good-bye.

Catalanotti had been right in what he'd written about Maria. She had an unpredictable personality. And at that moment Montalbano suddenly felt so sleepy he had to pull over. Seconds later he was asleep, head resting on his arms folded over the steering wheel.

It was at that hour of the morning, in the first faint, violet light, when the sky greets the earth, that street cleaner Totò Panzeca, sweeping here and sweeping there, ended up near a car stopped right at the bottom of the stone staircase of the Chiesa Madre, where it was strictly forbidden to park.

Totò took a look inside and saw that in the front seat lay a man curled up in the fetal position between the two doors. He couldn't see his face, because the man's left arm was folded over his head.

Totò tapped on the window, to wake the sleeping man.

He got no answer. The man did not move. Totò tried again, with no result. And so, feeling a little spooked, he shouted to his coworker Ninì Panaro, who was sweeping the street about ten yards away.

"Have a look in there," Totò said as soon as Ninì came up to him.

"So? What's the big deal? There's some guy sleeping."

"Then you try to wake him up!" Totò challenged him.

"All right," said Ninì. And, with the broom he'd carried along with him, he knocked loudly on the roof of the car.

The sleeping man did not move.

"Want to bet he's dead?" said Ninì, trying to force the car door open with both hands.

At this point, Totò, running quickly away, shouted: "Careful!"

"What's the matter with you?"

"The guy might be a terrorist with a time bomb!"

These words worked like a magic spell. In a flash both men turned as pale as corpses and embraced each other, trembling.

"What should we do?" asked Totò.

"Let's call the carabinieri."

Ten minutes later, Marshal Bonnici of the Royal Corps of Carabinieri came running, followed by a corporal-at-arms. Totò and Ninì immediately informed the officer of the situation.

Bonnici walked ever so slowly and carefully towards the car, keeping his head tucked down between his shoulders, as though expecting at any moment to be shot at. When he was two steps away from the car, he stopped and bent all the way forward to look inside. He, too, became convinced that the man in the car was dead.

He turned around and started walking back. When he reached the other three, he said: "It's clearly a trap. That corpse was put there to attract attention, and the moment anyone opens the car door, the car will explode. You stay here and keep people away. I'm going to call Montelusa at once and tell them to send the bomb squad."

As the marshal was speedily walking away, Father Stanzillà opened the great front door of the church for the six o'clock morning Mass, then came down the stairs to get a little fresh air.

"Get away from there!" shouted the carabinieri corporal. "Stand back! Stand back!"

The street cleaners added in tandem: "Run away! Run away! Run away!"

Father Stanzillà looked at them in shock.

"Why?"

"'Cause there's a bomb in that car."

In spite of their warnings, Father Stanzillà descended two more steps and, reaching the car, said: "But there's even a Christian soul inside!"

"He's dead! He's dead!" shouted everyone in chorus.

At this point Father Stanzillà got scared, turned around, ran back up the staircase, went into the church, and slammed the great door shut with a boom.

Then, as if on cue, a small truck full of fish stopped a short distance away from the car and a man inside the truck began to wake up the whole town with his amplified voice: "Come and see my fish dance! They're so fresh and alive they'll dance before your very eyes! Come and see the dancing fish!"

The corporal rushed over to the truck.

"Get away from here at once!"

"I'm completely legit," said the fishmonger, holding up a sheet of paper.

"Get away now! There's a bomb in that car!" the corporal shouted.

The little truck bounded forward as though onto the track at Indianapolis, and at the same time a powerful curse boomed over the loudspeaker, which the fishmonger had forgotten to turn off.

At that moment the car door opened and out came the man who everyone had thought was dead.

As the two street sweepers were running away in terror, the carabinieri corporal didn't hesitate for a second. He cocked his revolver and said: "Hands in the air!"

Montalbano, still half asleep, was under the impression he was still dreaming and instinctively held up his hands, thinking: *I'll wake up soon enough, I guess . . .*

The corporal, gun still trained on him, slowly approached, then, to his great surprise, recognized him.

"But . . . aren't you Inspector Montalbano?"

The inspector didn't even have time to say yes, when suddenly a man came running up behind him, shouting at the top of his lungs.

"*Matre santa! Matre santissima!* Wha' happen? Wha' happen? Why's the carabbineris pointin' 'eir gun a' my chief?"

It was Catarella, and he'd positioned himself in front of Montalbano, offering his body as a shield. Weighing his options, the corporal kept his gun pointed at them. Nobody moved. It looked like a freeze frame from a Tarantino movie.

At this point Marshal Bonnici came racing back.

"The bomb squad's on its w—" he started saying, then stopped, slack-jawed, at the sight of Montalbano.

When Montalbano finally got home, as he stepped out of the car he realized that having spent the night in so uncomfortable a position had made his legs as stiff as boards. He started cursing while unlocking the front door. Goddamn old age!

One way or another, he made his way into the dining room. Leaning with both hands against the table, he began doing a sort of gymnastic exercise, stretching first the right leg, then the left, a bit like a mule kicking out at someone.

After some ten minutes of this exercise, his legs began to feel a little less like boards. He took all his clothes off and got into the shower.

Then, beginning to enjoy himself, he got out, dripping wet, went into the kitchen, made himself a mug of coffee, and got back into the shower.

In short, it took more than an hour for his body to recover all its functions. But at this point another phenomenon occurred, owing certainly to his age: He felt sleepy again.

He grabbed the phone and rang Catarella.

"I've got stuff to do at home, Cat. Tell everybody I'll be coming in around eleven."

And then he went to bed.

As he was parking, he saw Scimè, the lawyer, come out of the station house. Montalbano got out of the car and called to him.

"Good morning, sir, I apologize for being late, but—"

"Yes, yes, I heard all about it," said the lawyer.

"I'm sorry, you heard all about *what*?" asked Montalbano, confused.

"About what happened to you this morning. Apparently you were mistaken for a terrorist! The whole town's been laughing about it."

Montalbano got pissed off and changed the subject.

"Did you bring the documents for me?"

"Yes. Unfortunately, I have to run to the courthouse in Montelusa now. I left them with the guard. You'll see the company's name on the folder: 'Trinacriarte.' At any rate, if you need any clarifications, you know where to find me."

They shook hands, and Montalbano went inside. Where he was instantly stopped by Catarella.

"Ahh, Chief, Chief! Ya feelin' better now? All recovered? Man, whatta scare I gat this mornin'! Man, whatta scare!"

Montalbano really didn't feel like hearing Catarella's blather, so he cut things short: "Gimme the documents that Scimè the lawyer left with you."

Catarella bent down and handed him a folder.

Montalbano took it and started walking towards his office. Halfway there, he crossed paths with Cumella, a beat cop, who looked at him and giggled. The withering glance the inspector shot at him quickly wiped the smile off his face.

As soon as he entered his office, Montalbano locked the door, tossed the folder onto his desk, and started pacing to and fro, cursing the saints. He needed to get the agitation out of his system. How was it possible that not a single hair could fall from a man's head in that goddamn town without everyone knowing about it immediately?

He opened the window, fired up a cigarette, smoked it, closed the window, sat down, and grabbed the folder.

Scimè had done a good job.

At first glance, the elements making up Trinacriarte seemed to break down into three categories: partners, subscribers, and staff. The first name on the list of partners belonged to the late Catalanotti, beside which Scimè had taken the trouble to inscribe a small cross. Next came the names of Scimè himself and the bank manager, Elena Saponaro, both of whom, together with Catalanotti, made up the directorate, and these were followed by those of the lead actress, the lead actor, and the administrator. The next list was longer and featured the names of the subscribers: six male actors, including Engineer Lo Savio, and six actresses.

The next and final group was the staff: a seamstress, prompters, lighting crew, electrician, set designer, costume designer, chief stagehand . . . All technical personnel, totaling seven people.

On another sheet of paper, Scimè explained the differences between the three categories. The partners were producers of a sort; they sought out financial support, covered the expenses of every production, and collected any proceeds there were to be had. The subscribers worked for free but had the right to a per diem if they went on tour. The technicians, on the other hand, were paid the union-approved minimum wage.

Scimè made a point of specifying that it was the directorate that decided which plays would be produced, which actors would take part in them, and whom to assign, on a case-by-case basis, the tasks of set and costume design.

For each of the names on the three lists, the lawyer had diligently written the address and telephone number.

Montalbano had just started rereading the pages for the addresses when there was a knock at the door.

"Come in," he said.

The door was pushed, but did not open.

Then he remembered he'd locked it.

He got up, opened the door, and found Fazio before him.

The inspector immediately felt grateful to him for not having a smirk on his face.

They sat down, as usual. Fazio got straight to the point.

"I've found out a few things about the Lo Bello family, Chief."

"Let's hear 'em."

"Apparently the quarrel that led to the girl leaving home was pretty serious. A neighbor woman told me that the girl's father literally threw her out of the house, right onto the street, then slammed the door on her. Then, as the girl was lying there, crying her eyes out, he started throwing her stuff out the window at her: dresses, panties, bras, shoes, and so on, followed by a big, empty suitcase, and then he said: 'Don't you ever show your face around here again!'

"At this point, Signora Nunziata—the neighbor—told me she went outside to console the poor girl. She gathered up all the stuff the father had thrown out the window, brought her inside, and calmed her down a little. The girl then called up her boyfriend, who rushed over there in about ten minutes, grabbed the suitcase, and drove away with her."

"A fine scene from the way things used to be," Montalbano commented.

"It gets worse," said Fazio. "Apparently this Tano Lo Bello is often violent with his family. Signora Nunziata also told me that two months ago, she even had to intervene because Lo Bello had beaten up his wife. Apparently—though I haven't confirmed it yet—he was called in by the carabinieri for his behavior."

"And what exactly is his gripe against his daughter? Did you find out?"

"His gripe is that she's been too long with a boyfriend who he says is a good-for-nothing."

"But the poor kid even goes down to the docks to unload fish . . ." Montalbano objected.

"Yeah, sure, but Signor Lo Bello doesn't see it the same way."

"What's the man do for a living, anyway?"

"In theory, he's a clerk at city hall."

"Why 'in theory'?"

"'Cause he seems to belong to that category of government employees who take turns going to work and punching each other in."

"And what's he do the rest of the time?"

"He goes to game rooms and plays video poker."

"Is Margherita an only child?"

"No. She's got an older brother, Gaspare, who's married with a one-year-old boy, and they all live with the parents."

"Does he have a job?"

"He did, but he just got laid off."

"All right," the inspector said by way of conclusion. "Do me a big favor and keep an eye on this Lo Bello."

"I will."

"And what can you tell me about the other two people?"

"Nothing, Chief. I haven't had time yet to start asking questions."

"Could you do me another favor?"

"At your service, Chief."

"Get up now, go out of the room, close the door behind you, wait a few seconds, then reopen the door, come in, and close it behind you again."

"And why all the rigamarole?"

"I'll explain afterwards."

Fazio got up and did exactly what Montalbano had asked him to do.

"Stop right there!" the inspector ordered him the moment he was back in the room. "Tell me precisely in what part of his leg Nico was injured."

"In his left calf."

"Have Forensics determined what direction the shot came from?"

"Yes, Chief: from the front."

"Excellent. You can sit back down. Now think carefully before answering: Tell me what your eyes saw as you opened the door."

Fazio thought about this for a moment.

"They saw you behind your desk, under the picture of the president."

"Now make another effort. Did you look immediately at me the moment you entered?"

"No, Chief."

"Feel like taking a little spin with me?"

"Sure."

"Good, then we'll take your car," said the inspector.

"Where are we going?"

"To Nico and his girlfriend's place."

Via Pignatelli was long and narrow, and there was almost nowhere to park, so Fazio practically had to go down the whole street before he could stop. They got out and retraced their path.

At number 57 was a small locked door.

"This is where Nico lives. Second floor," said Fazio.

It was a small, three-story apartment block.

"Do you know who's on the third floor?"

"It's vacant, Chief."

Only then did the inspector notice a sign saying FOR SALE. Just opposite the front door, across the street, was a haberdasher's shop with a metal shutter over its façade and a sign saying FOR RENT. To the right of it was another block of apartments, locked up.

The building opposite also featured two tall windows with iron grilles to the left of the door and two identical windows to the right.

"Okay," said Montalbano, "come with me."

He took a few steps and then stopped, with his back to the front door at number 57. Fazio came up beside him and did the same.

"Okay, imagine you're coming out the front door. What do you see?"

"I see the metal shutter of the haberdashery," said Fazio.

"And out of the corner of your eye?"

"I can see as far as the windows."

"Now turn your gaze a little to the left. What do you see?"

"The start of the building connected to it."

"Now turn to the right."

"Same thing. The other building."

"Conclusion?"

"Conclusion," said Fazio, "Nico had to have seen whoever it was that shot him. And when he recognized him, he turned around, not to close the front door, but to try to run back inside. Is that right?"

"That's right," replied the inspector. "And that's the part of the Mass that Nico neglected to sing to us."

"So what's our next move?"

"I'll tell you later. Now drive me to Enzo's."

There were few people in the trattoria, so Enzo came up to them almost immediately.

"Would you like a little seafood antipasto? It's very fresh today."

"I think we can make the sacrifice," replied the inspector.

Enzo was about to turn and go when he stopped and

bent down towards Montalbano, leaning his hands on the table.

"Could you tell me if you're making any progress on the Catalanotti murder?" he asked softly.

Montalbano did a double take.

"Why, did you know him?"

"Yeah, he was a customer."

"Really?"

"Yeah, he'd been coming out this way for the last three months. Always in the evening."

"Want to bet I can guess what evenings he came here?"

"Sure, go ahead."

"Tuesday, Thursday, and Saturday."

"You guessed right," said Enzo. "But did you already know?"

"No, but tell me something else. Did he come alone?"

"No, Inspector, he was always in the company of the same woman: blond, about forty, all dolled up and stuck up in the worst kind of way. A total, ball-busting pain in the ass. None of our dishes was ever good enough for her: sometimes it was overdone, other times it was underdone . . ."

"And how did Catalanotti act on those occasions?"

"I remember that one evening somebody called the restaurant to talk with Signor Catalanotti. When he came back to the table, the woman lit into him and made a big scene. 'How the hell do they know you're here? Who'd you tell we were coming to eat at this restaurant?'"

"And wha'd he do?"

"The poor guy got all confused and tried to tell her it wasn't an important phone call. But she was having none of it. At a certain point the woman, still yelling, got up and just left, leaving the guy in the lurch. Before sitting back down, poor Catalanotti felt obliged to apologize to the other customers in the restaurant for all the commotion she'd created."

"And they came back to eat here again after that?"

"You bet they did! They were back at their usual table two days later, all nice and well behaved."

"Do you know what this blonde's name is?"

"No, Inspector, I'm sorry, but I can't help you there. And I never saw anyone in here greet her, so I wouldn't know who to ask."

"Did you ever manage to notice whether they would come in the same car or two different cars?"

"I think they always came in one car."

"Why? How do you know?"

"Because on the evening of the big dustup, Catalanotti asked me to call him a taxi to take him home."

As Enzo walked away, it occurred to Montalbano that the trattoria was actually rather far from Catalanotti's place, which was on the opposite side of town. And it was also far from the warehouse where they held their rehearsals.

So it must have been a secret relationship, especially since neither the doorman of his building nor his housekeeper knew where he went on Tuesday, Thursday, and Saturday nights.

He had a substantial, satisfying meal. The walk out to the lighthouse at the end of the jetty was therefore slow and meditative.

As he sat down on the usual flat rock, the usual crab,

seeing him arrive, hid under the surface of the water. Apparently the animal wasn't in the mood for conversation.

Enzo's story added a further complication to the overall picture: now there was a mysterious woman in the middle of it all.

And so, as tradition would dictate, he should probably begin with the categorical imperative: *cherchez la femme*.

8

He'd just sat down at the desk when Mimì, his face one big frown, sat down without a word in the chair opposite him.

"Well, aren't you a sight for sore eyes!" said the inspector.

Mimì snapped angrily to attention.

"I've been busy on the case since yesterday."

"Which case?" Montalbano asked sarcastically.

"The case of our cadaver."

"Your cadaver, Mimì. That cadaver is all yours."

"Okay, okay . . . Look, I can't get any sleep anymore. I have no idea where they could have hidden him. How is it possible the body hasn't been found yet?"

"Tell me what you did."

"I went all the way to the port to ask the fishermen if they'd seen a body out at sea dressed up in trousers, jacket, and shoes. They told me that any bodies they find at sea they bring back to shore, no matter how they're dressed. Then I got wind that a dead body had been found in Fela. So I got in my car. It wasn't him."

"Stop right there," said Montalbano. "How could you know it wasn't him if you'd only barely touched him?"

"That was quite enough for me. And our cadaver—I mean, *my* cadaver—was wearing very fancy shoes. The dead guy in Fela was wearing shabby old peasant boots and his trousers were some kind of rough corduroy, whereas my guy's were fine fabric . . . Don't you think that's enough?"

"Listen, Mimì, stop tormenting yourself like this. Stop losing sleep over it. You can rest assured that, sooner or later, this cadaver of yours will resurface. In fact, I've been wanting to ask you to give me a hand on the other case."

"Sure, whatever you say."

"Let's start by saying that this Catalanotti was a moderate moneylender."

"What do you mean by 'moderate'?" asked Mimì, interrupting.

"I mean that he lent money at not terribly high rates of interest. He also owned some warehouses and apartments, worked as a stage actor and director for a company on whose board of directors he sat, and he was also an amateur psychologist."

"And what do you want from me?"

"On Tuesdays, Thursdays, and Saturdays he was in the custom of dining at Enzo's in the evening, in the company of a blond woman of about forty, all gussied up and very unpleasant in manner."

"So?" Mimì insisted.

"I was thinking you would be the most suitable person for trying to find out who this woman is."

Mimì's face brightened at once. He grinned.

"Well, I can try, at least," he said.

Then a moment later: "If he was an actor and a director, then the first thing to do would be to seek out the actresses in the troupe."

"I've got the list right here," said Montalbano, grabbing Scimè's folder and handing it to him.

Mimì took it, opened it, and then asked for a sheet of paper, on which he copied the names and addresses of the eight actresses.

When he'd finished, he stood up.

"I'll have some news for you soon," he said.

As if they'd planned in advance to take turns, as Mimì was pushing the door open on his way out, Fazio held it open and came in.

"Any news?"

"First I need to ask you something: How much did Sciacchitano owe Catalanotti?"

And who is this Sciacchitano? wondered Montalbano. Then, making a little effort, he recalled the register of Catalanotti's loans, where he'd seen the name, along with that of a woman, as two people who hadn't yet repaid their debts.

"I can't really remember," said the inspector, "but I think it was a small amount, maybe between two and three thousand euros."

Fazio raised an intelligent objection.

"A small amount depending on your point of view, Chief."

"What do you mean?"

"This Sciacchitano is fifty years old, with a dirty record for brawling, assault with a weapon, and other sundry offenses. He gets by robbing old folks and lives in a shack on the edge of town. For him, two or three thousand euros is a ton of money."

"You're right. And so? Do we call him in for questioning?"

"There's no need, Chief."

"Why not?"

"'Cause I already went to see him myself."

"And so? Do I have to pull the words out of you with pliers?"

"Nah, Chief, the fact is that Sciacchitano has been in the hospital for the past week. And he's pretty far gone, according to his wife."

Montalbano threw up his hands, then asked: "And what can you tell me about the other debtor? The woman?"

"Yeah, Saveria di Donato. I still haven't had the time. You'll have to be patient till tomorrow."

Then Fazio left, too.

Montalbano went to the window and smoked a cigarette. Then he sat back down and rang Scimè.

"Sorry to bother you, sir. Montalbano here."

"It's always a pleasure, Inspector. Thank you so much for calling."

"Thanks for what? I'm calling because I have a favor to ask of you . . ."

"Well, I'd really been hoping to hear from you. I need to talk to you."

Montalbano remained silent.

Scimè the lawyer continued. "I was just about to call you, believe me. I'm just so upset over my friend's death. There are so many questions I can't find any answers for . . ."

Montalbano was in the same situation.

"And so?" he asked.

"And so can we meet?" asked the lawyer.

"Of course. When?"

"This evening? After dinner?"

The inspector couldn't have asked for more. This way he could chow down without any disturbance.

"Perfect. Would you like to come to the station?"

"Whatever you think is best. Otherwise, if we don't

want to be disturbed, we could also meet at our place. There won't be anyone here."

It was as if the man could read his mind.

"Perfect. So, nine-thirty at Trinacriarte."

"Thank you. Thank you so much," said Scimè.

"Not at all. Thank *you*," said the inspector, hanging up.

He never found out whether it was Inspector Montalbano who needed information on the case, or Salvo the man who needed desperately to hear the woman's voice again.

"Ciao, Antonia, it's Montalbano. Am I interrupting?"

"No. What is it?"

A moment of silence.

"No . . . I just wanted to ask you . . . was it you who took Catalanotti's cell phone?"

"No. If we'd taken it, you would know. In fact, we left his computer there just so that you could work on it."

"So where do you think the cell phone could be?"

"Apparently the killer took it away with him. Any other questions?"

A couple of seconds of silence.

"At the moment . . ." said Montalbano.

"Then good-bye," said Antonia, hanging up.

Matre santa, was that woman ever rude!

Just to bother her a little more, Montalbano redialed the number.

"I'm sorry, Antonia, one last question . . ."

There was a slight note of forbearance in the woman's reply.

"Go ahead," she said.

"But didn't all that ricotta give you indigestion?"

She laughed, at long last!

"Come on, stop wasting my time," she said, and hung up.

But Montalbano had scored a point in his favor: Antonia's voice had sounded a little less surly. For his part, on the other hand, that strange feeling in the pit of his stomach felt more, not less, intense.

He went home early.

Adelina had defied Livia's instructions, cooking up, in fact, a very fine, indeed heavenly, casserole of *pasta 'ncasciata*.

The evening air was coolish, but tolerable, and so he set the table on the veranda and gobbled up enough pasta for two and more.

He cleared the table in a hurry. Feeling weighted down, he went onto the beach and began jogging along the water.

After less than three minutes of this, however, he had to stop, out of breath and feeling the pasta jumping up from his belly and into his throat.

And so he turned to go back home, head hanging as if he'd been to a funeral with Livia leading the ceremony.

Scimè was waiting for him outside the door of the Trinacriarte warehouse. After an exchange of greetings, the lawyer led him into the backstage area where, again through an arrangement of wooden screens, two bathrooms, four dressing rooms, and a rather spacious office had been created. On the door of the latter was a sign saying MANAGEMENT.

Scimè dug a pair of keys out of his pocket, opened the

door, turned on the light, showed the inspector inside, and invited him to sit down in a chair in front of the desk. He himself sat down in the chair behind the desk.

Montalbano was about to open his mouth, but the lawyer spoke first.

"I am so grateful to you for calling me, Inspector. Now I have a chance to talk about Carmelo's death."

"I'm sorry," said Montalbano, "but didn't you all talk about it among yourselves?"

"No, we've busied ourselves mostly with practical matters and haven't been able yet to face what actually happened—that our friend was brutally murdered."

"And how do you explain it?"

"Inspector, all I can really tell you is my impressions . . . You mustn't take what I say as anything more than suggestions, conjectures . . ."

"Don't worry about that, just tell me straight out."

"I had the feeling that our reticence to discuss the matter was due to a sort of mutual suspicion. As if every one of us was convinced that it was someone from our troupe who had killed Carmelo and so thought it best not to broach the subject."

"Excuse me, but was there any friction in your company between him and the others—any heated arguments, for example?"

"Of course there were, Inspector, but it was always stuff that had to do exclusively with our theater work, and it certainly wasn't ever violent enough to justify murder."

"Well, tell me about it anyway."

"I'm not entirely sure about it . . ."

"Why?"

"Because it's all . . . well, it was all just impulsive

stuff . . . But not off the wall, though. Do you know anything about the theater, Inspector?"

"I've seen a few plays."

"That's not enough. You should know that I got a degree from the National Academy of Dramatic Arts in Rome, and worked for two years with Gassman."

He stopped for a second, grinned, and then added: "Vittorio, that is. It was the legendary epoch of the avant-garde theater all over the world, and at the time you could see some astonishing productions, outstanding for the stage presence of the actors, their use of their bodies, the extraordinary versatility of their voices . . . Sorry to go into such detail, but it's absolutely essential that I explain to you that the method that Catalanotti devised for putting an actor in a condition to perform took all those theatrical theories based essentially on the emotions to their extreme conclusions . . ."

Montalbano stopped him.

"Lo Savio already mentioned that to me."

Scimè grimaced.

"Of course, Inspector, but, you see, Rosario never went so far as to audition for Carmelo, so he never went through the experience. Whereas I did."

"Then tell me about it."

"First of all, I should tell you that the test the actor had to take was never given here, but at an unexpected location. I, for example, was taken, by him, to an uninhabited apartment, an environment I was entirely unfamiliar with. And that's not all. It was night, and pitch-black. The moment we went inside, without saying a word to me, he disappeared. After feeling confused for about five minutes, I started calling his name. But Carmelo didn't answer. So I started moving about and tried to turn on the light. I flipped the switch, but nothing came on. I managed to stagger over to the door but was unable to open it, because it was locked. I still remember the terrible sense of uneasiness I felt, which turned slowly into out-and-out terror. Then I found a chair and sat down in it. Moments later I heard a very strange rustling sound, as if there was something moving along the floor. I thought, for whatever reason, that it might be rats coming towards me in a threatening manner, then I actually started hearing squeaks that grew louder and louder, and I couldn't take it any longer and suddenly yelled in despair. I jumped up and stood on the chair. And at that moment the light came on. Carmelo was right there, standing beside the light switch, staring at me and looking all serious. 'Why did you scream?' he asked me at once. I answered that I'd imagined . . . but then I couldn't speak anymore . . . '*You imagined what*?' he asked. 'Rats,' I stammered. 'Sit back down,' he said, pulling up a chair for himself as well. He sat down in front of me and then began a sort of psychoanalysis, according to which those rats became a representation of my secret fears. He had—I now recognize—an uncanny ability to penetrate deep into one's innermost, sometimes inadmissable, thoughts. To all intents and purposes, by the third audition—which was the worst one of all, and which I don't want even to go into any longer—I'd decided not to work with him anymore."

A moment later, Montalbano, who'd been listening with great interest to the lawyer's story, asked him: "Listen, can you tell me which were the actors Catalanotti preferred to work with?"

"You know what, Inspector? After a while, nobody wanted to work with him anymore. That was another reason there were a lot of quarrels within the troupe."

"Did these disputes occur with anyone in particular?"

"Yes, Inspector, with me. Things got very tense between us. Carmelo wanted to include in our group some people he'd met by chance and who'd shown themselves to be willing to go along with his experiments. Even people with no experience of the theater at all, but whom he needed anyway for his production—like Maria, whom you saw the other evening. Those of us in the troupe were totally against introducing random, throwaway elements into the group. I remember one time when he brought in a young girl, saying, 'I've found the real Ophelia!' She was little more than a child, Inspector, clearly with serious mental problems. We were speechless. There was no way she could take the stage. But, right up to the end, he stubbornly insisted that she was Ophelia, and the rest of us were incapable of understanding anything . . . The upshot, of course, was that we ended up never staging *Hamlet*."

Scimè paused.

"Would you like something to drink?" he asked.

"I would love a little whisky, but I doubt you—"

"Actually, I do have some," said Scimè, getting up, opening a small cabinet, and taking out two glasses and a bottle. He filled both glasses halfway, and before he could resume speaking, Montalbano asked:

"Tell me something. Lo Savio said that Catalanotti was getting ready to stage a new production. Do you know what it was?"

"Of course, Inspector. My introduction may have given you the idea that Carmelo only ever wanted to produce masterpieces and Greek tragedies. But that wasn't at all the case. He chose mostly twentieth-century drama. Said he found the bourgeois world fascinating. In fact, he was working on a British play by J. B. Priestley, *Dangerous Corner.* The author was noted for his excellent creations in the para-detective genre."

"And what's that?"

"It means the works seem to have mystery plots but in reality are profound investigations into the soul of contemporary man."

Montalbano reflected that there was no such thing as a good cop who wasn't also able to dig deep into the human soul.

Then he asked: "Do you know if there's a copy of this play available here?"

"We should have one around here somewhere."

Scimè got up and opened another shelf packed full of scripts. He poked around for a long time, then finally found what he was looking for on top of a stack of papers.

"Here it is," said Scimè. "But please be sure to give it back, because it's the only copy we own."

"Of course," said Montalbano.

Scimè went on: "I'm sorry we'll never see that production."

"When will you resume the rehearsals for *The Tempest*?"

"That's another problem. Because we're unable—" The lawyer interrupted himself, took a deep breath, and then said, "The fact of the matter is that we've been avoiding one another."

"Do you know what kind of work Catalanotti did for a living?"

"He didn't work. He lived on private means. He was a

relatively rich man. He owned houses and warehouses. If I'm not mistaken, he'd inherited from his mother and was able to manage the estate rather well . . ."

"And there was nothing else?"

"You know, Inspector, we were never actually friends outside the theater, so, as far as I know, no, there was nothing else. Why do you ask?"

"Because my findings show that he was also a moneylender."

Scimè seemed stunned. He opened his mouth, closed it, and opened his eyes wide. He was unable to speak. Then, little by little, he regained his composure. Taking a sizable sip of whisky, he grinned at the inspector.

"What are you thinking?" asked Montalbano.

"I'm thinking that, for us, at least, this is good news."

"Why?"

"Because a moneylender is certainly going to have a lot of enemies, and so the killer could easily be someone from outside our circle."

Montalbano changed the subject.

"Do you have a photo album of the actors?"

"Of course!"

Scimè opened a drawer in the desk and extracted a large album, which he handed to the inspector.

Montalbano started leafing through it.

There were photos of all eighteen members of the company. Among the eight women there wasn't anyone with blond hair, which meant that Catalanotti's dinner companion at Enzo's was not part of Trinacriarte. He closed the album, gave it back to Scimè, and asked him: "Tell me, in your opinion, who among these actors and actresses had the most intimate relationship with Catalanotti? I'm only asking you to save time. I could summon everyone into my office, but I'm sure there's no point. I would like to limit the investigation to those who were closest to him."

"There are two actors, a man and a woman, who worked on a production staged by Carmelo, Beckett's *Happy Days*, and they remained fairly close to him afterwards."

Scimè reopened the album and pointed them out.

"Here they are. They're Eleonora Ortolani, a character actress, and Ernesto Lopez, a colleague of mine, a fellow lawyer."

Montalbano made a mental note of both, then asked: "You told me that you yourself were not actually friends with Catalanotti, but do you by any chance know if he had any romantic attachments?"

"He probably did, but I don't know of any."

"He never talked about that sort of thing with you?"

"No, Inspector. Carmelo never let anyone get in a position to ask questions he might not want to answer. Maybe Eleonora or Ernesto could tell you more."

Montalbano, thinking the conversation was over, was about to get up when Scimè asked: "Have you got another ten minutes or so?"

"Yes, of course."

The lawyer's face changed completely. A big, toothy smile appeared as his eyes sparkled with contentment. Bending down, he opened the drawer on the left-hand side and took out three albums, all thicker than the one still on the table.

"I wanted to show you some photos of my bygone youth."

He stood up, went over, and sat beside Montalbano, then opened the first album to the first page. In the middle was a photo of Vittorio Gassman with the dedication: *To my dear friend, Antonio.*

On the second page was another photograph, this one of Scimè dressed up as a page.

"That," he said, "was taken during my performance exam at the academy. I was playing Page Fernando."

Montalbano studied the picture carefully. Scimè was very young in it, just a boy; almost nothing in the face he was looking at belonged to the lawyer's current face. After this introduction, three-quarters of the Italian theater world of the prior half century filed before the inspector's eyes. When, a good hour later, they finally got to the third album, Montalbano was in the throes of a deep depression.

He didn't own a single picture of himself as a youngster. Not one.

And so he had nothing with which to compare his present-day face. No doubt his youthful face would have been just as unrecognizable as Scimè's.

He slept little, but well.

His chat with Scimè had awakened the desire to kick the investigation into high gear, to give it a jolt of energy of a sort he hadn't felt for a long time.

As he was whistling in the shower, the springlike rebirth he felt inside had called forth, to his surprise, amid the fog of the hot water, an image of Antonia, as naked as him.

He turned off the tap and literally ran out of the bathroom.

9

He was drinking his customary mug of espresso when he got the idea to ring Fazio, who answered at once.

"What's up, Chief? Something happen?"

"No, no, no cause for alarm. I merely want you to call two people in for questioning. I'll see the first one at nine and the second one at eleven."

"And who are they?"

"Ernesto Lopez, who apparently is a lawyer, and Eleonora Ortolani."

"Have you got their phone numbers?"

"No, Fazio, but you'll find all the information you need in the Trinacriarte folder I left on my desk."

"Right, I remember."

"Good. I'll see you at the office."

He was on his way out when his cell phone rang. It was Livia. *Matre santa!* How long had it been since they'd spoken? He decided he'd better grab the upper hand before it was too late.

"Livia! Where on earth have you been?"

"You're asking me? Where on earth have you been, rather? . . . I called you repeatedly last night but got no answer. I started getting worried, and so I—"

"You did the right thing."

There wasn't anything else for him to say. He'd completely forgotten to call her.

"Is the investigation really taking up so much—"

"Yes, Livia, frankly, it is. I came home very late."

"Think it'll keep you busy for a long time to come?"

"I'm afraid it may, unfortunately. I still don't feel I have a good grasp on the case."

"Then I guess there's no point in me reserving a flight for Palermo . . ."

Her words stirred a feeling of tenderness in Montalbano. Not displeasure. He felt guilty and tried to make up for it.

"I promise that the minute I'm free," he said, "I'll come and see you in Boccadasse, and we'll go somewhere together."

"All right . . ." said Livia. She sounded disconsolate, but at least not resentful.

He found Fazio waiting for him at the office.

"What have you got to tell me?"

"Chief, Signora Ortolani will be here at nine, but Lopez, the lawyer, has to go to the courthouse, so he was wondering if he could come in the afternoon."

"Sure, fine."

"Okay, excuse me for just one minute, so I can inform Lopez," said Fazio.

He pulled out his cell phone, dialed a number, spoke briefly, hung up, then asked Montalbano: "Mind telling me who they are?"

The inspector remained silent for a moment, then started half singing, in a soft voice, the famous waltz from *The Merry Widow.*

"'Though I say not / what I may not / . . . it's true, it's true, / you love me so.'"

Montalbano's brain had traveled a path all by itself,

going from Signora Ortolani to Winnie, the character in Beckett's *Happy Days*, who at the end of the play intones the widow's song.

Fazio, saucer-eyed, just looked at him.

So Montalbano felt the need to explain. And explain he did.

"I've also got the information on Signora di Donato you asked me for," Fazio said when the inspector had finished.

"Tell me everything."

"What a sad scene, Inspector. Tragic, really. The lady's seventy years old and had a little grocery store in the old part of town. And like all these small-business people, she was going bankrupt. So she tried to save her business by borrowing some money from Catalanotti, which turned out to be pointless, since in the end she was forced to close her shop anyway. But, since she's an honest woman, she showed me the envelope in which she'd set aside nineteen thousand euros. She was getting ready to pay Catalanotti back. She even wanted to give me the money, since she didn't know anymore who to give it to."

"And wha'd you do? Did you take it?"

"No, Chief."

"So wha'd you say to her?"

Fazio didn't answer.

"What did you say to her?" the inspector pressed.

"I told her that for the time being, at least, she could keep the money, since at any rate nobody's gonna come around asking for it."

"You did the right thing," said Montalbano.

Fazio resumed speaking.

"Nico Dilicata was released from the hospital yesterday evening. What do we want to do?"

"What time did Lopez say he was coming in?"

"Four o'clock."

"Then have the kid come to the station at six."

"I'll call him right away, and if you haven't got any more orders, I'm gonna go to my office."

"Okay, see you later. But when Signora Ortolani gets here at nine, I want you present, too."

He'd been signing papers for an hour when the telephone rang.

"Chief, 'ere's a lady here say she's a 'orticultist or sum'n an' she wants a talk t'yiz poissonally in poisson 'cuz Fazio summonsed 'er. Whaddo I do?"

"Show her into my office and on your way here get Fazio."

The door opened, and Fazio stepped aside to let in a blond woman of about fifty, rather plump, all made up and coiffed, wearing a spotted overcoat that she'd probably borrowed from Cruella De Vil.

"Please sit down, signora," the inspector said, gallantly rising to his feet and gesturing towards a chair in front of his desk.

The woman walked with a sort of wobble, as though on a ship at sea.

She sat down on the edge of the chair, adjusted her skirt, looked at the inspector, and smiled. All things considered, if one forgot about the mask she was wearing, her face seemed to have a likable expression.

Fazio introduced himself and sat down in the other chair.

"You'll have to forgive me, but I feel awfully nervous," the woman said in a voice coming entirely from her head and as chirpy as a baby chick's.

She stood up. "Could I use the bathroom?" she asked.

"Show her the way," Montalbano said to Fazio.

The inspector felt bewildered. In the photo he'd seen the night before, the woman, like all of her colleagues, had decidedly dark hair.

So how was it she was now a blonde?

Might she be the woman who had been Catalanotti's companion for those evening meals on Tuesday, Thursday, and Saturday?

At first glance, however, she seemed to have a pleasant personality, unlike the quarrelsome character Enzo had described to him.

Signora Ortolani returned a short while later, followed by Fazio. She sat down, readjusting her skirt. The first question Montalbano asked caught her so much by surprise that the purse she was holding in her lap fell to the floor.

"How long have you been a blonde?"

"Excuse me?! . . ."

"Yesterday I saw a photo of you in which you had chestnut hair. I want to know how long it's been since you changed your hair color."

The woman sat there for a moment in silence, unable to speak, then, making an effort, she began to chirp.

"Sir . . . sir . . . yes, I know I made a mistake. My sister said the same thing. But with this sort of thing, it's not always easy to turn back . . ."

Montalbano stopped her.

"What are you saying, signora?"

"I know, I know, I should never have done it. But that day . . . I was desperate. I felt, well, like a stranger to myself. I simply had to do something extreme. So I got in my car and went out."

"Try to explain yourself a little better, Signora Ortolani. What was this extreme thing you did?" asked Montalbano.

The poor woman, sinking more and more into her chair, took a deep breath, emitted a chirping sound a little sadder than the others, and said: "It's all my own fault. I have no justification."

Fazio and Montalbano exchanged a glance.

Then Fazio took the plunge. "Are you talking about the murder of Catalanotti?"

"Whaaaaat????" the woman shrieked.

"Signora Ortolani," Fazio resumed, "you were telling us about something extreme you did . . ."

"Of course, I was talking about dyeing my hair blond."

Montalbano went over to the window, opened it, silently cursed the entire world outside, closed the window, and sat back down.

"Let me ask you the question again: How long have you been a blonde?"

"Thirty-three days."

Then she couldn't have been Catalanotti's dinner companion.

Signora Ortolani perked up and asked: "Blond hair doesn't suit me, does it, Inspector?"

"Signora," said Montalbano, changing the subject, "I called you in because Scimè the lawyer told me you played the protagonist's role in *Happy Days*, under Catala—"

The woman squirmed visibly in her chair like a chicken puffing up her feathers.

"Oh, what an unforgettable production! One of those that leave an indelible mark on an actress's life. So rare, so magical . . ."

"Okay, I wanted to know what method Catalanotti used to put you in the right state of mind for interpreting the role."

"I remember it as though it was yesterday. He took me to a splendid hotel by the sea. There were very few people there, because it was low season. We spent three beautiful days together. Or, at least I think we did . . ."

"What do you mean, at least you 'think'?"

"Well, on the first day he took me down to the beach, to a secluded spot. A lifeguard was following us with a shovel and a beach umbrella. Carmelo had him dig a deep hole, then asked me to get in it. The hole was then filled back up with sand, and only my head remained outside. Then they planted the big umbrella over my head.

"'Stay like that. I'll be back in half an hour,' Carmelo said. But you know what, Inspector? He didn't come back until the sun was already setting. I was exhausted, and I was terribly thirsty. Every so often I would cry out, but there wasn't anyone around to hear me. I must say, however, that it was also an amazing experience, being alone with myself. I remember eating with a tremendous appetite that evening. The following day Carmelo had another hole dug for me, but this time he left my bust and arms outside. He'd asked me to bring along my purse, which I did. When I later opened it, immersed in the sand as I was, I saw all the objects I normally keep in there in a completely different light. I started examining them one by one, as though seeing them for the first time. Just think, I couldn't even remember how to take the cap off my lipstick. They all seemed like unfamiliar, unknown objects. On the third day I had the most upsetting experience of all. Carmelo asked me to get back into the hole up to my chest again, and after the lifeguard left, he took a revolver out of his trouser pocket. And he said, 'Take it.' And so I took it, though I was terrified. I've always been scared to death of guns. 'Careful,' he said, 'it's loaded.' And then he left."

"And what happened?" asked Montalbano.

"It was so strange! Just think, after less than an hour of staring at the gun, studying it, I was no longer afraid of it. I took it in my hand and practically started caressing it. It was a high-caliber revolver. Very heavy, but all of a sudden it sort of became part of my hand. The desire to use it began to grow slowly inside me. Then at one point I tried to throw it far away. But I didn't throw it far enough, because I could still reach it. A few hours went by, and I started to dig out the sand around me; I wanted to come out of the hole, pick up the gun, and shoot it—at whom, I didn't know, maybe in the air, or at the first passerby. I'd dug down almost to my knees and would have been out of there before long, when suddenly Carmelo appeared and yelled: 'That's enough!' I froze. Then I saw that he had a pair of binoculars hanging from his neck and I realized he'd been watching me the whole time. So, anyway, these were the first auditions; he ended up needing quite a few more—five or six—and only at the end of it all did Carmelo tell me I was fit to take on the role. That made me very happy."

"That's a rather dangerous method," Montalbano observed.

"Well, but he did intervene at exactly the right moment, so he never put me in any real danger, since he was keeping an eye on me the whole time. On those days and during all the other auditions . . . And so it suddenly all became clear to me. I realized what the problem was for anyone trying to approach that play: Why does Winnie have a revolver?"

"Why does she?" Fazio and Montalbano asked in unison.

"Because she has reached a point in her existence where she could easily just kill herself and her partner or else start singing the waltz from *The Merry Widow*."

By the time she'd finished telling her story, her forehead was beaded with sweat and her hands were trembling slightly, so deeply had she been involved in her story.

"Would you like a little water?" Fazio asked her.

"Yes, thank you."

After avidly drinking down a glass, she resumed speaking.

"Well, it certainly was a system all his own. I remember, at first he wouldn't even let me read Beckett's entire text. He'd merely given me a sheet of paper with a few lines on it that I was supposed to repeat while I was buried in the sand."

"And when did he finally give you permission to read the whole play?" Montalbano asked.

"After he found Willie, my partner, whom he'd put through even harsher trials than mine. Only then did he let us read it, together, for the first time."

Montalbano thought of the printed sheets of paper in the folders in the closet of Catalanotti's home.

Apparently those excerpts of dialogue must have been lines from the play he was preparing.

"And afterwards, when he'd found the right actors, how did he go about getting ready for production?"

"Inspector, Carmelo would want to meet with each of us individually, even the costume designer, the lighting technician, and the set designer. He would keep us all intentionally apart. He even went so far as to forbid us to talk to one another. And, I must say, we all respected his wishes. When we were finally able to rehearse onstage, Carmelo would have us repeat the same line fifty, sixty times, until we were exhausted. After which we would have to come up with some kind of full-body improvisation on the line we'd been repeating. We would do two or three more improvisations, then go back to repeating the written line aloud. I'm not sure I'm being clear."

"That's about as clear as it gets. But what would Catalanotti himself do during these rehearsals? Did he intervene much? Would he interrupt you? Did he take notes?"

"He would interrupt us a lot, and, yes, he would also take notes."

"Tell me something, signora. Your theater company seems to be an amateur one, surely of great merit, but not professional. So I'm wondering: What was his justification for subjecting you to these terribly demanding trials?"

"I'll try to explain, Inspector. Carmelo had an uncanny ability to extract, from every one of us, everything—and I mean everything—we had inside. And to use it for dramatic purposes. It was a kind of therapy, a cure. Believe me, after every performance my boyfriend and I felt like breaking into a run, we felt so . . . so liberated, so unleashed. We had to pay a very high, overwhelming price for it, and some of our associates certainly weren't up to the task. It's not everyone who feels like confronting their innermost, hidden truths."

"Now I want you to think for a moment," said Montalbano, interrupting her again. "As far as you know, this talent of his for stripping people down naked and liberating them from their complexes, their excess baggage, their reticence, was it something Catalanotti used only for theatrical purposes?"

The woman remained silent for a moment.

"You have to believe me, Inspector, but even though he was able to achieve such a level of intimacy onstage, we would never see him outside of the theater. It was all played out on the floorboards. I don't even know where he lived, and I have no idea whether he had a family, a wife, children . . . I know nothing about him."

She paused ever so briefly, then looked the inspector in the eye.

"I'll even say more: I don't want the obscenity of Carmelo's death suddenly to reveal to me any aspects of his personality that we had willingly left out of the picture, out of some tacit agreement, when he was alive."

Montalbano looked at her in admiration. The woman who spoke like a chirping chick was worthy of the greatest respect.

"And I will honor your agreement," said the inspector, holding his hand out to her.

Fazio was opening the door to see her out when Montalbano said: "One more thing, signora. You know, I'm of the opinion that blond hair actually looks rather good on you."

Signora Ortolani very nearly fainted in Fazio's arms.

Fazio came back almost at once, but when he saw the inspector lost in thought, he simply sat down and said nothing.

Montalbano seemed not to have even noticed that he'd returned. But then two words uttered under his breath escaped from his lips: "Too bad."

Fazio now felt authorized to speak.

"Why?"

"I was thinking of Catalanotti. I would have liked to meet him and talk to him. Rarely have I come up against a personality as complex as his. We're clearly dealing with a real artist here. Maybe the only one in the troupe. And so I'm wondering: Which one was murdered? The artist or the moneylender?"

"I beg your pardon, Chief, but it seems a little weird to me that a real artist could also be a moneylender."

"But you're wrong, Fazio. There've been great artists who robbed, killed, and raped. Catalanotti was quite capable of keeping his activities separate, and in fact Signora Ortolani just told us she didn't know the first thing about his private life, and I believe her. And Scimè, too, didn't know about that side of him. And you know what, Fazio? The more we talk, the more I'm convinced that the key to it all lies precisely in my question: Which of the two was murdered?"

Fazio didn't know what to say.

"All right, then," said the inspector with a sigh, "let's move on to other things."

"Ah," said Fazio, "I forgot to tell you something. When I rang Nico Dilicata to summon him here this evening, he told me the doctors have forbidden him to walk, so he can't leave his home."

"No problem, that just means we'll go to him this evening."

The pile of papers waiting on his desk to be signed made him change his mind immediately.

"Actually, you know what I say? I say we go and see him right now."

"Okay," said Fazio, standing up.

As soon as Catarella realized they were on their way out, he stopped them.

"Ahh, Chief, Chief!!! Don' go! Iss th'end o' the woild! Iss rilly dangerous ousside, Chief! 'Ey e'en called for rinforcerments o' carabbinieri. Iss th'end o' the woild, Chief!"

"What are you talking about? What happened?"

"Chief, ya know the Bellofiore cement woiks? When the woikers went a woik 'iss mornin', 'ey foun' the gates to the factory closed. 'Ey was all sacked! Tree hunnert families 'at won't 'ave nuttin more to eat from now on."

"Let's go and have a look," Montalbano said to Fazio.

They went outside, but no sooner had they turned to the left than they could no longer see anything at all, finding themselves in front of a wall of smoke inside which they could hear shouts and explosions. Apparently the police were firing tear-gas bombs.

"Inspector," said Fazio, "I don't think this is a good idea."

At that moment they saw a man staggering out of the cloud as though drunk, holding one hand behind his neck and the other over his forehead. The man then fell forward onto his knees and started crawling towards them.

Montalbano sprang to his aid. The man had a gash over his right eye that was bleeding. He grabbed onto Fazio. He'd probably been clubbed by police.

"Let's bring him into the station," said Montalbano.

The man was groaning as tears ran down his face. They took him into the waiting room and laid him down on the sofa. Officer Cumella, who was also trained as a nurse, arrived with a first-aid kit, disinfected the wound, which luckily was not very deep, and dressed it.

Only then did the man look around as if slowly coming to. In a faint voice, he asked: "Where am I?"

"At the police station," said Fazio.

As if by instinct, the man crossed his arms over his face in a gesture of self-protection.

"Ahhh! You gonna keep beating up on me, eh?" he cried desperately. "I'm out of a job and you wanna bust my chops, too?! Who's gonna feed my three kids?"

Montalbano turned on his heels, went into his office, and locked himself inside. He was disgusted with himself, and with his chosen profession. Disgusted with the carabinieri, with law enforcement, with the government. Disgusted with the world, with the very order of the universe.

What kind of world was this that took away a person's right to work and earn an honest living?

So the state's answer, when these poor bastards dared to protest, was to greet them with billy clubs, tear gas, arrests, and convictions?

For how many years had he been a loyal servant of this state?

Had he worked honestly and respectfully with others?

Most of the time, yes, even if he didn't always succeed.

Apparently the majority of his colleagues had a different idea of what it meant to serve the state.

There was no escape.

He sat down, resigned, at his desk, grabbed the first paper from the pile, and signed it.

Around two o'clock, as he was practically drowning in paper and in need of air, the good guys came to the rescue in the nick of time, just like in an old 'Murcan movie.

They took the form of the door flying open and crashing against the wall with the usual boom.

But Montalbano barely heard it. The sound merely made him look up for a second at Catarella, who was standing in the doorway, carrying a paper tray with both hands.

"Beg yer pardon, Chief, but I hadda knock wit' my foot," he said, coming in and setting the tray down on the desk.

Under Catarella's self-satisfied gaze, Montalbano lifted the paper sheet covering the tray: sandwiches, *sfinciuni*, fritters, croquettes, *panelle*—manna from heaven!

"What are we celebrating, Cat?"

10

Catarella smiled. "We ain't cillibratin', Chief. I's jess a li'l worried 'at cuzza the diminstrations you migh' not get outta 'ere before dark, an' so I took a vantage of a moment o' calm an' ran into a bar an' bought everyting I cou' find."

"Well done, Cat . . ."

"Wait a secon' an' I'll bring yiz a li'l wine."

He went out and returned with half a flask of wine.

"Can you keep a secret, Cat? Come here and sit down with me. But you mustn't tell anyone else about our little feast."

"Ya wan me t'eat wit' yiz, Chief?" Catarella asked in a quavering voice, standing at attention, as stiff as a board.

"Of course. Now close the door, take two glasses out of the closet, and come over here."

Catarella did as he was told and sat down in front of the inspector, taking a little pizza for himself. And in the time it took him to make this movement—ever so slowly, with hesitation and almost fear—Montalbano was able to gobble down two whole sandwiches.

But then he had to get up in a hurry to help Catarella because a bite of pizza had gone down the wrong way and he was choking and coughing as his eyes filled with tears.

The inspector slapped him on the back with his open

hand and had him drink a little wine, but then Catarella stood back up.

"Ya gotta 'scuse me, Chief, but I can't manitch t'eat wit' yiz. Iss such a honor, iss too much. It chokes me up, an' I can't swallow!"

"Okay," said Montalbano, walking him to the door and opening it. "Oh, and how much did you spend?"

"Nah, nah, Chief, ya gotta 'scuse me, but iss on me."

Montalbano closed the door and conscientiously, with method and discipline, dispatched the rest of the food on the tray. After which he threw it into the wastebasket and leaned back in his chair, sighing with satisfaction. The door opened again, this time noiselessly, and the Archangel Catarella appeared with a steaming cup of coffee in hand, which he set down before the inspector. Without changing position, Montalbano brought two fingers to his lips and blew his assistant a kiss.

Catarella staggered and stumbled out of the room as if he'd taken a blow to the head. The inspector sipped his coffee, got up, went over to the window, opened it, and fired up a cigarette. He felt light and was digesting to perfection when, all of a sudden, Livia's note with her drawing of a death's-head came back to him.

Immediately he began to feel a great heaviness in his stomach. His digestion was henceforth irremediably blocked. He decided that as soon as he got home he would remove that piece of paper from the fridge and carefully hide it, to be retrieved only right before Livia's next visit.

There was a knock at the door, and Catarella reappeared.

"Chief, 'ere's some kine o' Spanish guy 'at came a li'l

oilier than aspected, cuz 'e was asposta come at four an' now iss only tree forty-five, an' so 'e ast if you cou' see 'im—"

"Tell me something: Is this Spaniard's name by any chance Lopez?"

"I tought it was Gomez, but 'at cou' be right, too."

"Is Fazio around?"

"Yeah, Chief, 'e's onna premisses."

"Okay, send me Fazio first, then you can show the Spanish gentleman in."

Fazio barely had time to sit down before Ernesto Lopez, lawyer, came in. It was impossible to assign an age to him: A balding redhead at least six foot three, as gaunt as death, he could have been anywhere between thirty and seventy years old. He was the one who had agreed with Maria del Castello during the commemoration. Today he'd tried to dress up for the occasion, without success: His tie was crooked and his jacket full of wrinkles. He walked as if swaying in a strong headwind, and Montalbano became immediately worried he might not make it as far as the desk. Luckily he did, but to sit down it took him a good ten seconds to descend from his height. He opened the discussion himself:

"I am at your service, Inspector," he said in a *basso profondo* voice. "I'm told you questioned Eleonora this morning."

"Yes," said Montalbano, "and she told us about the auditions for your production and Catalanotti's rather unusual methods. How did things go with yourself?"

Lopez gave a little laugh.

"As you probably know, Inspector, Willie, the Beckett character, is unable to walk and can only crawl along the ground. Before finally giving me the part, Carmelo had me drag along the ground for a whole month, explaining to me in detail the difference between the way a snake moves and the way a worm does. He wanted me to become a complete worm, even in my way of thinking. And since Willie is always wearing a suit, you can imagine the quarrels I had with my wife over the fact that I was ruining a jacket a week—"

Montalbano interrupted him.

"But do you know whether Catalanotti just pulled this method out of a hat, or was he inspired by something or someone else . . ."

"Inspector, as Eleonora probably told you, Carmelo didn't talk much about himself. One evening, however, during one of these individual auditions, when I specifically asked him about it, he replied that the idea had come to him many years earlier during a trip to Rome for work. He'd noticed that a theater there was devoting a whole week to Jerzy Grotowski, the Polish director, and his productions. So he went, and he was fascinated by what he'd seen. He managed to meet the main actors and talk with them at great length, but not with the director himself, who was not in town. Later he studied the man's theories in a book called *Towards a Poor Theatre*. I've read it myself, and if I had to give you my honest opinion, Inspector, I would say that Carmelo didn't have in fact the clearest grasp of its ideas, but he possessed an almost hypnotic power of pursuasion over actors. His system always managed in one way or another to work.

"Eleonora and I long remained very strangely attached to him. But he didn't feel the same way. He tried to avoid us. Once a show was staged, it no longer existed. He would do everything in his power to erase all trace of it. The very opposite of how people like us, theater people, feel about it.

For us, the photos and posters become a kind of documentation of a memory, a way not to forget. Carmelo, on the contrary, demanded oblivion. For him, the show's life ended the moment the curtain fell. And he was the same way about his private life. Which, I must admit, used to make me sort of angry. What is this? You can turn me inside out like a sock and I'm supposed to remain completely in the dark about your life? One time I happened to be walking past the big picture window of a café and I saw him inside. He was sitting down and speaking softly with a woman who had her back to me."

"Was she blond?" Montalbano asked with interest.

"No, no. I continued spying on him for a few minutes through the window. He seemed to have a strange rapport with the woman, because they kept their heads close together, like lovers in intimate conversation, but in fact, as I realized after a few minutes, they were in that pose so that nobody else would hear them. As I was making these observations he suddenly looked up and saw me. And was transformed: With an angry expression on his face, he stood up, grabbed the woman by the arm, and left the establishment without deigning even to glance at me. That was Carmelo."

"Was that the only time you ever saw him outside of rehearsals?" asked the inspector.

"Well . . . now that you mention it, I'm remembering another time we crossed paths, but only very briefly. It happened about three or four months ago. I'd gone to visit a friend who was in Montelusa hospital, and right in the entrance I practically ran straight into Carmelo. He recognized me, no doubt about that, but he didn't say hello and kept right on his way as if he didn't know me. And I guess that's all. I don't know what else to tell you . . ."

"I can tell you something you surely don't know," said Montalbano. "He was also a moneylender."

Lopez had no reaction.

"You're not surprised?"

"No."

"Why not?"

"I can't really explain. You see, I always thought that a man like him, who was able to unearth the innermost secrets of others, would be capable of anything. I think he derived a certain pleasure whenever . . ."

Signor Lopez fell silent.

"Go on," Montalbano encouraged him.

"Whenever he discovered some hidden cause for shame in one of us. There, I said it."

The inspector didn't feel like going any further down this path.

"Did you have discussions together, at least about the theater?"

"Yes, that we did. I myself have read quite a bit of dramatic theory, and one day I had to tell him that he was wrong, that he might well be applying Grotowski's method, but he was mixing it up with that of La Fura dels Baus."

"And what's that?"

"A Catalan troupe that does a physical kind of theater, resorting even to forceful, violent actions. Anyway, Carmelo replied that he wasn't looking for the sort of stage realism that basically everyone who works in theater aspires to. Realism over falseness. Verisimilitude. He didn't like this word, and so he turned it around and called it 'similveracity,' which was supposed to mean something different, but I could never quite figure out what."

"I'm sorry, but if you realized that Catalanotti's system was confused and maybe even, so to speak . . . unprofessional, why did you consent to such trying auditions?"

"I repeat: Carmelo had an exceptional gift for drawing people into his game, by knocking down our defenses little by little. He was a snake charmer."

Montalbano turned around to look at Fazio, as if to ask him if he had any questions. Fazio shook his head.

The inspector stood up, and so did the other two. He held out his hand to Lopez.

"I thank you for your information. You've been an immense help. I'll be in touch if I need to know anything else. Thank you again. Have a good day."

"Glad to be of service," said Lopez, taking leave of the inspector and heading off behind Fazio, who was leading the way.

By this point Montalbano felt he knew enough about Catalanotti's method. He decided to ring Maria del Castello, but as he was dialing he changed his mind. It would have been a waste of time; all the girl would have told him would have been more stories of abuse at the hands of the director. Never mind. Fazio returned almost immediately and sat down.

"Want to hear my opinion?"

"Absolutely."

"Chief, do you think it's possible Catalanotti was murdered in some kind of rebellion?"

"Explain what you mean."

"Chief, if that guy was capable of turning human

beings into his puppets, isn't it possible that one of these puppets could have rebelled during a particularly bizarre audition?"

"If what Lopez was saying is true, your hypothesis is certainly plausible. But it doesn't limit the area of investigation. On the contrary, it broadens it, because it wasn't necessarily one of the actors who rebelled; it could have been one of the many people he used to meet with to include in his productions."

As Fazio was listening to him, a furrow appeared on his brow.

"I'll explain," said the inspector. "When Catalanotti couldn't find a victim within the regular troupe, he would go looking for one outside, among common folks. The transcriptions of the auditions he did with them are in his bedroom."

"And how many are there?"

"About a hundred."

"Shit!"

"Exactly. There's work to be done."

"And where do we start?"

"At the moment I can't really say. I'll think it over tonight and get back to you on it tomorrow."

There was a knock at the door, and Mimì Augello came in.

"Hello there, Mimì. Got any news?"

"Enough. Before anything else I went and talked to Enzo."

Fazio gave a start in his chair.

"And what's Enzo got to do with any of this?"

Montalbano briefly filled him in on the story of

Catalanotti's dinners with the blonde on Tuesdays, Thursdays, and Saturdays.

"Well," Augello intervened, "that's not exactly correct."

"Meaning?"

"Meaning they didn't always eat together on those days. Sometimes they would skip it, sometimes they didn't go to Enzo's. Rather often, actually."

"What else did he tell you?"

"Enzo said the whole thing was of no importance, but when I pressed him, he remembered that he'd once heard Catalanotti call the blond woman Anita. That's as far as I got. I was hoping to bring you somewhat more concrete information. And what have you guys got to tell me?"

Montalbano gave him a quick résumé of what Ortolani and Lopez had said.

Mimì twisted up his mouth.

"A man like that is potentially very dangerous," he said.

"I agree," Montalbano concurred.

Mimì got up, said good-bye to both, and went out.

The inspector looked over at Fazio.

"What do you say? Is it too late, or do you think we can still drop in on Nico?"

"Let's go, Chief."

When they got to Via Pignatelli, Fazio rang the buzzer.

"Who is it?" asked a female voice.

"This is Inspector Montalbano."

"Ah, please come in and come upstairs," the voice said contentedly. It was clearly Margherita.

They climbed two flights of stairs. Margherita was waiting at the door with a big smile on her face.

"Come in, come in," she said.

They went in and found themselves in a dining room with at least ten people staring at them who then suddenly said, in chorus: "Good evening!"

Fazio and Montalbano stood speechless in the doorway, not knowing what to do.

Clearly they wouldn't be able to conduct any questioning with all those people around. The situation was almost comical: On one side of the dinner table sat Nico, with his leg propped up on a chair; and on the other side were two older people, who introduced themselves as Nico's parents. Then they were introduced to two male cousins of Nico's; then two female second cousins, of Nico's again; a distant uncle in the company of his wife; and, finally, Filippo, who was renting the extra room.

"Did you come to talk to me?" asked Nico.

"Not at all," Montalbano said casually. "We were in the neighborhood and wanted to see how you were doing."

"Thank you, Inspector, I'm feeling better. I still can't stand up, but I can tell I'm recovering fast."

"Good. My best to you all. Oh, and if I did need to talk to you alone, when do you think . . . ?"

"Tomorrow morning, maybe around ten."

"All right," said the inspector, taking leave of the whole company.

Then, as they were heading down the stairs, he muttered: "What a waste of time."

"What are you going to do now, Chief? Go back to your office or go home?"

"I'm going home. How about you?"

"I'd like to go back to the office for a bit."

"Then I'll take you there and continue on home afterwards."

Violent hunger pangs began to assail him when he was still about a mile from home. For him, having eaten a stuffed panino or a couple of sandwiches was like not having eaten at all. And so the first thing he did, once inside the house, was race into the kitchen, remove Livia's sign of warning and recommendations, and open the refrigerator. At a glance, he saw that it was empty. Slamming it shut, he turned in haste to the oven. O blessed be the heavens and all their little cherubs!

Adelina—who, as it was clear by now, didn't give a flying fuck about Livia's guidelines—had prepared for him a *sartù di riso* that the inspector had to restrain himself from eating right then and there, still cold. He lit the oven, took Livia's sheet of paper into the bedroom, put it on the bedside table, removed his jacket, turned on the television, opened the French door to the veranda, waited another five minutes, pacing back and forth, then finally took out the casserole, set it down on a plate, sat down at the kitchen table, and began eating.

After the first spoonful, he stopped and took a deep breath. The dish was truly excellent.

He heaved a big sigh, grateful to life for granting him moments like this. After the third spoonful, he realized he was keeping his eyes closed, the better to taste the food. Feeling satisfied, halfway through the *sartù* he got up and kept eating in front of the TV, sitting down to watch the evening news.

In Paris, pandemonium had broken out when an abandoned suitcase was believed to be full of explosives. Hungary and Poland were refusing to take in their quota of migrants; worse yet, they'd started building walls to keep them out. Meanwhile, pedophilia scandals were erupting within the refugee camps. In Italy, they'd been fortunate to shut down only seven factories. The danger suddenly became clear to Montalbano: He was beginning to lose his appetite. He changed the channel and found himself face-to-face with the beautiful dancer who looked just like Antonia.

This time he did not change channels, but continued to eat with renewed happiness.

When he was done, he got up to fill a small glass with whisky and then sat back down in front of the television. As he was sipping it one drop at a time, the TeleVigàta evening newscast began. The face of Pippo Ragonese, the news chief, appeared, and he opened with these words:

"And where does the investigation into the murder of Carmelo Catalanotti currently stand?"

Montalbano turned it off at once and felt gripped by a kind of remorse. With all the things he had to do, what the hell was he doing, sitting there watching a dancer?

No, he really had to get a move on.

He cleared the table unceremoniously, washed his face, put his jacket back on, checked his pockets to make sure he had the right keys, went out, got in the car, and drove off.

But he didn't go all the way to Via La Marmora. He stopped and parked about four streets before, so he could get his digestive juices flowing with a little walk, having eaten too much.

The streets were deserted. There was a bar closing up shop. He thought a coffee might help clear his head. Then, thinking that he had a great deal of work ahead of him, he went into a bar and had them make four coffees and put them in a small bottle. On the counter he also noticed some little tubs of orange rind covered in chocolate. He got a box of these. Then he noticed a couple of half-full bottles of whisky and bought them, too. Now he had enough provisions for a long night.

He had them put it all in a plastic bag and then left. When he came to the right door, he took out the keys and opened it. Again, because of the heavy feeling in his stomach, he went up the two flights of stairs on foot. A bit winded when he reached the door, he opened it slowly, closed it behind him, and turned on the light in the entranceway. And he turned into a pillar of salt.

He remembered perfectly well that he'd turned the lights out before leaving. So how was it that the lights in the study were on? He froze, and even held his breath. Want to bet the killer always returns to the scene of the crime? Damn! Not only was he unarmed, but the bag he was holding in his hand would make all movement difficult. And so, tiptoeing ever so lightly, and without making any noise, he made his way into the kitchen and set the bag down on the table. Weighing his options, he removed his jacket, rolled up his shirtsleeves, armed himself with the biggest knife he could find, and began to head for the study. Coming up beside the doorway, he flattened his back against the wall and was able to peer inside the room with one eye. And he didn't believe what he saw. He jerked his head back and ran a hand over his eyes. Ah, that must be it. The image from the TV must have remained imprinted on his retinas. He went through the same motions as before, ever so slowly. The confirmation of what he'd seen took his breath away.

Lying on the sofa, with her shoes off and three pillows behind her shoulders, was Antonia, wearing earphones and bobbing her head to the rhythm of the music. Around her a few folders and loan registers lay scattered. It was hard for Montalbano to take his eyes off her legs, since in that position her skirt had slid halfway up her belly. He bent over and set the knife down on the floor, stood back up, ran his fingers quickly through his hair, and, still on tiptoe, went all the way up to the sofa. Engrossed as she was in reading an open folder and listening to the music, Antonia didn't notice him there.

Montalbano raised one knee, rested it on the sofa, and then sat down beside her.

Antonia let out a muffled cry, shot to her feet, and turned to look at him.

"What the fuck are you doing here?" she asked angrily.

"I think the question is: What are *you* doing here?" was Montalbano's reply.

Unexpectedly, Antonia's face broke into a shy smile.

"Hello," she said.

"Hello to you," Montalbano replied. "Want some coffee?" he asked, walking out of the study and making his way around the apartment as if he were at home.

In the kitchen he blithely opened drawers and cupboards, found a tray with a picture of two birds on a branch, which seemed to him appropriate for the situation, set down on it two demitasses, two glasses, a bottle of whisky, the bottle with the coffee—which was still fairly warm—and a box of cookies belonging to the late lamented Carmelo Catalanotti.

Despite the precarious balance of everything on the tray, he managed to carry it all into the study with the light touch and elegance of a first-class waiter.

Antonia had remained on the sofa, still lying on her

back and leaning on the pillows, with her legs extended, except that now she'd pulled her skirt back down and put on a pair of glasses that made her look even more beautiful to Montalbano.

The woman patted the cushion beside her twice with her left hand, inviting the inspector to sit down. With great haste he laid the tray on the desk and sat down. But he ended up much closer to her than he would have liked.

"Do you realize what I've discovered? I took these documents and . . . Catalanotti was a loan shark! He lent money illegally at interest!"

The inspector looked at her, spellbound. *How is it possible? She puts on a pair of glasses and becomes more beautiful; then she starts ranting about Catalanotti, and this adds another, extra touch to her beauty?*

He was a million miles away from the case, happy to have Antonia beside him. He said nothing. All he did was draw nearer to her.

"And, as if that wasn't enough," Antonia resumed, "he wrote down all the dialogues he had with his debtors. Look here: I got this folder from the bedroom. There's a whole closet full of—"

"I know everything," said Montalano, cutting her off.

"They tell of a man who took his own life, probably because of his debts, in the most detached manner imaginable, almost indifferently . . . How is that possible?"

Montalbano rolled his eyes to share the girl's disdain, but in fact his body was inching closer to her all along without her realizing.

Soon they were pressed up against each other.

Antonia sat up, then bent over to pick up another folder,

but when she tried to return to her previous position, she was unable, because her place was now entirely taken by the inspector.

She had no choice. Either sit on the arm of the sofa or in Montalbano's lap.

11

Antonia said nothing but merely climbed over him and sat at the other end of the sofa, which was still vacant.

Montalbano, too, remained silent, as his body resumed, all on its own, its slow approach to the other side of the couch this time.

Antonia tried to move away but couldn't, because she would have fallen.

She looked him in the eye.

Salvo looked back at her.

It is all so simple,
yes, all so simple,
and so clear to see
that I can barely believe it.
Such is the body's purpose:
you either touch me or not,
embrace me or push me away.
The rest is for crazies.

They came out of the shower, all dripping wet.

They looked around but couldn't find even a hint of a towel.

"But where could they be?" asked Antonia.

At last Montalbano discovered a bathrobe hanging behind the door and grabbed it, and they began drying themselves off while still in each other's embrace. Then, all at once, they looked each other in the eye. They'd both had the same thought. They were using a dead man's home as they pleased. But the attraction their bodies felt had been stronger than any such consideration.

With their shared sense of embarrassment, a heavy silence descended on them.

It was broken by Antonia, who, looking at herself in the mirror, started laughing and said: "Look at what you've done to me! My skin's all red from your beard!"

"I'm sorry!" said Montalbano, not knowing what else to say.

They got dressed, still in silence.

It took them half an hour to finish the coffee, whisky, and cookies. They wolfed down even the crumbs. Then she stood up and, with an ever-so-serious face, said: "Inspector. We must get back to work."

"Gladly," said Montalbano. And he hopped to his feet, grabbing her and holding her tight, covering her with kisses.

She broke free.

"I meant, we must continue the investigation."

Montalbano tried feebly to resist.

"We've got all the time in the world."

"I said, we must get back to work," Antonia asserted resolutely, releasing herself from his embrace.

But it wasn't as if she herself was really so keen as she pretended. In fact, she immediately seemed to change her mind, and since the inspector had lain back down on the sofa, Antonia settled in beside him and embraced him. And, just like that, without realizing it, they both fell asleep.

Not until around five in the morning did Montalbano

open his mouth and ask: "Could you now explain to me why you came here?"

"I was overcome with a kind of regret," said Antonia. "We'd seen all the documents in the study, but hadn't been able to open the closet in the bedroom. Then we forgot all about it. Then this afternoon I remembered, and since I have copies of the house keys, I came and found what I found . . ."

"Look," said Montalbano, "we're dealing with two separate things. These registers concern the Catalanotti we could call the moneylender, whereas the folders in the bedroom closet contain records of the auditions he used to make his actors perform."

"What strange auditions . . ."

Montalbano proceeded to tell her about Catalanotti's methods.

"Tell you what," said Antonia. "I think it's too late to start looking at these documents now. Let's leave things as they are and go and get some sleep. We can come back here in the afternoon, around two."

"No," the inspector replied curtly.

"Why not?"

"Because I'll be eating at that hour. But if you wanted to come with me to Enzo's . . ."

"Of course I want to come with you to Enzo's."

> *What do I care if I'm not pretty? My love is a painter,*
> *and will paint me as bright as the city.*

And he whistled all the way home, to the point that he didn't notice three potholes in the road that nearly totaled his car, so high above the ground was he driving.

And he sang all the way home, to the point that when

he came to the turnoff to his house he kept right on going straight, and not until he saw the road sign to Montereale did he turn around, not cursing the saints as he might have done but with a doltish smile, and head back home to Marinella.

He felt not the slightest hunger, not the least bit sleepy.

Going into his bedroom, he undressed and then opened the armoire to take out some clean clothes.

The first shirt that came to hand had a slightly threadbare left cuff.

The second one had a collar that looked as if it had been through World War I.

The third one was a color that had gone out of fashion sometime before 1975.

How long had it been since he'd bought himself a new shirt? His eye fell on the clothes hanging in the armoire. The mere sight of them discouraged him. How could they all have that dusty, old, used-up look?

In a sudden fit of rage he emptied the armoire, throwing all the clothes with their hangers onto the bed. Then he sat down, feeling dejected. At this point it was inevitable that he caught sight of himself in the mirror: He had red eyes and a stubbly, prickly beard; from the arc of his eyebrows a few long white hairs were sprouting; and his spare tire was in the process of becoming a proper potbelly. He raised one arm, and the flesh quivered.

Matre santa! What was happening to him?

As if to dispel the image, he suddenly stood up and went into the bathroom to take a shower. He was about to turn on the water when he stopped and started sniffing the skin on his left arm.

Miracle!

There was still a little of Antonia's scent on it.

Wouldn't it be better, instead of taking a shower, to wash himself one body part at a time, without letting the water splash across his chest? That way, maybe a little of her scent would reach his nostrils during the morning hours.

While shaving, he remembered what Antonia had said. Indeed, it felt rather like sandpaper! Of course, with that cheapo shaving cream he'd bought at the smoke shop, what could he expect?

Back in the bedroom, he selected a pair of trousers and a jacket that seemed the best he could do. Then, before putting them on, he lay on the floor, belly down. No less than forty push-ups.

He got in his car and sped off to the center of town, where there was a big, sparkly perfumery that he'd never set foot in before.

Since it was still early, he had no problem finding a parking place.

Entering the store, he was immediately assailed by the sickly sweet, almost nauseating combination of scents stagnating in the air. Behind the counter were two very sharply done-up girls. The younger of the two turned to him and with a luminous smile asked if she could be of help. Montalbano felt a little awkward in that environment, which for all its fanciness utterly lacked elegance.

"I'm looking for some good shaving cream."

"Aerosol or brush?"

"Brush."

"Just one minute, please," said the girl.

She moved away from the counter and opened a small

glass display case, returning with three different packages of shaving soap.

"This one here is the best. It's French."

Montalbano, head increasingly numb from all the scents, said only: "All right, I'll take it."

But the girl, instead of packing it up, merely kept looking at him.

What on earth did she want? the inspector wondered.

"May I?" the salesgirl suddenly asked.

And she reached out with one hand, but Montalbano pulled away and stepped back.

"I'm sorry," she said, "I only wanted to . . ."

"No, I apologize," said the inspector, drawing near again.

The girl then ran her fingers delicately over his face, as if caressing it.

"Your skin is very dry. You need a good aftershave."

Resigned, Montalbano threw up his hands.

The girl went to another display case and came back to him.

She opened a box and unscrewed the cap on the bottle, which she then thrust under his nose.

"Smell how nice."

Montalbano sniffed. The scent was indeed pleasant.

"It's the same brand as the shaving soap. But I would like you also to try something else." The girl pulled a sparkly little tube out of a drawer and brought it to his nose. "What do you think?"

"What is it?" the inspector asked, feeling as if he'd suddenly entered a Buddhist temple.

"It's a liquid soap made with Dead Sea salts and pure Yemeni incense."

The inspector merely wanted to get out of that place as

quickly as possible. He told the salesgirl he liked the first one better.

As the girl went to prepare his package, a very elegant lady entered the store. The other salesgirl, who'd been sitting behind the counter all the while, greeted her.

"*Buongiorno*, Signora Geneviève."

Upon hearing her name the inspector turned to look her in the eye. The woman was doing the same. Feeling embarrassed at being caught in a perfume shop, Montalbano wished he could vanish from the face of the earth but gave in to his curiosity to see the woman who might be the one living a floor above Mimì's cadaver. At this point the woman smiled at him and said:

"You're the famous Inspector Montalbano, aren't you?"

Now, more than vanishing, he wished he could drop dead.

"Yes."

Then, rather bluntly: "I have the pleasure of knowing your second-in-command, Domenico Augello."

"Me, too," said Montalbano, immediately biting his tongue for the stupidity of what he'd just said.

Genoveffa—known to intimates as Geneviève—who apparently didn't know a thing about discretion, then asked: "Are you here to buy something for your companion?"

Montalbano didn't answer. He just turned to the salesgirl and said: "I'm sorry, I'm running late and have to go."

"That's all right, I'm all done," the girl said. "Here's your package. I also included some small samples of eye cream for men, which you're sure to like. And let me know how you like the shaving soap and aftershave."

Montalbano did not look up but only gave a half bow to Genoveffa, aka Geneviève, went over to the cash register, and, without even looking at the bill, paid with a credit card and left.

To shake off the embarrassment and the scent plaguing him, he headed for a café. Inside, he ordered, and as he was waiting at the bar, he opened the bag from the perfumery.

He took out the receipt, glanced at it, and very nearly fell on the floor.

He'd spent almost as much as for a dinner for two at the fanciest restaurant in Palermo. Then, thinking that when caressing his face Antonia might find soft skin instead of sandpaper, he decided it was worth it.

He got in his car and started up the engine to go to the office, when a doubt occurred to him. He turned off the engine to think it over. Wouldn't it be best, in fact, to resolve all his wardrobe problems that same morning? He'd come this far; he might as well go all the way.

He started the car back up, drove off, and miraculously found a parking spot right in front of the most elegant men's clothing shop in Vigàta.

Here there were no salesgirls. The personnel was . . . What kind of personnel was this, anyway? They were certainly male, but by the way they moved they seemed almost more feminine than the girls in the perfumery.

Montalbano told them he was looking for some shirts, and they sat him down in a red velvet armchair and then asked him what size collar he wore. He replied that he didn't know. The salesman then asked him to stand back up and ran a measuring tape around his neck. At that exact moment he heard a woman's voice cry out: "Oh, how wonderful, Inspector! It really must be fate! This must mean we're destined to become friends!"

It was Genoveffa, aka Geneviève.

The inspector cursed in his mind but managed a half smile on the outside.

The salesman returned, carrying a stack of shirts, which he then laid out on the counter. Displayed before Montalbano was a parade of colors reminiscent of a circus or a painted Sicilian cart: polka-dotted fabrics, shirts with pinstripes and fat stripes, with rainbows, with tiny giraffe prints or huge animals, with iridescent cuffs echoing the collar, with buttons each different from the other, or collarless, or with a seventies-style collar that came halfway down to your bellybutton. It was all too much for Montalbano, who was unable to say anything and just headed for the door.

Genoveffa, aka Geneviève, stopped him in his tracks.

"May I be of help?"

The inspector grabbed onto her as onto a life preserver.

"Yes, thank you."

"I think I've understood that you're looking for a shirt?"

"Yes, but not like those," Montalbano said disconsolately, indicating the items on the counter.

Genoveffa, aka Geneviève, said a few esoteric words to the salesman, who turned and left, and finally came back with a new stack of shirts. These looked wearable.

Together they selected three: white, sky-blue, and another, also sky-blue but with very fine pinstripes.

Now he'd spent the equivalent of almost four meals for two at the same fancy Palermo restaurant. He said goodbye to Genoveffa, aka Geneviève, thanking her again, then got in his car, put the shirts in the backseat, and headed for the office.

One minute later, he screeched to a halt.

What was the point of new shirts if his suits sucked?

He absolutely had to buy himself at least two new ones.

Going back into the same store as before was out of the question. He would find that big pain in the ass Genoveffa, aka Geneviève, still there. It occurred to him that at the far end of the corso was a clothing store with ready-to-wear suits.

He started up the car, but then shut it off again. The traffic had become more intense, he realized. He might not find another parking spot. So he got out of the car and headed off on foot.

Halfway down the corso, he noticed the sign for a barber shop. Looking in, he saw a free chair, so he went in and sat down.

He asked the barber to do a little trim on his hair and mustache. During the entire procedure he kept his eyes closed. Behind his eyelids, in fact, an image sequence was playing that ran from Antonia's left shoulder blade down to her right hip, then back again. The barber asked him if he wanted "the works"—that is, shampoo, pomade, and cream for the face and eyes . . . The inspector consented.

When he opened his eyes again and looked at himself in the mirror, he got a big surprise. He barely recognized himself. But the bit of himself he did recognize met with his approval.

Now he'd spent almost as much as a full fish dinner at the same Palermo restaurant. He went out and headed for the clothing store.

He wasted the rest of the morning there.

After seeing a great many suits and choosing two, he went and tried them on. But the sleeves of the first one were too long, and the trousers of the second one were too tight around the waist. A salesman came, took his exact measurements, and said he would have the suits ready for him the following afternoon. Tomorrow? But he needed them in less than two hours! And so, in addition to the ones he'd selected, he picked out two more items, a separate jacket and pair of trousers, which both fit.

Now he'd spent nearly the equivalent of a baptism celebration at the same restaurant.

Coming out of the store, he walked back up the corso, bought two packs of cigarettes and some breath mints, but then dropped the box. When he bent down to pick it up, he noticed that his shoes looked shabby.

Suddenly terrified that all the stores were about to close for lunch, he had no choice but to race into the shop of Umberto Amato, known for highway robbery, where he'd sworn he would never set foot.

Umberto Amato's fame proved almost too tame for the reality.

For a pair of English shoes, he made him pay almost as much as if he'd flown to England in a private jet to buy them.

Still, for whatever reason, he came out of the store all smiles, and headed in the direction of his car. At a certain point he saw a shop window featuring wonderful, elegant socks.

They certainly would look nice under his new trousers.

"Come on, man!" he said to himself with a note of masculine pride. "No socks! I'll keep my own!"

It was a little past one when he entered the police station.

He was immediately assailed by a shouting Catarella.

"Ahhh, Chief, Chief! Iss been all mornin'—"

Montalbano turned around, glared at him imperiously, and put his forefinger over his lips.

Catarella shut up at once.

The inspector was heading for the bathroom when Fazio stopped him.

"Where ya been, Chief? Your cell phone was turned off. I've been waiting for you all morning to go and see Nico Dilicata."

"How about that!" said Montalbano, smiling. "I'd completely forgotten about it. We can go tomorrow. What's the hurry, anyway? And now, my friend, I've got work to do. See you later."

And he resumed walking, followed by the flummoxed eyes of Fazio and Catarella, to the bathroom, where he locked himself in with all his packages and shopping bags.

It was twelve minutes to two when the bathroom door opened again.

Montalbano came out looking like a fashion plate: dressed to the nines, scented, and sporting shiny shoes.

The number of people in the corridor, meanwhile, had increased. Gallo and Galluzzo had joined Fazio and Catarella in their wait. They were all about to open their mouths to say something, but were left speechless at the sight of him.

Never in their lives had they seen the inspector so gussied up.

Montalbano had neither the time nor the desire to explain anything, and he communicated this fact to them by simply holding up the palm of his right hand to signal "stop."

He was like one of those star lawyers who, when confronted by journalists at the end of a crucial session, only answers their questions with a laconic "No comment."

It was ten minutes to two when he screeched to a halt outside of Enzo's trattoria.

He got out of the car and stood in the doorway of the restaurant, waiting for Antonia.

And he stayed that way for a good fifteen minutes.

There was no sign of Antonia.

It was two twenty-five when he decided to wait for her inside.

The moment he was in the restaurant, however, his eyes were drawn irresistibly to a scene that made him freeze: Antonia was sitting at a table with a man, and smiling at him!

Montalbano felt his heart give out.

Who was that man? He could see only his back. Then he recognized him. It was Enzo. And they were having a blast.

Smoldering with jealousy, Montalbano would have liked to go up to the table, take a napkin, swat Enzo across the face with it, and say: "Consider yourself challenged." But the joy of seeing Antonia again got the better of him.

He approached, bent down, kissed her almost on the lips, and, without out even deigning to look at Enzo, said: "Finally."

"You certainly made me wait," Antonia said frostily.

Meanwhile Enzo had stood up and, ceding his place to Montalbano, asked: "What can I bring you?"

Montalbano looked questioningly at Antonia, who said: "I'm so hungry I can barely see. You order for me."

The inspector ordered a few hearty antipasti and then, after Enzo had left, put his hand on Antonia's and smiled.

Antonia withdrew hers and did not return his smile.

"What's wrong?" he asked, alarmed.

"Nothing. What should be wrong?" said the woman. Then, shooting a quick glance at him, she added: "I liked you better before."

"Before when?"

"Before before. This haircut makes you look older, and, anyway, you're all . . . well, shiny . . . You look like you fell into a tub of brilliantine. And you smell funny. And that jacket . . ."

"What's wrong with the jacket?"

"It makes you look heavier."

What? He hadn't slept, he hadn't worked, he'd spent the morning shopping, he'd spent a small fortune, and all just to look older and fatter?

He was about to get up in a rage when she put her hand on his, caressed it, and, smiling, said: "Come on, don't take it so hard."

12

Luckily the *sarde a beccafico* arrived, followed by fried artichokes, then a baby-octopus-in-vinegar salad. But Montalbano's appetite had vanished.

Or at least he thought it had vanished. Because when he saw with what relish and satisfaction Antonia was dispatching one antipasto after another, he tried having a listless little bite himself, followed by another, and then another, until he realized that not only had his appetite not vanished, it was returning even more imperious than before.

And thus it all became one big exchange of smiles, and looks deep into each other's eyes, and toasts to their mutual happiness.

Under the table, Montalbano's legs instinctively sought out Antonia's, which curled around his like tree roots.

Well, that's a relief! Montalbano thought to himself. *She's over it.*

He'd barely finished formulating this thought when she extricated herself and said severely: "Let's try to be serious, Salvo. Remember, we're here to work on the case."

"Is that the only reason you're here?"

"Why else, if not?"

Montalbano lowered his head and started eating his *spaghetti alla carrettiera.* Then, all of a sudden, he stopped, fork in midair, when her legs returned in search of his. He raised his eyes from his plate and looked at her. She had an amused look on her face. Montalbano felt like he'd gotten on board a roller coaster and couldn't, or perhaps wouldn't, get off.

When it came time to pay the bill, Enzo said: "Already taken care of."

"Did you pay?" the inspector asked Antonia, ready to get angry.

"No, not me."

"If I may say so, it's on the house: an homage to beauty!" said Enzo, bowing to Antonia.

As Montalbano was driving towards Via La Marmora, he spontaneously put his hand on Antonia's left leg. Without a peep, she removed it and put it back on the steering wheel.

Man, what a sourpuss! Montalbano thought, feeling all of the hopes he'd put in the coming afternoon being dashed.

When he arrived at Catalanotti's building, he parked the car.

Antonia got out and, keys already in hand, headed for the front door. Montalbano had to lock the car in a hurry and ran to catch up to her. She'd already gone into the elevator, leaving the door open. Montalbano got in, pushed the button, and gave her a little smile. She, nothing.

Antonia was at the far end of the elevator, back against the wall, staring at the ceiling. There was about four or five feet's distance between them, but Antonia, in her present mind-set, was millions of miles away.

When they arrived at the right floor, Montalbano stepped aside for her, and she went out and opened the door, entering the apartment. He followed behind her, turned around to shut the door, turned again, and ran straight into a rigid

Antonia, who literally threw herself on him and forcefully pressed her lips against his.

Let my hands go free,
and my heart, let me go free!
Let my fingers travel
the roads of your body.
[. . .] Fire! Fire!

They dried themselves off with the same bathrobe and got dressed again.

Montalbano told her in brief everything they'd learned from the interrogations and the conclusions they'd drawn among themselves.

Then he added: "I have an idea. Let's now take these folders from the closet; there must be a good hundred of them. We'll split the load and, using the auditions as a base, and Catalanotti's comments especially, we'll try to get a handle on the character profiles. We're sure to find some more interesting than others. Those we'll put aside and then reexamine them together. All right?"

"All right," said Antonia, putting her glasses back on.

They got seriously down to work. In fact, when they finished, it was almost nine p.m.

They put the folders back in their place, leaving out only about ten.

They spoke a little about what they'd found and then Antonia asked: "And what will we do with these remaining folders: leave them here or take them to the station?"

"I'd leave them here," Montalbano said slyly. "In case we need to go over them together . . ."

"Okay," said Antonia.

The inspector then looked at her and, smiling, asked: "Shall we go out to dinner, or do you want to come to my place?"

"Neither," Antonia said brusquely. "I have to go home. Could you give me a ride to my car?"

Montalbano realized that the roller coaster had started up again. He nodded yes, and they gathered up their things and left Catalanotti's apartment.

As they were driving towards Enzo's parking lot, the inspector, without nourishing any hope, tried to make another move on Antonia: He put his right hand on her left leg, and she promptly removed it again and put it back on the steering wheel.

Q.E.D.

"So, what's the plan?" the inspector asked.

"I'll call you," said Antonia, getting out of the car without deigning to give him so much as a little kiss.

It was well past dinnertime, as his dully growling stomach was reminding him. To calm it down he put a hand on his belly, almost as if to caress it. He felt proud of his body: It might be well on in years and the worse for wear, but all things considered, it had performed well. Indeed it had acquitted itself beyond all expectation.

He turned onto the drive leading to his house but had

to brake suddenly, because he found the road blocked by three cars. For whatever reason, he thought it might be an ambush. In the darkness he saw three male figures and instinctively put the car in reverse to back up to the main road as his right hand quickly opened the glove compartment and grabbed his gun. At that moment he heard a voice.

"Salvo, it's Mimì."

Heaving a sigh of relief, he closed the glove compartment and resumed his forward progress. In the beam of the headlights he recognized not only Mimì but Gallo and Fazio.

He got out of the car.

"What the hell are you guys doing here?"

"And where the hell have you been yourself?" Mimì retorted. "This morning you came to the station for barely a few minutes, you got all dolled up, and then you disappeared for the rest of the day! With your cell phone off! And no answer on your home phone, either! Jesus Christ! Doesn't it occur to you that we might need you? At a certain point we even started to get worried."

"Worried about what?"

"Well, seeing you were in disguise and all."

"In disguise? Me?"

"Isn't that what you said to me, Fazio? You said he looked like something out of a fashion magazine. So we thought you were on some kind of secret mission."

"What the fuck are you guys thinking! Listen, if you want to chew me out, go right ahead. Otherwise, go back home or to the station."

"Good night," said Gallo, getting into his car and then executing a complicated maneuver to avoid the other cars blocking the way.

And since neither Fazio nor Augello showed the slightest intention of leaving, Montalbano made a decision.

"Park your cars properly, and then let's all go inside."

It was a pleasant enough evening, and so they sat out on the veranda. Montalbano went into the kitchen and in the oven found more than enough beef *involtini* with sauce and roast potatoes.

"Have you guys eaten?" he called loudly from the kitchen.

"No," the other two replied in chorus.

"Then set the table."

Augello and Fazio obeyed the order. As everything was warming up, Montalbano opened a bottle of wine and filled three glasses.

"So what good things have you got to tell me?"

"Salvo," Mimì said in an exasperated tone, "let's cut the charade. Now talk."

"I did something neither of you thought of doing. In Catalanotti's bedroom is a kind of closet containing over a hundred folders. I went through these, read them one after another, spent the whole day doing it. They're transcriptions of the auditions Catalanotti made his actors perform."

Mimì looked at him in admiration.

Montalbano continued: "There's about ten or so interesting documents that I've set aside. Tomorrow I'm gonna look at them more closely."

"Want me to come, too?" Fazio asked with great interest.

"Not on your life!" Montalbano blurted out, reacting instinctively.

Fazio looked at him, completely bewildered.

"Wha'd I do, Chief? Say something wrong?"

"No, no, I'm sorry. It's just that . . . I don't know how

to put it . . . I've come up with my own method, and I'd rather continue alone. What you should do tomorrow is instead inform Nico that we'll be at his place at ten-thirty."

"Okay, okay."

And, just to change the subject, he stood up and said: "I think the *involtini* are probably hot enough now."

He went into the kitchen and returned with the steaming casserole. He meted out the servings and then repeated: "So, what good things have you got to tell me?"

Fazio and Augello looked at each other, and Mimì spoke first.

"I still haven't been able to figure out who Catalanotti's blonde might be, but I think I may be on the right track."

"I, on the other hand," said Fazio, "have the keys!"

"The keys to what?" the inspector asked confusedly, stopping a forkful of potato in midair.

"The head of the agency is back, and I talked him into giving me the keys," said Fazio, sticking his hand in his pocket and taking them out.

"But what agency?" asked Montalbano, rotating the fork in his hand.

"Come on, Inspector! The keys to the apartment on Via Biancamano!!!" said Fazio, raising his voice and talking the way one does to children.

"My cadaver!" Augello jumped in.

This statement allowed Montalbano to do the math. And to save face, he said: "Well, it was about time!"

Then he fell silent again.

"I'll go myself," said Mimì. "That way I can also drop in and say hello to Geneviève."

"Nobody's going anywhere," said Montalbano, cutting things short. "Gimme those keys."

Fazio handed them to him, and at that exact moment the phone rang. It was Livia.

Mimì gestured to ask whether he wanted them to leave so he could talk undisturbed, but Montalbano shook his head.

"You'll have to forgive me, Livia, but I'm here with Fazio and Augello and we're discussing a very complicated case."

"No problem. Well, I wish you a good night."

"You sleep well, too," said Montalbano, and he went back out on the veranda.

"Now we have all the time we want to take stock of the situation."

He'd barely finished his sentence when the phone rang again. He got up reluctantly, thinking it was Livia who'd forgotten to tell him something.

"Hello," he said gruffly.

"It's me."

It was Antonia. Montalbano staggered and then said: "Could you wait just two seconds?"

"Of course."

He shot back out onto the veranda.

"Okay, guys, now you can do me the favor of leaving, pronto."

"But didn't you want to take stock . . . ?" said Mimì, not understanding.

"No! Now go."

After the two stood up, he practically pushed them into the house and then followed them, still pushing, all the way to the front door. Whispering for fear that Antonia might hear him over the phone, he said softly: "We'll talk tomorrow morning at the office."

He closed the door behind them and ran back to the phone.

"Are you still there?"

"Of course."

"I was afraid," said the inspector, feeling his body relax.

"Of what?"

"Afraid you'd hung up. But how did you get this number, anyway?"

"Inspector, I am the chief of the forensics lab. Don't forget that."

"In any case, it's wonderful to hear your voice," said Montalbano, his eyes closed, completely lost.

"Well, I certainly didn't call you so you could hear my voice."

"So why did you call, then?"

"To tell you I can't see you tomorrow."

Plop, went Montalbano's heart, falling to the floor.

But he didn't lose faith, and even managed to speak in a steady voice.

"Then let's see each other now."

"Come on, be serious. Tomorrow I have to go to Palermo and I don't know what time I'll be back."

"Then I'll call you in the evening . . ."

"No. I'll call you," she said, and hung up.

Montalbano stood there for a moment holding the receiver. Then he set it down, went out to the veranda, and started sadly clearing the table.

Then, feeling his eyelids drooping, he decided to go to bed and recover some of the sleep he'd lost the night before. As he took off his jacket, he noticed there was a set of keys in the pocket. He remembered that Fazio had given them to him, and they were to the apartment with Mimì's cadaver. Despite his fatigue he thought it might be a good idea to get in the car and go there straightaway, then he immediately had another idea that seemed much better to him: Why not ask Antonia tomorrow to go there with him? Into the bargain she might even be able to find some evidence on the deathbed that he hadn't noticed with the naked eye.

As soon as he hit the bed and closed his eyes, Antonia appeared before him. He sent a great big smile her way and fell asleep.

At ten-thirty the next morning, dressed in his new clothes, and with Fazio at his side, he rang the doorbell to Nico's apartment.

Margherita opened the door and welcomed them both.

"I was waiting for you," she said. "But you'll have to excuse me, I have to go out now."

"No problem at all," said Montalbano, holding his hand out to her.

They found Nico lying on the sofa.

"Come in, please, and make yourselves comfortable," he said.

Montalbano took two chairs, and they sat down beside him.

"Can I offer you anything?"

"No, no, thanks," they said in unison.

"These past few days," the inspector began, "I'm sure you've had a lot of time to think about what happened."

"Yes, I couldn't think of anything else."

"Good. Do you have anything new to tell us?"

"No, Inspector. And not only do I not know who it was that shot at me, but I can't even imagine why. I'm more and more convinced it was some kind of mistake."

"Mind if I have a look outside from your balcony?" asked Montalbano, standing up.

"Go right ahead," replied the young man.

The inspector went over to the French door, opened it, and went outside. The door to the street was directly below, and directly in front was the six-story building with the haberdashery on the ground floor. Since it was a nice sunny day, almost all the balconies in the building had laundry drying outside. Montalbano went back inside and sat down.

"So, in essence," he said, "you're confirming that, when you went out the door, you didn't see anyone, right?"

"Yes, that's right."

"But that's very strange."

"Why?"

"Because, when going out of your building, you couldn't help but catch at least a glimpse of whoever it was who shot you. The ballistics speak clearly. Your attacker was directly in front of you. So now, please, tell me who it was."

"I can't tell you, because I didn't see anybody."

"We have a witness," said Montalbano.

Though he was lying down, Nico visibly gave a start.

"That's impossible."

"Why? Haven't you ever noticed how many people live in the building right in front of you?"

"Could you tell me this person's name?"

"No. I can only tell you that she's coming in to the

station this afternoon, because she got a good look at your attacker and is going to help us make an artist's reconstruction of him."

Nico wiped his sweaty forehead with his arm.

"Are you sure you have nothing to tell us?" Montalbano insisted.

Nico's attitude changed suddenly.

"Inspector," he began, sitting up, "are you conducting an interrogation?"

"No. As you can see, nobody is writing down what's being said."

"So much the better."

"Why do you say that?"

"Because from this moment on I won't answer any more of your questions unless my lawyer is present, in accordance with the law."

It was a definitive statement, and so Montalbano stood up, signaled to Fazio to follow him, and giving a wave of the hand by way of good-bye, they went out, without deigning even to glance at Nico.

"And now," the inspector said once they were in the car, "I need for you to find me, before the morning is over, a photo of Tano Lo Bello."

"Do you think he did it?"

"It's possible, and I'm going to give it a try. But the trap has to be perfect."

"Meaning?"

"First I have to talk to Nico's girlfriend."

"When should I have her come in?"

"This evening around five."

He would cancel the meeting if Antonia called.

He'd started signing the first papers at the top of the stack on his left when he suddenly got the urge to use a green felt-tip pen, just to see how the higher-ups would react. Opening his upper drawer to look for the pen, he came across a sheaf of paper held together with a black plastic ring binding, and on its cover page were the words *Dangerous Corner.* What was this? He opened it and started reading. Nothing. All dialogues between people with English names. Then he remembered. This was a copy of the play Catalanotti had wanted to produce. He put the latest document back on top of the stack, and with a sigh of satisfaction at having found an excuse not to sign papers, he started reading.

Nearly two hours passed before he raised his eyes from the text. It was a beautiful play. And very possibly the key to everything lay in figuring out exactly how Catalanotti had been planning to stage it. He would surely have to talk this over with Mimì and Fazio, and so he decided to take a sheet of paper and write down a sort of summary.

> *Curtain down. Voices of a man and a woman talking about illusion and reality.*
>
> *Still in darkness, a gunshot rings out, followed by a woman's scream.*
>
> *The curtain rises. A middle-class interior with four women (Freda, Betty, Miss Mockridge, and Olwen), who've just finished listening to a play on the radio. They make a variety of comments.*
>
> *The men arrive. The couples pair off: Freda is married*

to Robert Caplan, Betty with Gordon Whitehouse (Freda's brother), and there is a third man, Stanton, who works at Robert's publishing house. Miss Mockridge is a writer, and Olwen also works with the publisher.

One learns that a year earlier, Martin, Robert's brother, after being accused of stealing 5,000 pounds sterling, committed suicide by shooting himself.

At a certain point Freda pulls out a cigar box that is also a music box. Olwen recognizes it, saying it used to belong to Martin. But in fact Olwen had no way of knowing it was Martin's. They ask her for an explanation; Olwen tries to make nothing of it.

Gordon looks for a danceable tune on the radio as a way of changing the subject. The radio stops working.

Robert, however, stubbornly wants to know more about the music box: How could Olwen possibly have known it belonged to Martin?

Robert wants to know the Truth.

Olwen is forced to admit that she went to see Martin in his cottage on the night of his suicide. Freda will also admit to having been there that same afternoon.

The unveiling of the Truth brings inadmissible loves and hatreds out into the open:

Olwen was in love with Robert (his own wife Freda will say so);

Freda had been having a relationship with her brother-in-law Martin for many years;

And Gordon, Betty's husband, was also in love with Martin.

Freda and Gordon, who are brother and sister, argue over which one was more loved by Martin, becoming a pair of hysterics quarreling over a dead man's body.

It is discovered that Stanton had set the two siblings against each other, by insinuating to Martin that it was Robert who'd stolen the 5,000 pounds, and then to Robert that it was Martin. The atmosphere grows increasingly tense.

Finally, at one point Olwen confesses that it was she who killed Martin, by accident, defending herself against a drug-fueled sexual aggression on his part. Stanton is not surprised by her confession, and communicates the three elements that had made him suspect Olwen all along.

Olwen reveals that after the incident with Martin, she went to Stanton's cottage and caught him in the act of making love with Betty.

Betty, who seems like the naïve airhead of the clique, is nothing of the sort, and is having an exclusively sexual relationship with Stanton. And in fact her husband, Gordon, doesn't deign pay her any attention.

They discover that in reality it was Stanton himself who stole the money, among other reasons to satisfy Betty's desires.

At this point Robert reveals his love for Betty, which Freda already knew about, and he is upset to discover that Betty is not the way he imagined.

The Truth is too much for everyone. They decide never to say anything to anyone about it.

Olwen, the one who pulled the trigger, seems to be the only person who comes out of this clean.

Robert is the most desperate, having realized that the reality in which he'd been living until then was only a world of illusion. The Truth is completely different. Freda reminds him that he was the one who started it all.

Darkness.

Light: Everyone's back in the same position as in the first act. The play begins anew, as the questions about the musical cigar box begin. Gordon succeeds in finding a good danceable tune on the radio, and everyone starts dancing.

The curtain falls.

Montalbano put the copy of the play back in his drawer and looked at his watch. It was time to go eat.

13

He came out of Enzo's feeling heavier. He took his customary stroll as far as the flat rock, sat down, and began thinking about the play he'd read. It was so well written that the inspector had no problem imagining the characters and their actions onstage.

But how had Catalanotti imagined them?

What kinds of auditions had he been planning for his actors?

Or perhaps even carried out?

Montalbano tried to remember the first lines in the play, the ones about reality and illusion.

He'd already read them somewhere before. But where?

Surely the folders he was going to review with Antonia would come to his aid.

But it was anyone's guess where, and with whom, Antonia was at that moment.

His cell phone rang. Hoping it was her, he tried to pull it out of his pocket, but as he was just about to succeed, the device slipped out of his hand and slid dangerously to the very edge of the rock. He leapt forward and grabbed it, getting all wet and slimy in the process.

"Hello! . . ."

It was Livia. His disappointment was profound. Why was she calling at that hour?

"What is it?" he asked rudely.

"I'm sorry, is this not a good time?"

"No, it's not. I'm in a meeting."

"Well, this won't take long. I just wanted to let you know that I'll be on the first flight to Palermo tomorrow morning, landing at ten."

"No!" Montalbano yelled.

"No, what? Is that too early? You can't come and pick me up? No problem, I'll just take the bus."

"No. You can't come."

"Oh, my God. Why not?"

Montalbano didn't know what to say.

He hung up. He would tell her they got cut off. Then, thinking she would try to reach him at the station, because he told her he was in a meeting, he steeled himself and dialed her number.

"I'm sorry, I just got out of the meeting. We can talk now."

"But what on earth got into you? Why can't I come?"

"Livia, I'll try to explain it all to you more calmly this evening. All I can tell you now is that it's really not a good idea for you to come. You wouldn't be able to find me."

It was, in fact, only half a lie, since it was true that if Livia did come, she would no longer find the Montalbano she used to know.

"All right, then. We'll talk this evening," she said.

When he returned to the office, he spent the first half hour simply dawdling about. Then he reread his summary of the play. He was about to fold the page in two when Fazio came in.

"Have a seat."

Without saying another word, he handed him the sheet

of paper with his synopsis of *Dangerous Corner.* Fazio read it, then asked him, as if in a daze: "And what is this gobbledygook?"

"It's the plot of the play that Catalanotti was preparing for production and looking for actors for."

Without saying anything, Fazio carefully reread the page and then looked at Montalbano inquisitively again.

"Do you remember that we'd conjectured that the killer might be someone who'd rebelled against the rather . . . er, cruel auditions Catalanotti put his actors through?"

"Mmm-hmm."

"Well, this play seems to give him a chance to unleash his fantasies to their most extreme conclusions and take them as far as they'll go."

"What are you trying to say?"

"Fazio, the play is about bourgeois, middle-class people, who have bourgeois jobs and lead bourgeois lives. They have no real problems, other than the fact that they live in a world of illusions. One evening, one of them, Robert, demands to know the truth about something apparently insignificant, and yet it's enough to open the floodgates to the point that somebody even dies. Maybe even two people."

"So that means you want to orient the investigation around the people Catalanotti was looking for to put in his play?"

"Exactly."

"Chief, there's also something else worth mentioning. It seems to me that in the play as well they talk about money that was stolen and not returned."

"And so?"

"And so you mustn't forget that Catalanotti was also a

moneylender. So, in my opinion, the field of investigation remains rather broad just the same."

Montalbano's cell phone rang. He took it out. It was Antonia.

How his heart leapt in his chest!

"Oh, joy! How nice to hear from you!"

Fazio bolted out of his chair and out of the office, closing the door behind him.

"Ciao, Salvo, I just wanted to let you know I'm on my way back to Montelusa."

"Excellent. What time can I come and pick you up?"

"I'm sorry, but to go where?"

"I don't know, we could go and have dinner together somewhere, and then . . ."

"No, Salvo. I'll see you in Via La Marmora, at nine-thirty."

"All right," said the inspector, disappointed. "See you then."

Antonia didn't return his good-bye. Apparently the roller coaster was starting up again. There was a discreet knock at the door.

"Come in."

Fazio appeared.

"Come in, come in."

"I just wanted to let you know that Margherita Lo Bello is here."

"Bring her in."

Fazio vanished and, one minute later, Margherita appeared in the doorway. Her face was ghostly white, her manner nervous, and the way she moved seemed to indicate that she was deeply worried.

"Please sit down," said the inspector, and before he could say anything else, she began speaking.

"I think it was a mistake for me to come here. Nico told me about your conversation this morning."

"So why do you think it was a mistake?"

"Because maybe I should have brought a lawyer with me."

"Look, let me reassure you straightaway: This is an informal discussion, as was my talk with your boyfriend."

"Okay."

"There are certain details, in your story and in Nico's, that don't add up. Can I go on?"

The girl nodded.

"First of all, both you and Nico have claimed you didn't hear the gunshot. But at six o'clock in the morning, the street was practically deserted. It's almost impossible you couldn't hear the shot."

"Maybe the gunman used a silencer," she said, interrupting him.

"But in that case we're talking about a professional killer, who certainly wouldn't have just shot Nico in the leg. On top of that, we have a witness who claims she heard the shot perfectly well."

Margherita's face grew chalkier by the second.

"If you'll allow me to speak frankly, I must say I don't understand why you feel the need to deny that you heard the gunshot. Unless . . ."

The inspector stopped.

"Unless . . . ?" Margherita said in a faint voice.

"Unless," Montalbano resumed, "the fact of not having heard the shot is the only way that you, Margherita, can uphold your version of events."

"I don't understand," said Margherita.

"I'll try to explain more clearly. The first time we spoke at the hospital, you told me you were about to open the balcony to say good-bye to Nico when you heard the buzzer ring. Do you remember?"

"Yes, that's right."

"Now, if you're in the process of opening the door to the balcony and you hear a gunshot, you know that your Nico is in the doorway of your building and so you would normally, instinctively, open the door and run onto the balcony to see what happened. But this isn't what happened, in your version of things, because you didn't hear the gunshot. You heard the buzzer. But, you see, between the gunshot and the ring of the buzzer, a fair amount of time would have to pass. Nico falls, tries to get back up, can't manage, then he finally succeeds, reaches the buzzer and intercom, and calls for help. And what about you? What are you doing all this time? Standing in front of the closed window to the balcony, not opening it? Do you realize that your story doesn't make sense?"

Margherita didn't know what to say. She merely hung her head and remained silent.

"Shall I go on?" asked the inspector. He paused a moment, weighing his options—because this time he was staking everything on a lie as big as a house. If he got it right, he was home free.

Margherita wearily threw her hands up.

"I'm giving you every chance to tell me the truth. But since you don't seem to want to take advantage of the opportunity, I have no choice but to tell you that next time you're called in, you'll have to bring your lawyer."

"Why?"

The girl's question was barely audible.

"Because my witness saw you on the balcony and heard you shout."

Margherita burst into tears. He'd been right on the money.

"All right, I'm done," said Montalbano. "You have twenty-four hours to think about it. Talk it over with your boyfriend. Fazio, please show the young lady out."

Fazio returned and they both sat there for a moment looking at each other in silence.

"Still have doubts?"

"No."

"It's clear that both Nico and Margherita saw perfectly well who it was that shot him, but don't want to reveal his name under any circumstances. Why not?"

"Because," said Fazio, "that name is Tano Lo Bello, Margherita's father."

"Did you find a photo?"

"Yessir."

"Is there anyone here who can draw an artist's reconstruction?"

"Yessir, Chief. There's Di Marzio."

"Then give him the photo at once and tell him to make the likeness pretty close."

He left the station, went to the store to pick up his new clothes, which were supposed to be ready by now, put them in the car without trying them on, and headed home. The moment he got inside, he opened the French door to the veranda and remained awestruck, looking out at the sunset, which was a thing of beauty.

The horizon line looked painted by Piero Guccione. Spellbound, Montalbano sat down. The red ball was sinking, ever so slowly, into the sea. Only when it was completely gone did his thoughts turn at once to Livia. Had their relationship also slowly declined and was it now setting once and for all, as the sun had just done? It had already happened once before, the time he fell in love with Marian and was on the verge of ending things with Livia when the tragic death of François changed the picture. But this time things were completely different. Antonia wasn't a replacement for Livia's setting sun; Antonia was the rising sun. Antonia gave him a chance to feel alive again. Or to feel reborn, perhaps for the last time in his life. So he couldn't afford to miss it.

But how had he and Livia come to such a pass? The distance between them, which used to strengthen their bond, turning absence into a kind of perpetual presence, was now only distance, absence. And neither of them had made any effort, any real effort, to try and fill that absence. Livia remained in Genoa, living her life there, and had only needed to get a dog to feel less alone. He'd continued working at his job in Vigàta, thinking things were fine that way, leading a life destined for a slow decline. By the sea, perhaps, but a decline nonetheless. But life actually has more imagination than we do. And he wanted to remain inside this fantasy for as long as possible, maybe forever. Whatever the case, he owed Livia an explanation before breaking things off. It was a complex matter, and a few phone calls weren't going to suffice. He absolutely had to find the courage to get on a plane and go to Boccadasse.

It was now dark outside. And, for whatever reason, all of a sudden the joy at the idea that he would soon be seeing Antonia began to be tinged with a subtle dose of melancholy.

He took immediate action. He got up, went inside, grabbed his new clothes, went into the bedroom, and began to get undressed. He put on the first suit and looked at himself in the mirror. He was ridiculous. Not that there was anything specificially wrong with the suit. It just didn't hang quite right. The sleeves were too wide, the trousers too short.

He felt like a puppet forced to wear armor that wasn't its own. He took the suit off in haste and tried on the second one. This time the armor actually looked like a sarcophagus. He threw everything on the floor and, since he'd started sweating, headed for the bathroom, but he made the mistake of looking at himself in the mirror. The only result of this was that he immediately started doing push-ups. When he could no longer bend his arms, he dragged himself into the shower.

When he'd finished, he decided to put on the suit he'd worn that day. He donned one of his newly bought shirts. Once he was dressed, he faced a dilemma: to eat or not to eat?

Maybe discovering what Adelina had made for him would help him to answer the question.

He opened the refrigerator: nothing.

He opened the oven: nothing.

On the table, however, was a pot with a dish over it.

When he tried to lift the dish, he was unable. It stuck so firmly it seemed glued. So before he could get all upset, he opened a drawer, took out a knife, slipped the blade between the dish and the pot, and . . . eureka! Caponata! The dilemma had been solved. Grabbing a fork, he was about to set to when a question occurred to him: Will Antonia have eaten or not?

Perhaps the only solution was to bring the caponata with him.

He sat down, felt happy, drank a glass of wine, then started to look for a container to carry the caponata in.

He opened the kitchen cupboard: nothing. A plastic container, but only a square lid. An aluminum pie pan, but no paper to cover it with. He found a wide-necked bottle, rinsed it out, stuck a funnel into the neck, and started pressing the caponata through with a spoon. Every so often the spoon would lose its way to the bottle and end up in his mouth.

Closing the bottle, he put it in a plastic bag. Before going out, he took a look at himself in the mirror and noticed that his new shirt was spotted with stains.

Amid a litany of curses, he went into the bathroom, washed himself, put on his last new shirt, and could finally leave the house.

In the car it occurred to him that they had nothing to drink. He would stop in at the bar again.

It was late at night. The street was rather broad, and the car advanced silently and ever so slowly, drifting past the other cars parked along the sidewalk. It seemed not to be rolling on wheels but sliding on butter.

All at once it stopped, lurched to the left, and went back up the same street in reverse.

It parked in front of a shop window full of colorful objects.

The driver's-side door opened and a man got out, carefully closing the door behind him.

It was Mimì Augello.

"Salvo, what are you doing here?"

Inspector Montalbano, who was in the process of paying for a bottle of wine, recognized the voice and felt a chill run up his spine.

How the hell was he going to answer that question? Planting a half smile on his lips, he retorted: "And what are you doing here?"

"I was on my way to your place when I saw you in the window."

"And why were you going to my place? Did you discover another corpse?"

Meanwhile they'd left the bar.

"Cut the shit, Salvo. Just the thought of our cadaver still makes me break out in a cold sweat."

"That cadaver is all yours, Mimì. Now tell me why you were going to my house."

"Because I know who the blonde is."

"What blonde? Catalanotti's?"

"You bet."

"Congratulations," the inspector said hastily. "You can tell me the whole story tomorrow."

"What are you saying, Salvo? This is big news. This is a bombshell. We need to talk about it immediately."

As if he'd grown deaf, Montalbano opened his car door and was about to get in, but Mimì put a hand on his shoulder and held him back.

"Look at me," said Mimì.

Montalbano turned around.

Mimì Augello looked deep into the inspector's eyes.

"Tell me the truth: Where are you going right now?"

Montalbano realized that from that moment on, Mimì was not going to let go of the bone. Better calm him down by tossing him a little meat.

"Okay, Mimì, no problem. Let's go inside, sit down, and you can tell me what you have to tell me."

Once inside, the barman warned them: "Hey, guys, I was just closing up."

"Give us five minutes and we'll clear out," said Mimì, still eyeing the inspector suspiciously. "You're not convincing me, Salvo: the wine, the new shirt, all spruced up like that . . ."

Montalbano didn't give him time for any more questions.

"So, are we gonna talk about this woman or not?" he said, turning around.

"Sure. Her name is Anita Pastore, and she's the sole proprietor of a family chocolate factory."

"And what else do you know?"

"Nothing. I've got her address and phone number and was coming to your place to ask how we should proceed."

"Couldn't we talk about this tomorrow morning? I was just on my way to Adelina's place, because her son Pasquale . . ."

Mimì threw up his hands.

"As you wish, sir!" he replied, getting up.

As he was opening his car door to get in, something occurred to the inspector. What if Mimì decided to follow him to find out where he was actually going?

And so he decided to head out in the opposite direction, away from Via La Marmora. After some ten minutes, when he was certain Mimì wasn't following him, he headed back in the right direction.

He found a parking spot near the front door. Getting out of the car, he looked at his watch. Between one thing and another, he'd lost forty-five minutes.

As he entered Catalanotti's apartment, he called out loudly: "It's me."

Like a husband coming home after work.

There was no answer. He noticed a light was on in the study. He left the bottles in the kitchen and headed for the study.

Antonia was sitting at the desk with her glasses on, in front of some sheets of paper scattered across the desktop.

Montalbano bent down to kiss her on the lips, but she turned away and offered her cheek. Another go-round on the roller coaster!

"Have you eaten?"

"No."

"I brought some caponata that's—"

"I'm not hungry," she said, cutting him off. Then: "Why are you so late?"

"I ran into Mimì Augello by chance and he made me waste a lot of time. Just think, he wanted to tell me—"

"Grab a chair and come over here beside me," said Antonia, paying no attention to what he was telling her.

Montalbano obeyed.

"Find anything interesting?" he asked.

"Yes. And I'd like to talk about it with you."

"Okay," said the inspector, "but I need to drink something first. You want anything?"

"No."

He went into the kitchen, uncorked the bottle of wine, looked longingly at the caponata, filled his glass, and brought it with him into the study.

As soon as he set it down on the desk, Antonia, without taking her eyes off what she was reading, reached out with one hand, grabbed the glass, and drank it down in one gulp.

Montalbano got back up and, without saying a word, went back into the kitchen with the empty glass and this time filled two.

The folder that Antonia opened for him contained a typewritten page that featured not, however, a series of questions and answers, but a sort of monologue instead. There was also a photograph of the full figure of a very thin man with a head that looked like a skull. On another sheet of paper, written in Catalanotti's hand, were the words:

Hannibal D'Amico, municipal bailiff, particularly neurotic. When properly provoked, he reacts unpredictably and uncontrollably. Probably too dangerous to deal with.

On the bottom right, two initials: HD.

"I wonder what these two letters mean?" asked Antonia.

"Maybe they're the initials of this Hannibal guy," replied the inspector.

"But what need was there to write his initials if he's got the whole name at the top?"

Montalbano recalled that he'd also seen initials in the documents he'd looked at the first time around. He stood up.

"Where are you going?" asked Antonia.

"I need to check something. I'll be right back."

He went into the bedroom and took out the two folders called "Maria" and "Giacomo," respectively. They both had the same initials on the bottom right: DC, which clearly didn't correspond with either of their names.

So what could it mean, then? Despite the fact that he hadn't eaten, despite the continuous ups and downs of his ride on Antonia's roller coaster, and despite, let's admit it, his increasing age, a light came on in his brain again: DC: *Dangerous Corner*!

He dashed back into the study.

"Antonia, HD doesn't stand for Hannibal D'Amico, but for *Happy Days*."

"What days do you mean?"

"It's the title of a play that Catalanotti produced."

"Oh, of course! Beckett. And so?"

"So we have to check all the most recent audition reports bearing the letters DC, the show he was preparing: *Dangerous Corner*."

"I don't know it," said Antonia.

"Let me tell you the plot," said Montalbano.

And, thanks to the fact that he hadn't given in and put on his new clothes but was wearing his normal trousers, he was able to pull out the sheet of paper on which he'd written his summary of the play. He began reading.

"What's that you're reading?"

"I wrote a sort of synopsis of it."

Taking the sheet out of his hands, Antonia said: "I'd rather read it myself."

Montalbano didn't breathe a word.

14

Moments later, Antonia said: "So, what now?"

"Now we have to change our method."

Without saying anything, Antonia stood up and grabbed a few folders. Montalbano took the rest and they went into the bedroom to put them all back and begin selecting all the others that bore the initials DC. This effort took them about half an hour. They returned to the study with a dozen folders under their arms.

Before starting to leaf through them, Antonia grabbed one of the two glasses and drank down the wine. Montalbano did the same. She then opened the first folder but then closed it almost at once and sat there, immobile, staring into space.

"What is it?" asked the inspector.

"Intermission," she said. Then, without saying anything else, she threw her arms around his neck and kissed him.

So, are you there? Straight from the still half-open
moment?
The net had only one hole in it. Your entry?
There is no end to my shock, to my silencing it.
Listen
How fast your heart beats for me.

"Let's get up."

"Come on, please wait. Let's just stay this way another two minutes."

"No. We've wasted too much time. I'm going."

Montalbano felt hurt. Or, rather, he wanted to feel hurt, but then told himself that the moments he was living were so wonderful that for no reason in the world would he ever ruin them with an unhappy word. And so he got up and followed her into the bathroom. They got dressed as best they could. Antonia took the first folder in hand and asked with a smile: "And now, Inspector, I await your orders. Tell me what this new method is."

Montalbano kissed her and began to speak.

"I could be wrong, but I am more and more convinced that there is a close connection between Catalanotti's murder and the production of *Dangerous Corner.* That's why we've taken only the reports related to that play. We have to locate a dozen or so actors, or so-called, who were going to play the parts of characters in some way ambiguous or decidedly guilty of a crime."

"Explain what you mean."

"In my opinion, we should use Catalanotti's observations as our guide, especially concerning two characters: Olwen, who turns out in the end to be the real killer, having committed the act during a sexual assault on her person; and Gordon, who, though married to Betty, is also in love with Martin. And I also wouldn't exclude two minor but highly complex characters, Stanton and Betty herself."

"What fun!" said Antonia. "I feel like I'm in some kind of Agatha Christie story: Call it 'Death on the Stage.'"

Then, as she was reading one report, Antonia's voice became fainter and fainter until it turned into a kind of murmur.

"What's that?" asked Montalbano.

Antonia didn't answer. The sheet of paper slipped out of her hand and onto the floor. Montalbano realized she had suddenly fallen asleep. And so he got up from the sofa, delicately took her almost in his arms, and laid her out comfortably. He sat down in one of the desk chairs and just stayed that way, staring at her, spellbound. Then he himself began to feel tired, laid one arm down on the desk, rested his forehead on it, and slowly drifted off to sleep.

They woke up to the ringing of Catalanotti's alarm clock, which he'd last set at 6:45.

"What a shame!" said Antonia. "I was having a very revealing dream."

"About the two of us?" the inspector asked, chuckling.

"What's left to reveal about us? I was dreaming about 'Death on the Stage.'"

"Whose death, Catalanotti's?"

"No, no. Even though I'd never seen him in person, I'm sure the dead man wasn't him, even though he was dressed like him."

"So tell me about it, don't be shy."

"Okay, just five minutes. Then we really have to leave before the doorman opens the building."

"Okay, promise."

Antonia told him she'd dreamt of a small theater that was all gilded and upholstered in velvet, and on the stage was a closed casket. She'd immediately imagined she was about to witness a magician's performance, but then the casket opened and a human form slowly began to take shape.

"But didn't you already say that there was a dead man?"

"Yes, but at first it wasn't clear. I was sure he was going to stand up, but in the end he didn't. After a while I realized, I don't remember how, that he was dead."

"And how did you realize that?"

"I'll try to explain, because it was very strange. I was the only person who realized he was dead. Everyone else in the audience remained perfectly calm. The man lying on the casket was all dressed up: black suit, tie, shiny shoes, and though I couldn't see his face, from my place in the audience I could see a bloodstain on his shirt."

Montalbano leapt to his feet.

"It sounds like you dreamt about Augello's cadaver!"

Antonia gawked at him.

"What cadaver? What's Augello got to do with this?"

"I'll explain."

"No, for now we're going to get dressed and out of this place."

Fifteen minutes later they were sitting and eating breakfast at a typical neighborhood café. Montalbano told her the whole story, not neglecting to mention that he'd also finally got hold of the keys to the apartment the day before.

"I want to see it," said Antonia.

Montalbano said okay, then made a timid attempt at inviting her out for lunch at Enzo's, but failed miserably. They left it that they would be in touch in the afternoon and decide when to go to Via Biancamano.

There was no time to go home, change clothes, and shave, so the inspector went directly to the office looking the way he did.

The moment he sat down there was a knock on the door and Fazio came in.

"Good morning, Chief. I've got the artist's reconstruction that Di Marzio made."

He set it down on the table beside the photo of Lo Bello.

"What do you think? Do they look enough alike?"

"Splendid!" said Montalbano, putting the image in his jacket pocket. "Any other news?"

"For now, none."

At that moment Mimì Augello appeared.

"Sorry, Salvo, I just wanted to let you know I took an initiative."

"What kind of initiative?"

"I rang Anita Pastore and called her in for three o'clock this afternoon."

"Well done. But now I've got stuff to do. I'll see you later."

Despite the fact that he'd eaten two brioches in the café, he felt a lot more hungry than sleepy. Irresistibly hungry. And he had a vision: the bottle of caponata on the kitchen table in Catalanotti's apartment.

He got in his car and drove to Via La Marmora.

"Good morning, Inspector," said Bruno the Bear. "Why so early today?"

"I have to get some important documents," said Montalbano, racing past the doorman's booth.

When he was inside Catalanotti's apartment, a problem occurred to him. How was he going to hide the bottle of caponata from the doorman? He thought about it for a few moments and came to the conclusion that the only solution was to eat it then and there. So he grabbed a plate and a fork, poured all the caponata out of the bottle, and got down to work. When he was done, he conscientiously set about washing the dishes. He cleaned and dried all the glasses before putting them back in the credenza.

His conscience was now clean, and he could go home and, as they say, sleep the sleep of the just.

The caponata, eaten so early in the morning, didn't sit well in his stomach. And so, when he woke up after one p.m., he decided it wouldn't be such a good idea to go to Enzo's. Feeling a little muddleheaded from sleeping off schedule, he stayed in the shower forever and wasted even more time goofing off in the bathroom, trying out the different samples the salesgirl had given him but too afraid to open the large tubes of cream that had cost him an arm and a leg. He decided to break in a new suit not by putting on the whole thing, but by donning the trousers and complementing them with . . . let's call it an older jacket. When he looked at himself in the mirror, it seemed a passable combination.

Though he hadn't eaten, it was now well into the afternoon, and so he rang Antonia, as agreed. But she didn't answer.

At ten minutes to three, he arrived at the office.

Mimì came in and informed him that Signora Pastore would be there momentarily.

"Call Fazio," Montalbano said to him. "I want him to be present."

He had just enough time to explain to Fazio who Anita Pastore was and why they'd called her in, when the telephone rang and Catarella said: "Chief, 'ere's a lady 'ere 'oo's some kinda lady pastor."

"Show her in."

Anita Pastore looked exactly the way Enzo had described her: done up and dolled up and sporting an air that seemed to say "don't touch me or I might fall apart."

Fazio ceded his place opposite the desk to her.

Signora Pastore immediately said in a shrill, resentful voice, "I don't understand why I was—"

"Quite simple, signora," Montalbano interrupted her. "You're here because we want to know about your frequent dealings with Carmelo Catalanotti, who, as you will have noticed, was murdered."

"Well, I certainly didn't do it," Signora Anita snarled.

She was a real pain in the ass, this lady.

"And I believe you. But I'd like to hear from you yourself what kind of relationship you had with him. You can respond freely, since this is just an informal conversation."

"So you called me in to the police station for an informal conversation? In that case we could have had a little chat in the bar right here across the street."

"We can make it more official, if you prefer."

"And what does that mean?"

"It means that you will choose a lawyer, then be summoned by the prosecutor, and he and I together will subject you to a rigorous interrogation. I should warn you in advance, however, that the Catalanotti case has been attracting a lot of morbid interest and that in the event that there were any leaks to the press, I wouldn't be able to guarantee the maintenance of investigative secrecy. There's always a chance your name and photo will end up in the papers."

Upon hearing these words, Signora Anita's attitude changed. She settled better into her chair, adjusted her hair slightly, and asked: "Do you want to know if our relationship was romantic in nature?"

"You tell us, signora."

"The answer is no. Far from it."

"So what kind of relationship was it?"

"It was a strange sort of work relationship."

Mimì cut in ironically: "I never knew that Catalanotti dealt in chocolate."

"That's not what I meant."

"Then please go on, signora."

"Well, I met Catalanotti about three months ago, when he was introduced to me by a girlfriend of mine. When, during the course of a conversation over dinner, he learned about my family's chocolate factory, he immediately overwhelmed me with questions. It was his intense curiosity that aroused my own."

"Explain what you mean," said the inspector.

"I sensed that his interest was genuine. He asked me out and I accepted."

The woman paused and then resumed speaking.

"Then our meetings became a habit. I'm not married, have no children, not many friends, and a lot of free time. I hardly ever talk about myself, and Carmelo had a gift for making me feel relaxed. Our dinners became almost regular appointments."

"So, it wasn't just a work relationship, but one of friendship as well?"

"Actual friendship I really wouldn't say. I don't know anything about Carmelo's life. We spoke almost exclusively about me, and essentially about my work. Carmelo wanted to know all about the dynamics of the factory, my relationships with my brothers, our employees, and our distributors. He even wanted to know about the everyday goings-on, and how things went from week to week."

"Did you ever wonder why he was so interested?"

"Yes, at first I thought my brother Paolo was right. He's the oldest, and is always thinking that everyone wants to cheat him. He suspected that Carmelo maybe wanted to steal some recipes or other business secrets . . ."

"And was he really like that?"

"No. Carmelo was attracted by the family dynamics, if you can call it that. He was curious about our work methods, how we shared responsibilities, what kinds of frictions and disagreements developed . . ."

"I'm sorry, but what was the point? Why all this interest?"

"Because he wanted to write a novel about a family business."

"Did he take notes?" Montalbano asked, remembering the folders.

"No," said Anita, "but he promised he would let me read a rough draft of the novel, which made me feel very proud. While waiting I said nothing to anyone about it."

"Excuse me, but you speak of a family business. Who else is involved in it? Is it just you and your brother Paolo?"

"Up until a couple of years ago, my brother Giovanni was also involved. But now there's just Paolo and me left. Giovanni can't be a part of anything anymore. He's dead."

Anita Pastore sighed, looked at the inspector, and said: "But by now it doesn't make much difference . . . he killed himself."

A bell started ringing in Montalbano's head.

"I'm sorry," said the inspector, "but do you know why?"

"Why he killed himself? Because he was a fragile man, unprepared to face the problems of life, and so he chose to take himself out of the picture."

Her answer was intended to close the subject, but now that the inspector knew why Catalanotti was so interested in her, he didn't want to give up the bone.

"So you're saying your brother was the weakest of you three?"

"I'm sorry, but what does that have to do with Carmelo's death?" the woman asked, gripping the arms of her chair and looking him straight in the eye.

"I'll be the one to decide about that," Montalbano replied brusquely.

Anita settled back into her chair.

"Look, Inspector, it's a sad, complicated story. There was a sudden, huge shortage of cash. Paolo was convinced that it was Giovanni who'd stolen it. I, a bit less so. Giovanni became, well, indignant and demoralized and didn't really defend himself, and so his suicide seemed to me like a tacit admission of guilt."

"And did Catalanotti ask you any questions about your brother's suicide?" Montalbano asked.

"Yes, many. He even wanted a photo of Giovanni. And he said he'd also had a brother who committed suicide."

Too bad Catalanotti was an only child, thought the inspector.

Then he asked: "But did Giovanni ever respond to your and your brother's accusations?"

"He always claimed he was innocent but never produced any evidence."

"A lack of evidence isn't always a confirmation of guilt."

"What are you trying to say, Inspector?"

"That his death might have been a reaction to being falsely accused by his brother and sister."

Upon hearing these words, Anita became furious, leapt

to her feet, and said in a voice more penetrating than an electric drill: "How dare you! I'm not staying in this office one more minute!"

And she headed for the door.

Fazio stood up to stop her, but Montalbano signaled to him to let her go. The woman opened the door and then slammed it behind her.

"Why'd you let her go?" asked Augello.

"Because, Mimì, I realized the real reason why Catalanotti was interested in her."

"Then please let us in on it."

Fazio resumed his place in front of the desk.

"The plot of the play Catalanotti wanted to stage has many similarities to the story of what happened to the Pastore family business."

"And what play is this?" asked Augello.

Montalbano didn't feel like recounting the plot of *Dangerous Corner* yet again.

"Have Fazio fill you in on it. I have to go out now. There's something important I have to do."

He got up, went out of the building, and headed for the nearest café. His hunger was making its needs felt, since he'd skipped lunch at Enzo's. The bar had some ham and cheese sandwiches. He ate four in a row. And washed it all down with a medium-sized beer.

Back in the office, he called for Fazio at once.

"The twenty-four hours we gave Nico and Margherita are up," he said.

"Should I have them come here, or should we go there?"

Montalbano didn't answer, but just sat there, lost in thought.

"Chief, what should we do?" Fazio ventured again a few moments later.

"I was just thinking that those two kids will either never admit that the gunman was their respective father and future father-in-law, or if they do, they'll regret it for the rest of their lives. They're good kids, after all."

"So what are we gonna do?"

"Have you got the home phone number of Lo Bello?"

"Yessir, I do."

"Then give him a ring and turn on the speakerphone. We'll call Lo Bello in immediately for a chat. If he isn't at home, see if you can find out where he is. And if they tell you, go and get him in person and bring him here. Let's go!"

Fazio took a handful of scraps of paper out of his pocket, selected one, and started dialing.

"Hello, is this the Lo Bello residence?"

"Yes," replied a male voice.

"Am I speaking with Signor Gaetano Lo Bello?"

"Yes. Mind telling me who the fuck you are?"

"Yes, I'm calling from the police commissariat of Vigàta. Chief Inspector Montalbano wants to see you at once."

"Nice to hear, but at the moment I'm busy, so don't bust my chops."

"All right, then, I'll be at your place in five minutes and will drag you in to the police station in handcuffs."

A litany of curses came through the receiver.

Then the man hung up.

"We'd better go and get him before he escapes," Montalbano said to Fazio, who in the meantime had stood up and was putting on his jacket as he hurried towards the door.

At that moment Augello came back in.

"Salvo, I went onto the internet to read part of the text of *Dangerous Corner.* Damn! The similarities with the Pastore family are indeed very striking: the two brothers, one of whom commits suicide . . . One thing is certain: This Catalanotti was one really strange guy."

"In what sense, Mimì?"

"Well, to me, at least, more than a moneylender or a man of the theater, he seems to have been an out-and-out cop. Or, better yet, a truffle dog! How the hell did he manage to find a family that corresponded perfectly with the one in the play? Salvo, do you know whether or not he was really writing a novel?"

"Gimme a break! A novel, yeah, right! You see, Mimì, Catalanotti's theatrical method was always to start with a concrete fact; in this case, it was a real find for him to encounter a family in which almost the same things happened as in the play."

"So what need was there to have concrete fact just to stage an imagined story?"

"I'll try to sum it up for you, Mimì. Catalanotti had a theory that was based not on realism, not on verisimilitude, but on something he called similveracity. And I'll leave it at that. All I can tell you is that on this basis, he would dig into people's minds, in search of that concrete reality in anyone wishing to act in his play. And that's why he turned them inside out and outside in like socks. This is what I was able to gather from reading his notes in the folders."

"Speaking of which, Salvo, how far along are you in your reading?"

"It's a long and complicated process, Mimì," said the inspector, also thinking of his affair with Antonia, "but I think I'm on the right track. I've managed to isolate the audition reports for the actors trying out for *Dangerous Corner.*"

"And who plays Olwen?" Mimì immediately asked.

"I don't know yet. There are two or three possible actresses who . . ."

The little march that his cell phone began playing made Montalbano give a start in his chair.

He took out the phone. It was Antonia.

For a moment he couldn't make up his mind. Should he answer? What if Mimì managed to figure things out?

"Well? You gonna answer it or not?" said Augello.

Montalbano summoned his courage and said in a flat voice: "Hello."

Antonia seemed to understand at once.

"You're not alone?"

"Yes, I'm in a meeting," Montalbano informed her.

"I'm confirming for this evening. Give me the address."

Montalbano felt lost. There was no way he could pronounce the name "Biancamano" in front of Mimì.

"I can't."

"I understand. And so?"

"Can I call you back?"

"I'm about to go into a meeting myself."

"I could come and pick you up at home. Could you give me the address?"

Antonia giggled and then took revenge.

"I can't."

"All right, I'll find it on my own. I'll be there at eight. Okay?"

"Oh, my, if you find out where I live!" said Antonia, laughing, as she hung up.

"What a mysterious phone call, Inspector Montalbano," Mimì Augello commented slyly. "I smell a woman."

"Mind your own business, Mimì."

"Fine, fine. Just promise me that when it's my turn, you don't start in with your fucking moralizing . . ."

"Let's get back to Catalanotti," said the inspector, changing the subject.

"Can I ask a question?" asked Augello.

"Go right ahead."

"Why are you so jealously guarding Catalanotti's folders?"

"What do you mean?"

"You're keeping them all to yourself like some kind of secret. If you'd talk to us about them or bring them here to the office, we might be able to help you."

"You're right," Montalbano conceded.

What he was jealously guarding, of course, was the secret of Antonia.

15

The door flew violently open. The gust sent two sheets of paper that had been on the desk fluttering to the ground. As Montalbano bent down to pick them up, he froze.

An ogre had appeared in the doorway.

A real fairy-tale ogre: a mountain of a man, dressed in rags, head resting directly on the shoulders, hair a dense, tangled forest, teeth—or those remaining—all yellow and black, face dirty and oily as if he'd just finished eating Tom Thumb.

Montalbano breathed a sigh of relief when he saw that the guy was handcuffed.

A shove from Fazio, who along with two uniformed cops was behind the man, pushed him into the middle of the room.

In the photograph and the artist's reconstruction the ogre had looked relatively civilized, and so the images in the end hardly resembled the man before them at all.

Only then did Montalbano notice that Fazio was holding a blood-reddened handkerchief against his mouth.

"What happened?" he asked.

"This bastard reacted and punched me in the face, so I had to handcuff him."

"Tha'ss right," the man said, "but tell 'im the whole story. First he kicked me in the balls and then—"

"Okay, okay," Montalbano said, cutting him off. "Signor Lo Bello, do you realize that by forcefully resisting arrest by a public official you've already reserved a few years in jail for yourself?"

"Oh, you can imagine how scared I am!" said the ogre with a mocking grin.

"Well, I wanted to let you know that this is just the beginning. We have a witness who saw you shoot your daughter's boyfriend."

"I didn't shoot nobody."

"You can tell that to the prosecutor. As of this moment, you are under arrest for attempted murder."

And without saying anything else, Montalbano signaled to the others to put him in a holding cell.

It wasn't an easy task, however. The man put up a fierce resistance, and they practically needed a capstan to move him an inch. Fazio and the two cops were forced to push him to the door, with the ogre sneering all the while: "I really wanna see this witness o' yours!"

And he went on, saying that in any case he would be free again the following day, that justice was for assholes and he wasn't an asshole, and these four shitty policemen were only good for TV.

The litany continued well into the corridor, and then the ogre suddenly fell silent.

"What the fuck are you doing here?" his voice rang out a moment later, as if he couldn't believe his eyes.

Hearing these words, Montalbano got up and went out to see what was happening.

Standing in front of the ogre was a man of about thirty next to a woman and a younger woman holding a baby in her arms.

The policemen dragged the ogre towards the holding cell as the brute resumed his yelling.

"Get back home, you big whore!"

The inspector went up to the new arrivals and asked: "And who are you, may I ask?"

The first to speak was the young man.

"I'm Gaspare Lo Bello, and this is my mother, Nunziata; my wife, Caterina; and my son, Tanino."

"Please come into my office," said Montalbano, leading the way.

They all went in. Fazio sat the two women and the baby down on the little sofa and gave up his usual chair to Gaspare.

Gaspare was again the first to speak.

"I'm Gaetano Lo Bello's son. We're here to report him for repeated domestic violence."

The mother started crying.

The daughter-in-law put her arm around the woman's shoulders, hugged her, and whispered: "C'mon, Mama, don't cry."

Montalbano observed a few seconds of silence, wondering how such a nasty ogre could have sired a pair of children as honest and polite as Gaspare and Margherita. The answer was that the credit could only have been the wife's.

"I realize," said the inspector, "how hard it must be for you to file this report, and I thank you for the courage you've shown. But before we proceed any further, I have to ask you an even more difficult question. I'm referring to the attempted murder of Margherita's boyfriend."

Apparently the Lo Bellos were expecting this question. They all looked down at the floor and remained silent.

"There's one thing I want to know: Did any of you see him leave the house that morning?"

"Not me or Caterina," said Gaspare.

The inspector then directly addressed the mother, who covered her face with her hands.

"If you like, you can answer me with a nod or a shake of the head. Did your husband tell you what he intended to do before going out?"

The woman shook her head.

"Did you have any idea of what he had in mind?"

The woman nodded and started weeping convulsively.

Gaspare spoke again.

"Mama told us she saw him open the closet and take out a box."

"Was there a weapon in the box?" asked the inspector.

This time it was the young man who nodded.

"Okay, that'll be enough," said Montalbano. "Thank you for your help."

Then, to Fazio: "Take these people into your office, draft a statement of their accusation for domestic violence, and write out everything that's been said here."

Montalbano stood up, shook hands with all three, stroked the baby's cheek, then went and sat back down.

When his office was at last empty, the inspector told himself that the ogre absolutely had to be sent to jail, because if the children and the wife had succeeded in overcoming every resistance they might have to admitting to something so devastating as domestic violence, it meant that all limits had been exceeded in that household and the next step the brute might take could well turn out to be a tragic one.

He wondered curiously about Nico and Margherita, who still hadn't given any signs of life.

The phone rang.

"Ahh, Chief, Chief, 'ere's a couple a youngsters 'ere.

One's the dilicate kid 'at got shot but wasn't killed. Remember?"

Speak of the devil.

"Yes, of course," Montalbano said curtly. "Send them in."

The moment he saw them the inspector was convinced that they had no intention of talking. He sat them down and asked brusquely: "So, what have you got to say to me?"

The kid spoke first.

"Inspector, if you really want to know the truth, Margherita and I haven't even discussed the incident since the last time."

"So you think it's normal for someone to shoot at you?"

"That's not what I meant, Inspector. Of course it's not normal. It's just that we have nothing to add to what we've already each told you separately. Neither I nor Margherita saw the person who shot me."

Without saying a word, Montalbano stuck a hand in his jacket pocket and pulled out a small sheet of paper. He set it down on the desk and said to the two: "Have a good look at this. The artist's reconstruction was made on the basis of the witness's description. Have you anything to say?"

This time it was Margherita who spoke.

"Yes, it looks a little like Papa, but it's not him."

"There's something I should tell you: At this point you could both be charged with giving false testimony."

The young couple turned pale.

Montalbano continued. "All I can do now is advise you to find a good lawyer; you've painted yourselves into a corner. It will be rather hard to defend your position. You'll be summoned directly by the prosecutor. That'll be all, thanks. Good-bye."

The two seemed disappointed. They'd probably planned to deliver a longer, more convincing argument.

But then, at that moment, a baby was heard crying in the corridor.

Montalbano leapt at the opportunity. He sprang to his feet, rushed out of the office, and said: "Please come in here for a moment, Gaspare."

Before the stunned saucer-eyes of the couple, the man appeared with Tanino in his arms, trying to comfort the baby.

Gaspare, Margherita, and Nico all stared at one another in astonishment for a few moments, then Margherita asked in a faint voice: "What are you doing here?"

"I didn't come alone. Caterina and Mama are here, too. It's time to tell the truth, Margherì."

Margherita looked at him almost hatefully.

"Why did you do it?"

"Because I don't want this child to live through what we've had to live through."

Gaspare laid the baby in her arms and, putting a hand on her shoulder, said: "Come, I'll take you to Mama."

Without saying a word, Margherita stood up and followed him out.

Nico remained seated.

"Now, do you want to tell me what really happened?" Montalbano asked him.

And Nico spoke.

"Inspector, Margherita and I have been together for two years. We wanted to get married right away, but we were never able to find even the flimsiest jobs that might allow us to raise a family. I have a university degree and earn a little cash unloading crates of fish at the docks. Margherita also quickly got a degree, but she's in the same fix as me. How are we going to get on in life if there's no work? It's getting harder and harder for me to bring home the little we need to eat and still have the strength to start over again the next day. Luckily, at least I don't have to pay for the apartment."

The inspector—who, faced with what he was hearing, could only feel ashamed at the fucked-up world that he, too, had handed down to this kid—decided to change the subject.

"Tell me about Lo Bello," he said.

"After I started going out with Margherita, Tano almost immediately started tormenting his daughter. He wanted her to leave me and find somebody who could promise her some kind of future. Their arguments got more and more heated, to the point that a couple of times Tano actually raised a hand against her. So I finally decided to go and talk to Tano, but after just a few words he wouldn't listen to reason and said that if Margherita didn't leave me immediately, he would throw her out of the house. He kept his word: Margherita stayed with me, and he threw her out. But then, when Margherita moved in with me, Tano sort of lost his mind. Then one morning as I was coming out of my building I saw him standing there with a gun in his hand. Realizing what he was about to do, I made a move to go back inside, but he didn't give me the time. He said, 'This'll help you to understand that you're not gonna see my daughter no more,' then he fired and ran away. What could I do? Margherita made me swear that I would never implicate her father. So I did what she asked of me."

Montalbano remained silent.

His silence disturbed Nico.

"Look, Inspector, I told you the truth this time."

"I know," said Montalbano. "But I was trying to think of a way to leave you and Margherita out of this. I'm gonna need some time. You're a good kid, Nico. You should all go home now and take advantage of the fact that Tano's away. Spend some time together in peace and quiet, and you, Nico, try to calm everyone down."

The young man stood up.

"I don't know how to thank you, sir."

"Never mind about that." Montalbano patted him on the shoulder, and the lad went out.

Fazio came in. "All done," he said.

"There's something I wanted to tell you," said the inspector. "Keep those verbal transcripts on hold for now."

"Why? What do you want to do?"

"I want to keep Margherita's and Nico's names from appearing as witnesses to the shooting. I'm trying to figure out how to proceed."

"That's not gonna be easy, Chief."

"I know, and what I'm afraid of most is that if Nico claims that he never saw his attacker, Tano Lo Bello could actually say, just to hurt the kid, that not only did Nico get a good look at him, but he even spoke to Nico."

"And how do you think you're gonna get Tano to say what you want him to say?"

"I'm not even thinking about that. The only hope would be to threaten him with an increased sentence if he doesn't do something. Tell you what. While we're waiting for me to come up with an idea, let's keep him on ice all night, and maybe that'll give him a chance to think about how badly he's fucked up. Then tomorrow morning I'll go and talk to him. You, in the meanwhile, do me a favor and go to Lo Bello's house and confiscate his revolver."

As Fazio was leaving the office, Montalbano realized that he had no idea whatsoever how to resolve the situation. He only felt he owed something to the two kids, to whom he'd bequeathed a fucked-up world. In one way or another, he had to think of a solution.

He glanced at his watch. It was late. He called Catarella, who materialized a couple of seconds later.

"Yer orders, sah."

"Close the door."

"An' lack it, Chief?"

"Yeah. Now come closer."

Catarella, who'd realized that he was about to be entrusted with a personal task, started turkey-strutting as he always did whenever Montalbano asked for his help: legs stiff as a puppet's, arms stretched downwards and held slightly away from the body, hands with fingers slightly apart like webbed feet, eyes bugged out, face red as a bell pepper, teeth clenched.

"I need for you to do me a favor, but you mustn't tell anyone about it."

Catarella brought the index and middle fingers of his right hand to his lips and kissed them front and back.

"I's silent as the grave, Chief, an' 'a'ss a slalom oat'."

"Before five minutes are up, you absolutely must find the address of the new chief of Forensics."

"She's a woman, Chief."

"So? Does the fact that she's a woman somehow make it more difficult?"

"Nah, Chief, I jess wannit a let yi' know 'at she's a

woman o' the female pirsuasion an' 'ey say she's goo' lookin', too."

"Okay, okay," said Montalbano, cutting things short. "Just find me that address."

Catarella went out. The inspector walked over to the window, opened it, and fired up a cigarette. He hadn't yet smoked half of it when the telephone rang.

"Chief, Chief, I talked wit' Cicco de Cicco. You wan' me to tell it t'yiz o'er the phone, or shou' I come in poisson?"

"Come in person."

Catarella materialized with a scrap of paper in his hand.

"I writ it down 'ere. Ya wan' me to read it?"

"No, thanks. You can go now."

But Catarella in the meantime had turned into some kind of Egyptian mummy, and it took him a good five minutes to reach the door, open it, and close it behind him.

Montalbano got up, took the keys to Via Biancamano out of the drawer, put them in his pocket, and left the building.

Before entering Montelusa he pulled over for a minute to look at the scrap of paper Catarella had given him. It wasn't a residential address but rather a hotel that luckily wasn't very far away. And so at eight o'clock sharp he was able to enter the lobby of the small but well-kept hotel.

"Could you please tell Signorina Nicoletti that Inspector Montalbano is waiting for her?"

The desk manager picked up the phone, spoke a few words, and then said: "She'll be right down."

Montalbano remained standing and studied a poster for

the Valley of the Temples. He felt troubled but didn't know why. Then all at once he understood: If Antonia had taken up residence in a hotel, it meant she wouldn't be staying in Montelusa for very long.

First one, then a hundred, then a thousand thoughts flooded his brain.

Then one rose to the surface from the very depths of his body: He should request a transfer to Ancona. But would they ever grant him this on the eve, or almost, of his retirement? Or would he have to resign?

At any rate, all these thoughts twisted his heart into a knot. Ever so slowly, a wave of melancholy engulfed him, but luckily at a crucial moment he heard Antonia's voice, and suddenly every concern, every dark thought vanished as if by magic in the light of her smile.

"Ciao. I never doubted for a moment that you would manage to find my address."

Montalbano noticed she was carrying a small suitcase, and, like an idiot, he panicked and asked: "What, are you leaving already?"

"Why would I be leaving?" said the woman. "I just brought some tools for taking samples. Isn't that what we're going there to do?"

"Yes, of course," said Montalbano, relieved.

Once they were outside the hotel, the inspector tried to kiss her, but Antonia pulled away and said: "Not here."

As they were heading to his car, Montalbano asked: "Wouldn't it be better if we went out to eat first?"

"All right," Antonia consented. "But let's make it quick."

"Do you know any restaurants in the neighborhood?"

"Yes," she said. "There's one nearby. We can walk there."

Montalbano took the little suitcase out of her hand, and

less than ten minutes later they were sitting in a glittery new restaurant. They were the only customers.

"But how's the food here?" the inspector asked, feeling doubtful.

"It sucks, but the service is quick. This shouldn't take more than half an hour."

They ordered steaks and salad.

As soon as the waiter left, Antonia got up slightly from her chair and kissed Montalbano on the lips. He held her there, keeping his hands on her cheeks, and was just returning her kiss when his cell phone rang.

It was Livia.

He didn't answer at first. Getting up, he excused himself to Antonia and went outside. Only then did he open communications.

As soon as he said "Hello," he was immediately assailed by an angry Livia.

"Do you mind telling me what's become of you? You said you would call, but there hasn't been a peep out of you! What the hell is up with you? Would you please explain it to me once and for all?"

"This isn't the right time."

"No, actually it is. I'm sick and tired of this. If there's anything wrong, have the courage to tell me openly."

"I said this isn't the right time. I'm with other people. I haven't any time to waste."

"So you're telling me that talking to me is a waste of time?"

"I repeat: I can't talk right now."

"All right," Livia conceded. "Then tell me when I can call back."

"At the moment I really can't say."

"You know what I say? I say that since you can't talk, I'll do the talking. I'm tired of waiting around for your phone calls, your visits, or any kind of promise at all from you. All I ever do is wait . . . and wait . . . I've been waiting all my life, suspended between your work and what is supposed to happen at some future date that never arrives. Do you think it's normal that you haven't tried to get in touch with me for days? That you don't ask me how I am, what I'm doing, how I feel? Salvo, there's only one thing that could explain your behavior: You don't love me anymore. Or at least not enough to do anything for my sake. And so now I'm fed up with always giving priority to what's best for you. I want to think about myself. I'm sorry. Maybe it's not right to tell you these things over the phone, but I'm really at the end of my rope. As far as I'm concerned, it's over between us."

They both remained silent for ten long seconds.

Then Livia, almost incredulous, asked: "Haven't you got anything to say?"

"No," said Montalbano, hanging up.

He didn't go back into the restaurant right away, because he needed to brace his whole body against a wall. He stayed that way for several minutes, feeling completely empty. He lit a cigarette, but the taste disgusted him and he threw it away at once Then he took a deep breath and went inside.

As soon as he sat down, Antonia looked at him in silence and then said: "Bad news?"

"Yes, I'm afraid so."

At that moment the steaks arrived, but Montalbano no longer felt the least bit hungry.

Antonia realized something was wrong.

"This meat is disgusting," she said. "Do you mind if we leave?"

Montalbano paid and they went out. They walked to the car without talking.

At last they pulled up outside the entrance to Via Biancamano.

"There's a slight problem," said the inspector. "You know that mistress of Mimì's that I mentioned to you? I really want to avoid running into her."

"Don't worry. I'll take care of it. I'll go on ahead and leave the main door open for you. Just count to a hundred and then come in."

Antonia got out, stuck the key in the front door, and disappeared.

When he got to a hundred, Montalbano brusquely opened the car door, which promptly got stuck against the sidewalk, leaving only the narrowest of fissures, through which he would never fit.

Cursing the saints, he grabbed the door with both hands to try to close it, but was unable to. For whatever reason, it seemed to have become cemented to the paving stone. He opened the door on the other side, got out, walked around the car, and tried to shut the goddamn door from the outside. This time he finally succeeded. He circled around the car again, got back in from the passenger's side, started the engine, and realized that he had barely a few centimeters in which to maneuver between the car in front and the car behind.

It took him a good five minutes to move the car a little farther away from the sidewalk. At last he got out and crossed the street. He stopped outside the front door to the building, which, in the meantime, for whatever reason, was no longer open. He started ringing, but nobody answered. He'd wasted too much time.

The only hope was to call her on the phone. He pulled out his cell phone and dialed.

"What on earth happened to you?" Antonia asked.

"I had a little problem!"

"Another bad-news phone call?" asked Antonia.

"Are you going to open the door for me or not?"

"Okay, okay."

Finally inside, the inspector raced up the stairs and catapulted into the apartment.

16

When he closed the door, the darkness in the room was complete.

"Before turning the lights on, let's make sure all the shutters are firmly closed," Antonia's voice said in the dark.

Montalbano went and checked the only window in the room.

"This one's sealed tight," he said. And he turned the light on.

They said nothing, but only looked each other in the eye and felt the need to embrace. Then Antonia stepped back and said: "Let's go."

They inspected the whole apartment from top to bottom. It had clearly been unoccupied for a while. There was one room that struck them in particular: The walls were all lined with bookshelves made of wooden planks, except that on the shelves were not books but hundreds of seashells that ranged from gigantic to an infinity of tiny ones.

Not that he knew the least thing about the subject, but Montalbano had the strong impression that it was a valuable collection. Which was why Aurisicchio wanted only the head of the real estate agency to have a set of keys.

"Let's go back into the bedroom," said Antonia.

It was the first one on the right, and corresponded, as Mimì had said, exactly with the bedroom of Genoveffa, aka Geneviève.

As soon as they went in, the inspector closed the

shutters. They turned on the light and were finally able to see the bedroom of Mimì Augello's cadaver.

The furnishings consisted of a pair of chairs and a double bed with two mattresses on it, covered by a sheet. There was also one pillow.

Antonia set her little suitcase down on a nightstand and said to the inspector: "Sit down somewhere and let me work."

Montalbano sat down in the nearest chair and began to watch her.

She moved with a natural elegance that enchanted him.

The first thing she pulled out of her case was a sort of magnifying glass with a little light inside, and she used this to examine the bedsheet centimeter by square centimeter. Then, setting the magnifying glass aside, she took out another tool that looked like a telescope. She worked in silence, methodical and precise.

A short while later she put down the telescope and took out a small sort of scraper and a little transparent plastic envelope. She ran the tool ever so lightly over the fabric, then put whatever substances had stuck to the blade into the envelope.

After about half an hour of this silent labor, Antonia stopped to examine part of the sheet that was under the pillow. She took up her magnifying glass again, looked very closely at the fabric, and finally turned and said to the inspector: "There's a tiny drop of something here that may well be blood. But with the tools I've got with me at the moment, I'm unable to study it properly. What should I do? Think it's okay to cut off a part of the sheet?"

"Of course it is," said Montalbano. "There are very few other people who know about Augello's cadaver."

Antonia pulled a small pair of scissors out of the case,

cut out a little piece of sheet, and put it in another plastic envelope.

"Okay, I'm done," she said to the inspector.

"So, what can you tell me?"

"Well, to begin, there's a total anomaly: a corpse lying on a sheet and pillow like this is definitely going to leave an impression. Here there's some imprint, but not enough to be made by the weight of a dead body that was set down on it. It should have left a deep furrow, a much more visible concavity."

"But several days have already gone by . . ." Montalbano commented.

"Of course, but, believe me, it should have left a much clearer sign. Here it's barely visible."

"So what does that mean?"

"Well, right now, without further study, I can't say. I need to examine the samples I took in the lab."

"So what do we do now?" asked the inspector, feeling a little disappointed.

"Now, if you want, we can go back to Via La Marmora and finish working on those folders."

Montalbano looked at his watch. Not yet ten o'clock . . .

"Listen," he said, "all right, but first let's stop somewhere and eat something."

"Ouf!" said Antonia. "Always thinking about food . . . At this hour we'll have to content ourselves with a few stale sandwiches in a bar . . ."

"No," said the inspector, cutting her off. "I have a better idea. What if we went and ate at my house?"

"At home? What, are we going to start cooking now? We don't have all this time, you know . . ."

"Come on! There's no need to cook anything! I'm

lucky enough to have a housekeeper who's a fabulous cook. You won't be disappointed."

"Oh, all right," said Antonia.

When they got to Marinella and Antonia sat down on the veranda, she couldn't believe her eyes.

"What a fantastic place!" she said.

Montalbano felt proud.

"I'll go and see what Adelina cooked up."

There was nothing in the refrigerator. To make up for it, however, in the oven . . . there was a dish he'd never seen before!

Almost as if she'd foreseen that he would have an important guest to dinner that evening, Adelina had prepared a *timballo di maccheroni in crosta*.

It was exactly like the one described in Lampedusa's *The Leopard*: a *timballo* fit for a prince! And when Montalbano set it on a tray with two plates, two forks, two glasses, and a bottle of wine, and took it all out to the veranda, Antonia was thoroughly charmed. Neither of them had the heart to break the pastry crust, but when the knight in shining armor Montalbano raised his knife to do so, he released a head-spinning scent of sugar and cinnamon. Inside they found all manner of good things.

Antonia and Salvo looked at each other with contentment, and, at the same time, started eating directly from the pan.

For at least three minutes all they did was exchange smiles and mumbles of pleasure. Then Antonia asked: "But does Adelina always cook like this?"

"No," said Montalbano. "Maybe she sensed that tonight was going to be a special evening."

"I can't eat another bite," Antonia said at a certain moment, setting her fork down.

Montalbano thought it wouldn't be right to keep eating alone, even though he felt he could clean the pan. And so, to avoid giving in to temptation, he stood up and took the *timballo* into the kitchen. He returned to the veranda with two glasses and a bottle of whisky. They started sipping it slowly, without talking.

Montalbano felt his heart slowly opening up, happy just to be beside this creature, who for him was like a gift that had fallen from the heavens at a time when he'd been sure that no such miracles could ever occur in his life anymore. It couldn't be true. And so, just to be sure that the moment was real, he put an arm around Antonia's shoulders and squeezed her. And she let herself go. His physical contact with her gave him the courage to speak.

"You probably noticed that I was very upset by the phone call at the restaurant."

"Yes, but don't worry about that. You're under no obligation to tell me—"

"But, the fact is, I really want to talk to you about it. The whole thing concerns you directly."

Antonia looked surprised.

"Concerns me directly?" she said, pulling back.

"Yes. The phone call was from Livia, my girlfriend. I'd mentioned to you, I think, that I wasn't single."

"I remember perfectly well."

"I've been with her for a very long time. Livia lives in Liguria—"

"There's no better way to make a relationship last," Antonia cut in, interrupting him.

"No better way than what?"

"Being together without being physically together. But please go on. I'm very curious to know how this phone call concerns me directly."

Montalbano had a moment of hesitation. He thought he heard a note of sarcasm in her last words. But, at any rate, he went on.

"Livia is an extremely important person to me. She's a wife, a companion, and we've been together for so long I can't even tell you how long it's been. It's just that . . ."

"It's just what?"

"It's just that our relationship has changed. The distance, which at first acted as a spur for us to see each other as soon as we could, is now just distance. Our passion has become a fraternal love. We no longer feel the need to spend time together. In short, I think it's over between me and Livia."

"And what, if I may ask, have I to do with any of it?"

"You have a lot to do with it, Antonia, because meeting you was the real litmus test. With you, I feel alive again. I want to be near you at all times, I feel the physical need to have you beside me. I want to be with you. I feel happy with you."

Antonia looked at him as though shaken and confused.

"But I'll soon be leaving. I don't . . ."

"I'll come with you, Antonia. I'll request a transfer, or submit my resignation, but I don't want to lose you. I want us to go somewhere and live together."

Antonia at this point stood up, went over to the balustrade of the veranda, then came back, took a gulp of whisky, and sat down again.

"Just one question, Salvo."

"Ask me anything."

"But have you, for even an instant, asked yourself what *I* might want? Have you asked yourself if *I* want to live with you? If I feel the same way about you? If I also want you by my side in the future?"

She stopped, took another sip of whisky, and, with the anger in her voice mounting, continued.

"Why? I'm wondering why you would think that a young, more or less pretty woman, with her career going reasonably well, should be so anxious to have a man by her side? Maybe you're also thinking that I can't wait to get married and have children so I can stop working? Hasn't it ever occurred to you that if I'm single it might just be because I want to be single? That it's not because I'm a misanthropist or a lesbian, or because my father raped me as a girl, or because I'm an old maid deep inside, and not even because men have let me down in life? That it's simply because I like it this way? I'm just fine having no obligations to others, to a husband, to a child. I'm fine the way I am. Period."

To Montalbano these words had the same effect as a hundred knife-thrusts to the heart. Because he suddenly realized that his passion had so blinded him that he couldn't see the reality of the person he had before him. He'd already considered her a thing of his own, and this was a terrible mistake, due, perhaps, to his advancing age. Or perhaps only to fear. How many years was he older than this girl, after all?

He hadn't realized that for Antonia theirs was only a

passing encounter, whereas he had believed that their meeting might be the culmination of his existence, not bothering, for even a second, to ask himself what the whole thing might mean to her.

In spite of everything, Montalbano not only still desired her, but he now held her in higher esteem than ever, having had occasion to appreciate her honesty and sincerity.

He remained silent until Antonia said: "But are you really so sure it's all over with Livia?"

Montalbano smiled tensely and didn't answer. Only after a pause did he speak.

"Thank you for helping me to understand a great many things. I apologize. We can go now, if you want."

Montalbano used the time that it took to drive to Via La Marmora to tell Antonia what Anita Pastore had told him and the conclusions that he had drawn with the help of Fazio and Augello. Antonia remained silent all the while, just listening and not saying a word.

They sat down on the usual little sofa. The twelve folders were still there, stacked on top of one another.

"I'm more and more convinced," said the inspector, "that the killer's name is in one of these."

"I was thinking something else," said Antonia.

"And what's that?"

"If I've understood correctly from what you've told me, nobody, in theory, had access to the Via Biancamano apartment, because the owner had left the keys at the real estate agency. So I asked myself: Then how did they get in? How were they able to take the body away? Clearly there must be another set of keys somewhere, which somebody used to open the door. Can I make a suggestion?"

"You can say whatever you like to me," the inspector replied with a smile. Antonia gave him a little push and then continued.

"I would go and have a little chat with this real estate agent if I were you," she said.

"You're right," said Montalbano. "So, shall we get to work on these folders?"

"That's what we're here for. I thought of a way to save time, however."

"And what's that?"

"The whole time I was working in my office in Montelusa, all I did was think about this case. I even downloaded and read the play. I'm very struck by the personality of this Carmelo Catalanotti. He seems like a man who really liked to play with fire."

"In what sense?"

"In the sense that he would go looking for, and finding, men and women with either something to hide or huge personal problems. And he even succeeded in making them tell him their—"

"More than that"—Montalbano cut her off—"he wasn't satisfied merely with their stories: First he would make them confess and then, at the right time, reopen the old wounds with his scalpel and make them bleed again."

"You're right," Antonia resumed. "He had a very sharp sort of sixth sense, a kind of diviner's skill for finding borderline personalities, people whose reactions weren't always predictable. Reactions which he, of course, intentionally provoked himself. So, anyway, I have the impression, who knows why, that he was, well, the victim of what you might call an accident in the workplace . . ."

Montalbano remained pensive for a moment.

"So you've come to the same conclusion as me."

Antonia continued: "If Catalanotti's model for the mise-en-scène was Signora Pastore's chocolate business, clearly the information she gave him was both revealing but also limiting to him."

"What do you mean?"

"I mean that while everyone at the Pastore business is convinced they're looking at a suicide, in the play there's a further twist: That is, they discover that Robert, the victim, was murdered, if you can call it that, by Olwen, who killed him while fighting off his attempted rape. The death was accidental. He'd threatened her with a revolver to make her give in to his desires and in the struggle she inadvertently made the gun go off, killing him."

"That's exactly right," said Montalbano.

"So, if Catalanotti was following that plot every step of the way, clearly we should find the woman who killed him in one of the twelve folders we've set aside."

"Can you see that we've come to the same conclusion?"

"Come on, let me finish. To save time, I would advise you to focus only on the women—on the possible Olwen."

As she was speaking, an idea began to surface in Montalbano's head, and since he didn't want to add more doubts to those he already had, he spoke openly.

"Thank you, Antonia, you've made a detailed, intelligent argument. You've given me some very valuable tips, but there's something I want to ask you, and I hope you'll answer my question sincerely. Does what you're saying mean you won't be involved any further in the case?"

"Yes, Salvo, my contribution ends here. I have one last task: to get you the results of the tests on the samples I took at Via Biancamano as quickly as possible."

What else could he say?

Any other statement on his part would have aggravated the situation between them. All he could do was accept the reality. Damn the obviousness of that reality!

How hard it was to swallow reality at that moment in his life. And yet he had no other choice. To close his eyes and swallow and swallow. Down to the dregs.

"All right," he said, springing to his feet. "We can go, if you like."

"Let's go," she said.

The inspector grabbed the folders, stuck them under his arm, and ten minutes later they were in the car.

"I'll take you home."

"Of course. How else did you think I would get there?"

Montalbano felt torn. On the one hand he wished he could drop Antonia off at her hotel as quickly as possible so he could go and flagellate himself in solitude; on the other he was tempted to drive as slow as a snail just so he could be with her a few minutes longer. He couldn't resist, and ended up going at such a crawl that at one point she asked: "Everything all right?"

"It's just the engine . . ." he muttered.

It took forever. Before getting out of the car, Antonia leaned over and kissed him on the cheek.

"We'll talk later," she said.

She got out. Montalbano followed her with his eyes, watching her until the hotel door closed behind her.

Some ten minutes passed with him sitting there motionless, feeling that something odd was happening in his veins. It was as though someone had injected ice into them. Yes, that was it: He felt like an ice cube. Frozen, lifeless. He was unable to move the amount it would have taken to start up the car. Finally he managed, and then the car shot off like a rocket to get him to his lair in Marinella as quickly as possible, as if fleeing to a safe, inviolable refuge in which to hide.

Going to bed was out of the question. He opened the French door and sat down on the veranda, but after just a few minutes he got up. The night felt too cold. He took the folders he'd put on the table and placed them next to the armchair, in front of the television. He sat down. Grabbing the first folder, he set it on his lap and opened it. One second later, he closed it. He hadn't the slightest desire to work on the case. A great many thoughts were swirling about in his head, but they were all entangled like snakes. He fired up a cigarette and sat there smoking it, looking at the blank television screen. Then the phone gave the briefest of rings and immediately broke off. Montalbano's heart stopped beating for a second. The only person calling him at that hour would have to be Livia . . . or else Antonia. But there were no other rings. It had to have been a momentary contact. He suddenly had an overwhelming urge to call Livia. He got up, put his hand on the receiver . . . and stopped. He shook his head. And sat back down.

And he asked himself: Why had he felt the need to call Livia? What would he or could he have possibly said to her? What would or could Livia have possibly said to him, after what she'd already clearly told him over the telephone?

She'd shouted to him that she didn't want to wait anymore.

All I ever do is wait . . . and wait . . . I've been waiting all my life, suspended between your work and what is supposed to happen at some future date that never arrives.

Future? But did he want to have a future with Livia?

For years he'd lived their life as a couple as though it were suspended in time and space. His work had always taken precedence over their relationship. Their plans were always made on the fly. Whenever a chance to "take responsibility," so to speak, for their relationship presented itself—as with François—he'd always erected barriers of defense. He'd never really asked Livia to marry him or to live with him. Every time they would begin to discuss it he'd let the subject drop into that frozen bubble of space and time. As if his relationship with Livia were too ironclad to be affected by space and time . . . Considered a sure thing . . . taken for granted . . . Also taken for granted were the phone calls making small talk, the evenings spent together on the sofa saying hardly anything to each other, or lying in bed in each other's arms without kissing.

Was that somehow love?

He had no doubt: Yes, it was love. Old and threadbare like a worn-out suit, with a few holes here and there, patched up as best one could, tired, but still love.

But then, hearing the word in his head, his heart gave a tug, and another name surfaced: Antonia. With Antonia, on the other hand, he'd immediately made plans for the future: He'd confided to her, without embarrassment, that he wanted to stay with her forever, that he would retire for her, that he would follow her to the ends of the earth. And yet, with Antonia, nothing was certain. Their conversations were not taken for granted, nor was their lovemaking, nor was the time and place of their next encounter. Their whole relationship was uncertain. It was at the mercy of space and time.

And was this somehow love?

Once again, he had no doubt: Yes, it was love.

The only solution was to set to the bottle of whisky. Which he did.

When at last he lay down, he plunged into a black abyss, and for this reason he didn't know how or what time it was when he finally made up his mind to undress and get into bed without bothering to shower.

Some time later the insistent ringing of the telephone forced him to make the effort to open his eyes. He immediately closed them again, wounded by the first light of dawn.

This, he thought as he was getting up to answer the phone, *is surely going to be that pain in the ass Catarella, needing to inform me of the latest murder.*

His mouth was still all gluey with whisky, and his "Hello" came out as a kind of grunt. The voice that replied brought him immediately to his senses: lucid and perfectly alert.

"What were you doing, sleeping?" asked Antonia.

And while his mind had clearly woken up, his voice betrayed him.

"Nzzz ngrt."

"Tell you what," the girl said, thinking practically. "Go and take a shower, and I'll call you back in ten minutes."

17

Montalbano got down to business with such speed that he moved like Larry Semon in a silent film. Before the phone started ringing again, he'd managed to shower, comb his hair, shave, douse his face in sandalwood-scented after-shave, and put the coffeepot on the burner.

"Hello," he said, this time in a clear voice. "How is it you're so—?"

"I'm sorry, you're right. It's probably too early to call, but I've been working all night."

"You worked all through the night? Where?"

"After you took me back to the hotel I wasn't sleepy, so I went to the lab and analyzed the samples."

"So have you got any news? If you like, I can come to you and we can have breakfast together. That way you can tell me everything," said Montalbano, taking off in fifth gear.

"No, I'm sorry, but I need to get some sleep."

"Then tell me now," said the inspector, shifting down to third.

"There are no organic traces."

"What are you saying? What about that little bloodstain?"

"Special effects."

"Meaning?"

"It's fake blood. Artificial. Made of a chemical compound used for special effects in movies."

Montalbano was momentarily confused.

"What about the other samples?"

"Nothing of importance. Just blends of esters, alcohols, saturated acids . . ."

"Meaning?" Montalbano repeated.

"Wax."

"Excuse me?"

"Wax, Salvo. Common wax."

"And what does that mean?"

"I don't know."

"Could it possibly be from candles that were placed around the body?"

"No, I really don't think so. They were all tiny little scales of wax, pale pink, blue, and black . . ."

Montalbano remained silent. He was truly stunned.

"Well, since you have nothing to say," said Antonia, "I'm going to bed."

"Thanks. But when can we . . ."

Beep . . . beep . . . beep . . .

She'd already hung up.

What could this new complication mean?

He didn't feel like thinking about it anymore, and put the question off for later. The important thing he had to do right away was what Antonia herself had suggested: go and talk to the boss of the real estate agency.

As soon as he saw the inspector come in with his arms full of folders, Catarella raced out of his closet and relieved him of his burden.

"Fazio and Augello in?"

"Yeah, Chief, 'ey're onna premisses," said Catarella, setting the folders down on the desk.

"Send 'em both to me."

Five minutes later, the meeting began in Montalbano's office.

"So these are the famous folders?" asked Mimì.

"Yes," replied Montalbano. "They are the product of a long, careful evaluation we've been doing—"

"*We?*" Mimì interrupted him.

"That *I've* been doing," the inspector corrected himself. "Anyway, here are the folders I've set aside. And here are the profiles of those who showed some psychological or psychic anomalies, or a natural inclination to all kinds of transgression. That is, those most likely to have rebelled against Catalanotti's demands. Is all that clear?"

"Quite clear," said Fazio.

"In each folder you'll also find a photo taken, in my opinion, without the subject knowing. But good old Catalanotti didn't make our job any easier, leaving out the surnames of the auditioners, as well as their addresses and phone numbers. Start with the second folder, however, because I'm already quite familiar with the first one. So your task will be to see if you can perform the miracle of identifying them. Now I've got something else to do. Fazio, do you have the keys to the holding cell?"

"Yessir, I do."

"Gimme 'em."

Fazio pulled them out and handed them over. Montalbano got up.

"I'll see you guys in five minutes," he said.

He went out, walked down to the end of the corridor,

opened the door to the holding cell, and closed it behind him.

Tano Lo Bello was sitting on a straw mattress, elbows propped on his knees and head in his hands. Montalbano remained standing in front of him. Tano raised his head. He no longer had those animal eyes of the day before. He now looked like a beaten dog. They looked each other in the eye for a moment, then Montalbano pulled a scrap of paper out of his pocket and held it in front of Tano's face.

"Now listen closely. If you agree to my offer, this piece of paper will remain a piece of paper in my pocket. But if you don't agree, this piece of paper will turn into a little envelope. And do you know what's in the envelope?"

"No, sir."

"There's a good dose of cocaine. And do you know where we found this little envelope?"

"No, sir," replied the ogre, who by now seemed almost tame.

"We found it in your pocket, together with another ten or so identical envelopes. Got that?"

"Yes, sir. I got it."

"Do I need to go on?"

"No, sir. Just tell me your offer."

"It's quite simple: Nico and your daughter must be left out of the story of the shooting."

"Explain what you mean."

"Nico has always maintained that he never saw your face as you were shooting. You must confirm his testimony. Is that clear?"

"Perfectly clear. And what do I get in exchange?"

"In exchange, your assault on a police officer will be dismissed, we'll pretend we never found your drugs, and you'll only be charged with attempted murder. In other words, you get a few years less in jail. Need time to think it over?"

"No, sir," said the ogre.

"Good-bye, then," said Montalbano.

He opened the door of the holding cell, went out, and locked it behind him. He felt ashamed of himself for having resorted to blackmail. But he had no other choice. He went back to his office. He turned to Fazio.

"Do you remember that I told you to keep Nico's and Margherita's depositions in a drawer?"

"Yeah, Chief."

"Well, now make them disappear. Nico never saw the face of the man who shot him."

Fazio understood everything at once.

"But can we trust Tano?" he asked while taking the keys Montalbano was handing back to him.

"Yes. Do me a favor: Let the Lo Bello family know that they needn't worry any longer. And I'll see you again in a couple of hours."

He went out. Before reaching the door, however, he was stopped by Catarella.

"Ahh, Chief, Chief, Dacter Pasquano's onna line wantin' a talk t'yiz all oigent-like."

Matre santa! He'd completely forgotten about the autopsy! He grabbed the receiver out of the switchboard operator's hand but only had time to say "Hello" before he was assailed by a deluge of expletives and insults.

"Has your head gone completely up your ass, you old fart? Is your memory completely gone? Can't you see you just can't cut it anymore, with all those years piling up on you? Why, I've been wondering the last few days, has he not been busting my chops to know the findings from Catalanotti's autopsy? Or would you rather I spoke to Catarella about it? Maybe he's more likely to solve the case? All these questions and not a single answer? Maybe you can help me . . ."

"I'm terribly sorry, Dr. Pasquano, but haven't you heard the news?"

"What news?"

"They've been reporting, on the TV, on the radio, that there have been some cases of severe poisoning stemming from a batch of cannoli ricotta gone bad, and so I was afraid to contact you."

"Would you please just go fuck yourself?"

"Doctor, I apologize for going missing. You're right, I'm just a poor old fart. Now speak."

"Well, listen carefully, because the situation's an odd one, to say the least. At first glance, it looks like the cause of death was a fatal stab wound with a letter opener. Except that, when I looked at the wound to the heart, I realized that there was another very serious lesion there, inflicted just prior to the other one."

Montalbano balked.

"Do you mean to tell me that he was stabbed twice?"

"No. I didn't say another stab wound. I beg you to activate that small bit of brain you've still got left. I repeat—listen very carefully. I mentioned a wound to the heart, caused by the letter opener; the grave lesion I was referring to was caused instead by a heart attack. Therefore at the moment of the stabbing, the man was already dead."

Montalbano was so bewildered that he couldn't say a word.

Pasquano went on. "At this point you should be asking me: But how did you figure that out? And I would answer: Since the man's blood was no longer circulating, there was no infiltration from the skin laceration—that is, the one caused by the letter opener. And, given your inability to take part in this conversation, I would also add that the heart attack was caused by an excess of sexual stimulants. That's probably the only aspect of this whole discussion you can grasp. And now listen up: Seeing that you're still in a catatonic state, I suggest you set the receiver down now, so we can end this fine conversation."

Like an automaton, Montalbano obeyed, and then just stood there staring at Catarella.

"Ya feel okay, Chief?"

Five more seconds of silence, then the inspector returned to reality.

"I feel fine, fine," he said. And he headed for his car.

The real estate agency, according to Fazio's information, was located near the end of the main corso. The only problem was that, halfway there, he was stopped by a traffic cop who knew him.

"Inspector, I'm sorry, but the street is momentarily closed, because a manhole cover just blew."

"And so?"

"And so you'll have to go all the way around."

Cursing the saints, he put the car in reverse, and when he reached the first cross street, he turned right, then turned left at the first opportunity. Now he found himself in a rather narrow little street, in the middle of which a small van sat immobile. He honked, but to no avail. There was nobody inside the van. He waited for a few more minutes, as a long line of cars began to form behind him. And soon a concert of car horns, shouts, and curses was struck up.

To his left was a small church with its main doors wide open. Moments later a man came out, cupped his hands to his mouth, and said: "Just be patient for five more minutes while we load the saint."

Montalbano decided that his only option was to get out of the car, and so he did. At that moment two men came out of the church carrying a life-size statue of a saint as a third person steadied the statue from behind.

Once they reached the van, they set the saint gently down on the ground.

Montalbano grew curious and asked one of them:

"What are you guys doing?"

"We're taking St. Anthony the Abbot to get repaired."

"Why? What happened to him?"

"A lit torch fell and melted the saint's right hand, as you can see."

"What do you mean, melted?"

"It melted! He's made of wax."

Hearing this, Montalbano froze.

Meanwhile, the three men, with great effort, had succeeded in loading the saint on top of the van and were busy tying him down with elastic straps.

Montalbano recovered his senses.

"I'm sorry," he said, "but where are you taking him to be repaired?"

"To Fela. There's a waxworks there that makes statues."

The van finally drove off, but the chorus of curses and car horns resumed even louder than before. Indeed, the inspector didn't realize that he was standing as still as a lamppost in the middle of the street. Then he felt someone grab him by the arm and shake him violently.

"Hey! You gonna wake up or what?"

"I'm sorry, I'm sorry," he replied confusedly.

He got back in his car and started driving. After just a few yards, however, he pulled over to the sidewalk, stopped, and got out.

He was unable to drive.

So there was a wax-statue factory in Fela?

". . . Just blends of esters, alcohols, saturated acids . . ."

"Meaning?" Montalbano repeated.

"Wax."

"Excuse me?"

"Wax, Salvo. Common wax."

He sat down in the first free chair he found in a bar.

"What can I get for you?" asked the waiter.

"Please bring me a strong coffee. Very strong," said the inspector.

The Casamica real estate agency consisted of a rather large room with two desks in it. One was empty, and at the other sat a well-dressed man of about fifty, talking on the telephone. On the walls hung hundreds of color photos of apartments and homes, each with its respective floor plan beside it, and beneath each photo was a small sign with the word BARGAIN! on it. The man on the phone signaled to Montalbano to have a seat in the chair opposite his desk. While the man kept on talking, the inspector started looking around. The empty desk was in perfect order. Apparently its occupant was late to work or out with a client.

The man ended his phone conversation, smiled at the inspector, and held out his hand.

"Hello, I'm Michele Tudesco, the owner of this agency. What can I do for you?"

With the question of the waxen saint firmly lodged in one half of Montalbano's brain, he decided it was best to get straight to the point. He weighed his options.

"I'm Inspector Montalbano, police," he said.

"Oh, I'm sorry," said the owner, "I didn't recognize you."

"Not a problem. I need some information from you concerning the apartment belonging to Signor Aurisicchio in Via Biancamano."

Michele Tudesco looked confused.

"But I gave the keys to one of your men just the other day."

"Yes, in fact, I've got them right here in my pocket."

He pulled them out and set them down on the desk.

"But I don't understand why—" Tudesco began.

Montalbano interrupted him and began to improvise.

"Look, I'm here because there've been two reports to the police."

"Two reports? About what?"

"Signora Genoveffa Recchia, who owns the apartment just above Aurisicchio's, which she knows is currently uninhabited, heard some strange noises from below for several nights in a row, including some muffled cries of a woman's voice."

"But when are you talking about? I know nothing about this. I'm just back from vacation."

"Please let me finish. We'll try to clear everything up afterwards. I wanted first to talk to you about the second report, which is considerably more serious. But I need to know something first: Have you been in that apartment?"

"Of course I have."

"Have you seen the room with the seashell collection?"

"Obviously, yes, it's very valuable. That's why Aurisicchio asked me always to be present when potential buyers visited the place."

"Anyway," the inspector continued, "something aroused my suspicion. And so I photographed the collection and sent the photos to the owner, who immediately noticed that a good fifteen or so of the most valuable shells were missing and so officially reported a burglary."

Tudesco turned as pale as a corpse, opened and closed his mouth a few times, then managed to say: "But are you sure that . . . that . . . the door wasn't forced?"

"Absolutely certain. There was no sign of a break-in."

At this point a female voice behind them called out: "Good morning, everyone!"

Montalbano turned around, and for a moment his blood stopped coursing through his veins. The girl standing in the doorway, smiling, was none other than Maria del Castello, the Maria of Catalanotti's first folder! The Maria of the evening of commemoration at Trinacriarte!

"Hello, Inspector," the young woman said to Montalbano. Then she went and sat at the empty desk and got down to work.

"And therefore," the inspector continued as if he hadn't recognized the girl, but raising his voice a little so that she, too, could hear him, "it's clear that someone got hold of the keys to Aurisicchio's apartment in order to steal those shells."

While speaking he was watching her out of the corner of his eye. Upon hearing the words "keys" and "Aurisicchio," he saw her sit straight up in her chair and turn three-quarters towards them, as if to hear them better.

"So if it wasn't you who did it," Montalbano went on, "it could have been someone else who took the keys when you were out. Mind telling me where you kept them?"

"Right here, in this drawer," said Tudesco, opening the first drawer on the left side of his desk.

"Was it locked?"

"Of course it was locked."

"Then please do me a favor. Take these keys," said Montalbano, handing him the set, "put them in the drawer, and then lock the drawer."

Tudesco did as he was asked. Montalbano got up, went and stood in front of the drawer, and then, turning to Maria, who by now was completely turned towards them and watching the scene, said: "Have you by any chance got a hairpin?"

"Sure," said Maria, sticking a hand in her hair and taking one out.

"Could you do me a favor? Please come here beside me."

"What do you want me to do?"

"Try and see if you can pick this lock with your hairpin."

"But I've never . . ."

"Just stick it in the lock and try turning clockwise . . ."

Maria did as he said, and they immediately heard a click in the drawer lock.

"Thank you," said Montalbano. "That'll be all."

As the girl put the pin back in her hair, the inspector noticed that her hands were trembling and her face had turned pale. She went and sat back down at her desk.

Montalbano bent down slightly, put one hand under the drawer, and pulled it out.

"See how easy that was?" he said to Tudesco.

"Yes, I see. And that gives me great relief."

"What do you mean?"

"Well, since I wasn't here, just about anyone could have opened that drawer and taken the keys."

"How many employees do you have at this agency?"

"Just one. Signorina Maria del Castello."

"Well, *I* certainly didn't . . ." the girl protested firmly.

"I don't doubt you for a minute," said the inspector. "It could have been the cleaning lady."

At this point he realized that the best thing would be to let the two stew in their own juices for a bit. He slapped himself in the forehead:

"Sorry, but I have to go now. Have a good day."

And he went out, leaving the two of them there immobile, like statues of salt. Or, better yet, two statues of wax.

"You know what, Mimì? I get the feeling your dalliance with Genoveffa has numbed your brain."

"What are you talking about?"

"Well, it seems to me you haven't understood a goddamn thing about all that's happened."

"Such as?" Augello asked in an offended tone.

"Such as, your cadaver didn't die of a stab wound, he was shot."

". . . But it was so dark in there . . . Come on, how could I . . . ?"

"But since you did put your hand on his forehead, you could have noticed something else . . ."

"Such as?" Augello repeated, this time sounding more worried than offended.

"Such as the fact that the cadaver in Via Biancamano wasn't a real corpse."

"What the fuck are you saying . . . ?"

"Shut up, Mimì, you'll be better off. Your cadaver was a puppet made out of wax."

To avoid falling out of the chair he was sitting in, Augello grabbed Fazio, who was sitting beside him.

"Who on earth told you that . . . ?"

"Mimì, I just now got back from the Palumbo waxworks in Fela. It was they who created your cadaver: a good-looking man, life-size, nicely painted and groomed, all dressed up and shot in the heart. He looked like a man but in fact was a real work of art. Just think, all we see is a very fine layer of wax, laid over a gridwork of very fine resin wire. He was light as a feather! And he could be broken down into two parts."

"But why all this song and dance? Why all this play-acting?"

"Because, Mimì, we are indeed dealing with the theater," said the inspector. "Catalanotti had the waxworks make him a dummy for his auditions. The fake corpse was supposed to be Martin."

At that moment the telephone rang.

"Ahh, Chief, Chief! 'Ere's summon onna line's got two discos, but I din't unnastan' a woid 'e said, 'cept fer the fac' 'at 'e wants a talk t'yiz poissonally in poisson."

"And did you hear disco music in the background?"

"Nah, Chief, nuttin' like 'at."

"Okay, put him through."

"Hello, Inspector, this is Michele Tudesco."

Montalbano put the speakerphone on at once.

"What can I do for you, sir?"

"Following your visit here I came to the conclusion that the only person who could have used the keys to Via Biancamano is my assistant, Maria. I put some pressure on her and she confessed. I fired her on the spot."

"Tell me something," said Montalbano. "Did she explain why she needed that apartment?"

"Yes, to meet her lover there. Maria didn't want to bring him home because she was afraid the neighbors would gossip."

"She must have been very upset to have been found out. I'd like to speak to her. Do you know where I could find her?"

"Very upset, I wouldn't say, not at all. She was merely keen on repeating to me that she was not a thief and didn't touch a single shell. If you want to know the truth, I think this job was just a way to pay her rent more than anything else. Her real passion is the theater."

18

Montalbano smiled. Tudesco continued. "Maria's an actress, or at least she considers herself one. She used to repeat to me often that as soon as she was able, she would drop everything and go and register at the academy in Rome. Just think, this very evening she's debuting in a new show at the Satyricon Theater in Montelusa. I'd promised her I would go . . . but, with everything that's happened, now I can luckily spare myself."

That was enough for Montalbano.

"Thank you so much for your help. It's been precious. I'll keep you posted."

As soon as he hung up, he was assailed with questions from Fazio and Augello.

"So who's this Maria? More stuff to do with the theater? Why are you keeping us in the dark about everything?"

It took Montalbano a good ten minutes to tell them about Maria del Castello and the surprising conclusion that Pasquano had come to. He gave them her address and phone number and then added: "Mimì, I don't feel up to it myself, but I want you now to go to the prosecutor and ask for a warrant to search the girl's apartment."

"And what about you?" asked Fazio.

"Well, seeing what time it is, I'm gonna go and eat."

In the car he started thinking that the Catalanotti murder case was now drawing to a conclusion.

For whatever reason, instead of feeling pleased by this, the thought merely triggered a bout of melancholy. Not only was he coming to the conclusion of the case, he was coming to the conclusion of his affair with Antonia.

He suddenly felt an overwhelming need to hear her voice.

He pulled the car over, took out his cell phone, and dialed her number, hoping she would answer.

"Ciao, Salvo, I was about to call you."

Silence.

"Salvo . . ."

He finally drew enough breath to speak.

"To tell me something?"

"To say good-bye. I'm leaving tomorrow."

"What do you mean, 'leaving'?"

"Leaving. I'm going away. I've been transferred, effective immediately. They say it's urgent."

Silence.

"Salvo . . ."

"Can I see you?" asked Montalbano in a faint voice.

"Well, that's why I was going to call you. It's sort of a problem. I haven't got time. Somebody's coming to pick me up in an hour, to take me to Catania. My former boss has organized a sort of going-away party for me this evening and—"

"Can I come and say good-bye to you in Catania?"

"No, Salvo. I don't see why you—"

"It really means a lot to me."

"Oh, all right. My train leaves tomorrow evening at eight o'clock."

"Then I'll see you at the Catania station tomorrow at seven-thirty. Okay?"

"Okay."

His appetite was completely gone.

He got back in the car and headed for the port.

When he got out, he started the long walk out to the flat rock under the lighthouse.

Sitting down, he fired up a cigarette, feeling completely empty inside. He couldn't even remain seated and had to lie down on the rock. The cigarette left a bitter taste in his mouth, so he tossed it into the sea and closed his eyes.

Ah! How much better it would have been to be not a man in flesh and blood but a wax puppet made in Fela!

A wax puppet, with no brain, and therefore no past, no present, no future.

A thing. A thing that, if a wave bigger than the rest suddenly came crashing down on it, would be dragged out to sea.

He had to make an enormous effort to sit back up. Running his hands over his face, he realized his cheeks were wet. And not with seawater.

And so he did something strange: He stuck out his tongue and started licking his hands, cleaning them of his tears, then rubbed his hands on his trousers to dry them.

He'd thought that by his age such tears should never have fallen from his eyes. But those tears gave him strength and dignity, or at least just enough to head for his car—at a crawl, it was true, but at least he was a man again.

"The prosecutor," said Mimì, "didn't make any fuss and gave me the warrant immediately. You want it?"

"Yes," said the inspector, taking it and putting it in his jacket pocket.

"So when are we gonna go there?" asked Fazio.

"My idea is to go and search the apartment when we're absolutely sure the girl isn't at home. And since we know she has a performance in Montelusa this evening, we'll plan accordingly."

"Meaning?"

"Meaning that as of this moment, you're going to start watching her building. As soon as she goes out, give me a ring and I'll come."

"But are you going to stay here at the office in the meantime?"

"Yes. I want to make this big stack of papers disappear."

"What about me?" asked Mimì.

"Mimì, you've already done what you had to do. Thank you, and good-bye."

Sign on the dotted line. Sign, sign, sign. Let's go, Montalbà, sign until you become an automaton. That way, you won't think of anything.

Salvo Montalbano. Salvo Montalbano.

That's it, keep signing, drown yourself in a sea of paper, Montalbà. And even if your arm starts hurting, fuck it, keep signing, keep signing . . .

The telephone rang.

Montalbano looked at his watch. Half past six. He picked up the phone.

"Chief," said Fazio. "The girl just left. She got in her car and drove off in the direction of Montelusa. I think the coast is clear."

"I'll be right there."

He pulled up outside Maria's building, and Fazio opened the car door.

"What's the situation?" the inspector asked.

"No doorman. The girl lives on the fourth floor. Sorry to say, there's no elevator. I had a look at the lock. It looks pretty easy."

"Let's go."

It was a studio apartment. Everything was contained in a space of just a few square feet: alcove kitchen, double bed, a fine bookcase full of theatrical works, and on the wall against which stood a tiny little desk, a huge photo-portrait of Maria in beautiful seventeenth-century dress.

They opened the armoire, and it took them twenty minutes to realize that there was nothing of any remote interest to them in that apartment.

Just a moment before they were about to leave in disappointment, Montalbano heeded the call of nature.

He went into the little bathroom, and as he was relieving himself, he noticed that the ceiling in the room was lower than in the others. Looking a little closer, he spotted a double ceiling with a trapdoor the same color.

He called Fazio, who wasted no time, grabbing a chair, climbing up, and opening the trapdoor with a strong shove.

He then reached in with one hand and pulled out a light, foldable aluminum ladder.

"Be my guest," he said to the inspector.

"No, you go," said Montalbano.

Fazio disappeared. And a moment later Montalbano heard his voice shout in triumph.

"Augello's cadaver's here! Inside a box. What should I do? Bring it down?"

"No," said the inspector, "leave it there and come down."

Fazio put the little ladder back in place and closed the trapdoor.

"And that brings things to a close. You can go back to the station or wherever you want to go."

Fazio looked at him uncomprehendingly.

"Want to tell me what you have in mind to do?"

"I'll tell you tomorrow."

The Satyricon wasn't a proper theater. One descended two steps and entered a kind of cellar. There wasn't even a ticket booth. Montalbano saw only an elderly woman sitting behind a shabby wooden table.

"May I help you?" she asked.

"A ticket for the show, please."

The woman threw her hands up.

"Unfortunately, there's not going to be any show tonight."

"Why not?"

"Because there's no audience."

"What about me?"

Reluctantly, the woman stood up.

"Excuse me for just a moment," she said. She took four steps, opened a curtain, and called into the darkness. "Marì, there's a man here. Whattya decided? You gonna do the show or not?"

"Yes," said a female voice in the distance.

The elderly woman returned and rudely tore off one ticket. Montalbano paid six euros and went in.

The theater consisted of some forty-odd wicker chairs and a stage that was probably no larger than fifteen feet wide by ten feet deep. There was no curtain, and no décor. All he saw was a small table with a 1930s-style telephone and an ashtray on it, and a half-collapsed armchair beside it. Montalbano sat down in the first row, and a spotlight came on onstage, falling perfectly on the area comprising the little table and armchair. Then Maria appeared, barefoot and wearing a skirt. She came forward and, shading her eyes with one hand, looked out at the sole member of the audience. Montalbano had the impression that the girl's face suddenly seemed to cheer up. She had a stage presence and authority that commanded attention. A little smile appeared on her lips. She then stepped back and sat down in the armchair. She began:

"This evening I was supposed to present Jean Cocteau's *The Human Voice*, but given the fact that we have a very special guest in the audience, I will improvise for him, and him alone."

Montalbano nodded, almost as if to say, "Please go ahead."

"I became a woman when there were still men around. I was brought up with the principle that males always want to do only one thing: fuck. Men were kind to women for one reason alone, men went out with women for the same reason, and sometimes they got married to women, again for the same, sole reason. To fuck them."

The girl's voice had become transformed. She was clearly speaking a truth, but using phrasings, tones, and colors that made her words seem more a thing of the theater than of real life.

"And so, for a long time, I tried in every way to be a respected, respectable girl, as my family had taught me. Never, however, respecting myself. I tried to hide my femininity so much that no man ever took any notice of me. Only onstage"—and she pressed her bare feet harder into the floorboards—"have I had a chance to be the real me, by interpreting the characters of women different from me: free women, who knew what they wanted, and went out and took it. In real life I remained Maria del Castello, a virgin, ready to defend myself from men. Then Carmelo, my demiurge, came into my life, and he explained to me that there was a way for me to be myself even off the stage. And I put my blind trust in him. Or rather, I let him mold me. And he was so good at making me really feel like Ophelia, and then Theodora, and then Irina and Nora. And, most of all, it was he who made me a woman."

At this point her voice became deeper and more pained.

"Only once, however, did he make me a woman. It lasted just a few minutes, in the car. Afterwards, and I never knew why, he rejected me. But that one time, and the hope that there would be others, was enough to make me become his slave, his prisoner. Dependent on him, totally subject to his will, and especially to the desire that he would make me his again. And Carmelo took advantage of this. And how. As if to punish me for my submission, he stopped allowing me to take the stage. I did not rebel. I was always there wondering why he didn't want me, why he rejected me. Had I not made love to him? Had I not done it well? Had I not done what he wanted of me? Why had everyone always told me that men want only that one thing, when he himself didn't want it from me? Why did he leave me at the very moment I found myself as a woman, begging for his body, for a simple caress and embrace from him?

"Then came *Dangerous Corner.* He said maybe I could play Olwen. Olwen was my last chance. She's a secondary character. Nobody even notices her until Martin, perhaps only because of drugs, decides he wants to possess her. And by refusing him and killing him, Olwen emerges from her anonymity. I wanted to be Olwen. But Carmelo quickly changed his mind: 'You'll never manage,' he said. 'How are you ever going to be able to pull on a man's cock? And then actually shoot him? No, Maria, come on, forget about it. I'm going to get someone else for the part.'

"I begged him to let me audition. Carmelo then challenged me: If I really wanted that part, I had to show him I was ready to do anything. He asked me to find a venue in which to audition, because he didn't feel like bringing me to his place. And so I stole the keys to that apartment from the agency. He asked me to dress up as Olwen. And so I became an anonymous secretary: thick, flesh-tone stockings, loafers, skirt down to the knee, the commonest of blouses, white gloves, and a briefcase for work. I had to go around dressed like that, at all times. We went to the Via Biancamano apartment a first time, then a second time. He asked me to leave him the keys to the place. We were going to meet there the following evening after dinner. When I arrived, I rang the doorbell, but then I noticed that the door was ajar, and so I went in. Carmelo didn't answer when I called his name. Walking in the dark, I entered the bedroom and got a glimpse of a corpse on the bed. I thought it was him, and I started screaming. I screamed so loudly that Carmelo turned on the light and showed me that it was just a wax puppet. But I was very upset. 'I told you you'd never manage. You're afraid of a wax puppet; how would you ever be capable of killing someone? Come on, Maria. Forget about it.'

"I didn't know what else I could do. I got down on my knees and unbuckled his trousers; I wanted to show him I was a real woman. But Carmelo not only did not get aroused, he started laughing. With a mocking smile on his face. Then he said he had no more time to waste and was leaving. He ordered me to put everything back the way it was, explained to me how to dismantle the puppet and put it back in the box that was on the bed, and then repeated to me not to come around anymore. But I implored him to take me with him, and despite his refusals, I followed him all the way to his house, still dressed the way I was. 'All right, Maria,' he then said, 'we can do this, but then you have to promise you'll leave. I'll give you a gift—actually, my cock will give you one last gift.' And he searched through his pockets, took out some pills, searched again, took out some more, and swallowed them. Then he said: 'I'm going to lie down, because I'm tired. Put your hand on my pants, and when you see that it's ready, you can climb on top and do what you need to do.'

"I remember this image of myself: me sitting on the bed next to him, my white gloves on his fly, and him lying there, resting. At a certain point his face broke into an idiotic smile, and I thought the medication had taken effect. But nothing doing. Just that doltish smile still floating on his lips. Would you believe that it was that smile, Inspector, that liberated me from him? As I was looking at him I realized that I hated him, I detested him, and that I would indeed have been capable of killing him. And so, on impulse, without thinking, I grabbed a letter opener that was on the nightstand and thrust it into his heart. Carmelo didn't move, didn't try to stop me . . . He just kept on smiling, and I kept pressing the knife deeper.

"Afterwards, I felt free. Free at last. I left him there on the bed. There can't have been any traces of me in that apartment, since Carmelo had never allowed me to call on him there. Then I went back to the Via Biancamano apartment, cleaned everything that had to be cleaned, put the wax puppet back in its box, and took it away with me. I didn't touch anything else, Inspector. I assure you I didn't steal those shells. Then, once out of the apartment, I threw away those horrible Olwen clothes. But believe me: I regret nothing, not even for a moment. Is it possible to kill a man and not feel guilty, but only free?"

Having finished, she collapsed, drained of strength, against the back of the armchair. Montalbano got up, approached the stage, and called to her softly: "Maria . . ."

The girl raised her head and looked at him. Montalbano noticed that her cheeks were dry. Not a single tear had fallen from her eyes.

"Would you give me another five minutes before arresting me?" she asked.

"I have no intention of arresting you," Montalbano replied.

The girl gave a sudden start. She stood up and shouted: "But everything I've just told you is true! I am a murderess. Carmelo didn't think me capable of it, but I actually did it, in reality, not in some simulated reality, some similveracity like he wanted."

"Listen to me," the inspector said patiently. "The autopsy has shown that when you stabbed him he was already dead of a heart attack from a few seconds before. So, I'm sorry to say, you didn't murder him."

Maria staggered. Her legs gave out, and she fell into the armchair and this time burst into convulsive, uncontrollable weeping.

Montalbano let her get it out of her system, and when he noticed she seemed a little calmer, he said: "I'll expect you at the police station at ten o'clock tomorrow morning."

Unable to speak, Maria merely nodded assent.

"Try to get some sleep tonight," he said, then turned around and left the theater. Once in the car, he rang Fazio.

"Sorry to bother you, but the girl has confessed, and I told her that in any case Catalanotti was already dead. I summoned her to appear tomorrow morning at ten. Make a transcript of her report, then take her to the prosecutor, who will already have received Pasquano's report. She should get off pretty lightly."

"I'm sorry, Chief," said Fazio, "but aren't you coming to work tomorrow?"

"No, I've got an engagement. I'll be out of town all day. Listen, I wish you a good night. See you soon."

He started up the car and drove off.

When he got in the car the following morning to drive to Catania, he congratulated himself. He'd managed to make the previous evening, night, and morning pass just by wasting as much time as possible.

Starting up the engine, he figured he would get there too early for his rendezvous. But he immediately found a solution. Once he got to Fela, he turned off in the direction of Piazza Armerina. But when he reached the town, he simply couldn't get over the fact that he was alone in appreciating such wondrous beauty. He saw not a soul anywhere near the villa's mosaics and enchanting allées. How the hell was it possible that in the country containing the greatest quantity of the world's cultural treasures, the administration was incapable of organizing a tourist industry to feed everyone, instead of leaving them just poor and insane?

Despite these thoughts, as he drove away his heart felt a little less heavy.

He arrived exactly on time, and there was Antonia, waiting for him on the platform. She had only one suitcase, and not a very large one at that. Maybe she'd already sent on her more cumbersome stuff. There were few travelers about. The train hadn't arrived yet. Montalbano felt momentarily awkward, seeing the young woman standing before him, smiling. Should he shake her hand, kiss her on the cheek, or just say hello? Antonia realized his embarrassment and went up to him and embraced him.

"Thank you for coming," she said.

Then something terrible happened: They couldn't find anything to say to each other.

Antonia was the first to speak.

"Where are you on the Catalanotti case?"

"It's been solved. You were right: It was the girl trying out for Olwen's part in the play who did it. I even had a bit of luck: She practically confessed on her own initiative. But she wasn't what killed him."

Antonia balked and looked at him uncomprehendingly.

"What do you mean?"

Montalbano told her everything that had happened in the meantime, including the bit about the wax puppet.

Finally her train announced its arrival with a long whistle and then came to a stop. Montalbano bent down to pick up her suitcase, but instead of the bag's handle, his hand grasped hers, which had preceded his.

And it was as if those two hands would never come unstuck again. They both stayed that way, half crouching, holding each other's hands and lost in each other's eyes.

"All aboard! . . ."

They seemed not to have heard. They kept on looking at each other without speaking. Squeezing each other's hands tighter and tighter. Neither one felt like letting go.

The train started slowly moving.

They didn't even see it leave.

All of a sudden they found themselves in an unreal silence. As though enclosed in a bubble outside of space and time.

Letting go of the suitcase, they immediately found themselves in each other's arms, in a convulsive embrace.

"What now?" Montalbano managed to ask.

"Now we're here."

The blaze that raged all night
and seared you to your deepest roots
died out at dawn's first light, lost force and vigor,
its guttural roar become
but a stuttering crackle.
Then it fell silent, forever.

It was, you knew, the final flame
the gods allowed you in your late autumn.
But will an Everest of ashes now suffice
to bury that handful of embers
still stubbornly burning?

Author's Note

The poetry quoted here is by Patrizia Cavalli, Pablo Neruda, and Wislawa Szymborska, respectively.

I will repeat to the end that the characters, names, and situations, not to mention their thought processes and personal realities, are all products of my imagination.

Not produced by my imagination, on the other hand, are certain political facts that have now become reality but at the time of the novel's writing seemed only a nightmare to Montalbano.

I thank General Enrico Cataldi for his precious advice.

And thanks, as always, to Valentina for her incomparable contributions.

Notes

15–16 the comic who'd founded the Vaffanculo Day party: A reference to the Movimento Cinque Stelle, the "Five-Star Movement," an independent populist party founded by the comic Beppe Grillo, originally to protest the policies of the Berlusconi government in power at the time. The party is left-wing on many issues but has little vision as to how to govern, and recently allied itself with the far right on the problem of foreign migrants to the country. In 2007, the party established "Vaffanculo Day" (roughly translated as "Fuck You Day"), also called "Vaffa Day" and "V Day," a day for "the people" to get together to air their discontent.

36 "*pasta con le sarde* . . . octopus *a strascinasale*": *Pasta con le sarde* (literally "pasta with sardines") is a classic Sicilian dish made with fresh sardines, onions, fresh wild fennel tops, sultana raisins, pine nuts, and saffron and usually served on bucatini pasta. *A strascinasale* means simmered in salted water and served simply with lemon and olive oil.

42–43 *Bruno Ammazzalorso, the killer of the brown bear of the Abbruzzi!*: The *orso bruno marsicano*, also called the *orso bruno degli Abbruzzi*, is the Marsican brown bear, an endangered small brown bear native to the Apennine mountains of central Italy. *Ammazzare* in Italian means "to kill," and Ammazzalorso, the man's surname, therefore means "bear killer."

63 Trinacriarte: Trinacria was the ancient Greek name for the island of Sicily, which the Romans also used. The word means "three-pointed," reflecting the island's geography, and is represented by a proto-heraldic symbol of a three-legged head, an emblem still used today by Sicilians. *Arte*, in Italian, of course. means "art."

65 Gassman: Vittorio Gassman (1922–2000), known to most as a great screen actor, was originally a major figure of the Italian stage, figuring prominently in serious and avant-garde drama. He didn't discover his comic talents until he began working in the cinema.

115 "he was working on a British play by J. B. Priestley, *Dangerous Corner*": The lines of dialogue quoted from *Dangerous Corner* are from an Italian adaptation of said play that shortened and revised much of the text. While the plot remains basically the same as in the original, the text is not the same. Therefore, the quoted passages from *Dangerous Corner* in this edition are translations from the Italian adaptation of the play, and not direct quotes from the original.

133 *sfinciuni . . . panelle*: *Sfinciuni* (also written *sfincione)* is a kind of Sicilian pizza; *panelle* (sing. *panella*) are chickpea cakes.

144 *sartù di riso*: A Neapolitan rice timbale with a great many ingredients that can include peas, meat, chicken, sausages, cheese, eggs, and a variety of flavorings.

158 a parade of colors reminiscent of a circus or a painted Sicilian cart: Sicily has a long popular tradition of colorfully painted, inlaid, and decorated carts, usually drawn by a donkey or horse. The decorations are partly abstract but also often narrative, and can feature stories from Greek mythology, medieval romance (usually from the Carolingian cycle), or more recent history or legend.

159 the corso: In small Italian cities, the corso is the main street in town. Larger cities often have several *corsi*: Rome, for example, has the Via del Corso, the Corso Vittorio Emanuele, Corso Trieste, etc.

164 *spaghetti alla carrettiera*: A simple dish of pasta with a spicy tomato sauce containing a great deal of garlic, hot pepper, and parsley.

169 *involtini*: Roulades.

220 Valley of the Temples: The fictional city of Montelusa is modeled after the real Sicilian city of Agrigento, outside of which stands the famous Valley of the Temples, a major archaeological site of Sicilian Greek architecture. There are seven temples, all in the Doric style, mostly from the fifth century BC.

228 *timballo di maccheroni in crosta*: A rich traditional Sicilian pastry timbale containing pasta, ground meat (usually pork and veal), eggs, peas, tomatoes, cheese, béchamel, flavorings, and spices.

266 Piazza Armerina . . . the town . . . the villa's mosaics: Piazza Armerina is an ancient Sicilian town whose original settlement dates back to the pre-Greek era, but which underwent extensive development in the Middle Ages when large influxes of Normans and Lombards settled on the island. The town's main attraction, however, is a vast Roman villa complex, the Villa Romana del Casale, which features major mosaic works.

269 certain political facts that have now become a reality but at the time of the novel's writing seemed only a nightmare to Montalbano: That is, the Movimento Cinque Stelle ("Five-Star Movement"; see note to pages 15–16) has since gained power in Italy and was briefly, at a little over 30 percent of the vote, the strongest political party in Italy. Its star, so to speak, has fallen a little in the past year or two, but it is still one of Italy's biggest political formations.

Notes by Stephen Sartarelli

"Camilleri is as crafty and charming a writer as his protagonist is an investigator."

—*The Washington Post Book World*

For a complete list of titles,

please visit www.prh.com/andreacamilleri